"Romantic, voicy, and full of ██████████████████████ uiz is a master at putting beautifu███████████████████ lly compelling situations. If you v███████████████████ no further than this one."

—Ali Hazelwood, *New York Times* bestselling author
of *Love, Theoretically*

"Gritty, complex, and real. I could not put this down!"

—Abby Jimenez, *New York Times* bestselling author
of *Part of Your World*

"*Luck and Last Resorts* is my favorite sort of love story—one where the feelings are as strong and complicated and euphoric and messy as they can be in real life, and one where the characters, in all their flawed and frustrating humanity, are given the space to experience them all. Sarah Grunder Ruiz's writing is absorbing and affecting, perfectly tuned to the voices that populate this story."

—Kate Clayborn, author of *Georgie, All Along*

"This book has the perfect ingredients of flawed but lovable characters; warm-hearted humor; and gorgeous, swoony romance, with a generous side helping of witty banter. I defy anyone not to fall in love with Nina and Ollie; this is the vacation read you NEED to pack."

—Freya Sampson, *USA Today* bestselling author of *The Lost Ticket*

"*Luck and Last Resorts* has every ingredient for the perfect contemporary romance—engaging writing, delicious heat, charming and complicated characters who face deeply felt questions of how much love to gamble on life's risks."

—Emily Wibberley & Austin Siegemund-Broka, authors
of *Never Vacation with Your Ex*

"*Luck and Last Resorts* hits every beat of a second-chance romance to perfection.... Both funny and deeply emotional, this is a lovely, utterly memorable romance."

—Martha Waters, author of *To Swoon and to Spar*

"Expertly crafted and brimming with wit and emotion, *Luck and Last Resorts* is a beautiful romance that is nothing short of chef's-kiss-incredible."　　　　—Libby Hubscher, author of *Play for Me*

"This is a deeply satisfying romance at the same time it's a compelling novel about the reality of 'starting over' and the tenacity of love in the face of a person's obvious flaws. People may not be perfect, but this is a perfect romance."

—Elizabeth Everett, author of *A Love by Design*

"With a perfectly saucy heroine and a delightfully grumpy Irish hero, it's easy to fall head over heels for Sarah Grunder Ruiz's lovable leads. *Luck and Last Resorts* is full of yearning, hope, and hard-earned romance."　　　—Bridget Morrissey, author of *That Summer Feeling*

### PRAISE FOR *LOVE, LISTS, AND FANCY SHIPS*

"*Love, Lists, and Fancy Ships* is a delightful love story about setting and settling goals, about the journeys of the heart, and about how you have to let go of the past in order to move forward. You'll be rooting for Jo from the first page."

—Jodi Picoult, #1 *New York Times* bestselling author of *Mad Honey*

"This book is a love letter to letting yourself feel your feelings instead of pushing them away, or pushing away those who want to love you through it. Sweet, beachy, and emotional, you will want to read this one with a box of tissues."

—Sarah Hogle, author of *Just Like Magic*

"*Love, Lists, and Fancy Ships* is funny, touching, swoony, and brimming with heart. Sarah Grunder Ruiz writes characters you'll cheer for and fall in love with, and leaves you wanting more."

—Trish Doller, author of *Off the Map*

"An incredibly moving and beautifully told story about the importance of being open even after encountering loss. Sarah Grunder Ruiz masterfully weaves together heartbreaking moments with lighthearted fun as Jo attempts to move forward and complete her bucket list. I laughed, I cried, and I became super invested in Jo's delightfully slow-burn romance with the single dad known as Hot Yacht Chef. This is the perfect beach read, as long as your beach bag contains a box of tissues."

—Kerry Winfrey, author of *Just Another Love Song*

"Charming and hopeful, with a tenderness that underscores every scene. I adored headstrong, secretly vulnerable Jo, her chaotic teenage nieces, and Hot Yacht Chef, all of them beautifully written, fully realized characters trying to make sense of their own heartbreak. This debut is utterly irresistible—the kind of book that's impossible not to hug to your chest after finishing."

—Rachel Lynn Solomon, *New York Times* bestselling author
of *Weather Girl*

"Sarah Grunder Ruiz's *Love, Lists, and Fancy Ships* is a book with enormous heart, and one that balances family grief with truly delightful witty banter. It made me laugh, it made me cry, and it made me swoon from all the delicious pining between Jo and Alex. It's a wonderful debut, and I can't wait to read more from her."

—Olivia Dade, author of *Ship Wrecked*

"Sometimes hilarious, sometimes devastating, and always heartwarming, *Love, Lists, and Fancy Ships* is an amazing debut about picking up the pieces after loss. With a complicated (but ultimately loving) family, fully realized friends, and a very handsome chef, this beautiful book shows how being generous with your heart can help mend it. I loved it!"        —Farah Heron, author of *Jana Goes Wild*

"Ruiz captures the complexities of grief and guilt through many different lenses . . . and tackles them all with sensitivity and skill. Readers are sure to fall for this heartwarming and emotional novel."

—*Kirkus Reviews* (starred review)

"Ruiz debuts with a touching, hilarious rom-com that finds Florida yacht steward Jo Walker striving to cross 30 items off her bucket list by her 30th birthday. . . . The sunny setting; chaste, endearing romance; and heartwarming themes of familial devotion will leave readers hungry for more from Ruiz."

—*Publishers Weekly* (starred review)

Also by Sarah Grunder Ruiz

LOVE, LISTS, AND FANCY SHIPS

LUCK AND LAST RESORTS

# Last Call at the Local

## SARAH GRUNDER RUIZ

BERKLEY ROMANCE

NEW YORK

BERKLEY ROMANCE
Published by Berkley
An imprint of Penguin Random House LLC
penguinrandomhouse.com

Library of Congress Cataloging-in-Publication Data

Names: Ruiz, Sarah Grunder, author.
Title: Last call at the Local / Sarah Grunder Ruiz.
Description: First edition. | New York : Berkley Romance, 2024.
Identifiers: LCCN 2023019634 (print) | LCCN 2023019635 (ebook) |
ISBN 9780593549063 (trade paperback) | ISBN 9780593549070 (ebook)
Subjects: LCGFT: Romance fiction. | Novels.
Classification: LCC PS3618.U55 L37 2024 (print) | LCC PS3618.U55 (ebook) |
DDC 813/.6—dc23/eng/20230512
LC record available at https://lccn.loc.gov/2023019634
LC ebook record available at https://lccn.loc.gov/2023019635

First Edition: January 2024

Printed in the United States of America
2nd Printing

Book design by George Towne

To Raven, Danielle, and Emelia.

And to you, dear reader. You deserve every good thing,
even when you're having dark thoughts.
You deserve to be happy, even when you aren't well.

And love—you deserve that too.

# Last Call
## at the Local

# JANUARY

# One

RAINE

When I step inside the pub, the first thing I notice is the music. It's punchy, with layered vocals and a thrumming bass that makes me want to hum along, even though I don't know the words. The Local is emptier than I'd expect for a pub on a Friday night in Ireland, but maybe this is normal. The only thing I know about Cobh is that it was the last port of call for the *Titanic* before it sank. That and, according to a woman I met in Dublin who makes her living hula-hooping, the cruise ship terminal is an excellent spot for busking.

I cross the pub, take a seat at the bar, and after ordering a Guinness from a polite but grumpy-looking bartender, pull my phone from the pocket of my coat to use my song-finder app. When the screen doesn't illuminate, I instinctively reach for the giant backpack I always keep by my side, only to remember that I no longer have my backpack. Or my guitar. Or the travel case I use to carry my gear. Or any of my gear, for that matter. No street amp. No microphone stand. No phone charger.

I am usually calm in a crisis, probably because I'm so good at getting into one. But my face is numb after searching for my stolen things in the January cold, and I am one wrong turn from snapping like a too-tight guitar string.

The problem: I am stuck in this town I know nothing about, with nothing to my name but the contents of my pockets. Lip balm. My train ticket to Cobh from Dublin. A Ziploc bag with some cash from my guitar case. A foot tambourine. Old napkins with scribbled lyrics. Old receipts with scribbled lyrics. A piece of chewed gum inside of a crumpled receipt. (A lot of receipts, really.) My passport and phone, thank God.

The solution? Yet to be determined.

When the song ends, I'm resigned to the fact that I will never know the name of it. Just as I am resigned to the fact that after a year abroad, I will likely be moving back to Boston sooner than I planned.

The bartender fills my pint glass halfway, then sets it aside and disappears through a door to the kitchen. While I wait, I peer around the pub. It's clean and well-lit but sparsely decorated. Other than two Irish flags on the ceiling, a chalkboard menu, and some black-and-white photos of boats and buildings, it's not decorated at all. And speaking of sparse, there's hardly anyone else here. I wish I'd stumbled upon somewhere livelier to take my mind off of things, but now that I'm seated, I simply don't have the will to get up.

The bartender returns a few minutes later and sets my Guinness before me. "There you are, love," he says.

I thank him, but he only grunts and disappears to the kitchen again.

As I drink my pint, I prod my dead phone with a finger. I don't *want* to call my parents, but I need to. There's only so long I can put it off. I try to focus on the music playing overhead, but I'm stuck in a loop of negative thoughts. The humiliation of calling my parents and asking for help. The humiliation of returning home and moving in with them until I can get back on my feet. The humiliation of *I told you so.*

I've just finished my beer and am working up the motivation to hunt down a store that sells phone chargers when I'm startled by a blur of movement to my right. When I turn, I find the largest black cat I've ever seen perched on the barstool beside me.

"Oh, hello," I say. The cat swishes its tail lazily behind it, staring at me with its large green eyes.

It might just be the beer, but I'm already in love with this cat. I dangle my hand in front of it and say, "Aren't you incredibly floofy? You're a little late though. I've already had all my bad luck for the day. At least, I hope I have."

The cat blinks at me, then makes a trilling sound, almost like a bird.

"I bet you get the bad-luck thing all the time, don't you? I'm sure it's not true. You're probably a very lucky cat."

The cat chirps again. It rubs its face against my hand, so I give it a scratch beneath its chin. "Speaking of luck, you don't happen to have a phone charger, do you, floofy boy? Or girl. I don't want to assume."

I nearly fall off my stool when a voice answers me. "He doesn't, but there's usually one behind the bar."

When I look up, a man is lowering himself onto the stool on the other side of the cat. He swipes the beanie from his head and stuffs it into the pocket of his coat, then runs a hand through his dark hair. When he faces me, I decide that I was right, this cat is lucky, because with clear blue eyes and an easy expression, this man is . . . *hot.*

He props an elbow on the bar, posture confident and casual, like he owns the place. He's sex on a stool, and I bet he knows it. I take in the swoop of hair that falls into his eyes, the black peacoat and black jeans and black wingtip boots, and decide that this sophisticated-bad-boy look really does it for me.

"I like your . . ." *Everything*, I think. "Boots," I say, and immediately want to punch myself in the face. Of all the things that shoot out of my mouth, I couldn't find something more charming than *I like your boots*? Seems I haven't become any more worldly since leaving home.

"Thank you," the man says.

He gives me a bemused smile, and I soon realize the cat has pulled away from me and I've been scratching at nothing but air for the last few seconds. I grab my pint glass and take a sip, but it's empty except for a few drops of liquid. Any game I had (minuscule, tiny, almost nonexistent) has abandoned me in my time of need.

The man pushes the hair from his eyes and looks at my dingy brown hiking boots with faded red laces. "I like your boots too," he says.

I can't tell if he's serious or not. These boots have taken a beating. I really need a new pair, though I probably won't need hiking boots much back home. My parents will use their connections to get me an office job at a clinic or something, and instead of hiking boots, I'll be buying *something sensible*, though I don't see how heels and pointy-toed flats are more sensible than traction and arch support.

The man nods to the cat. "He's a boy, but you can call him whatever you like. He doesn't care. Isn't that right, Princess Ugly?"

I wiggle my toes in my perfectly sensible, if dingy, hiking boots. "That's quite the name."

He shoots me a playful smile. "His real name is Sebastian, but floofy boy works too."

I've fantasized plenty of times about meeting a cute local and falling into a whirlwind travel romance, but none of those fantasies ever began with the cute local catching me in conversation with a cat. "You can't deny he's very floofy," I say. "It's scientific."

"Ah, yes. What we have here is the magnificent *Felis floofyis*, the fiercest and, dare I say, floofiest of felines." When Sebastian chirps at him, he gives the cat a scratch between its ears before lifting his eyes to mine. "So the phone charger. Do you want to borrow it?"

*Right.* I tap my fingers along the screen of my dead phone with a sigh. "I don't want to be a bother."

"I know the owner," the man says. "He won't mind." Before I can tell him not to worry about it, he reaches behind the bar, face twisting in concentration as he gropes blindly for the charger.

"Really, don't trouble yourself. I'll just—"

"There," he says, a victorious look on his face when he sits back down, phone charger in hand.

I look from him to the charger. I don't make a habit of borrowing other people's things without asking. Hell, I won't even touch them, not even if said thing is in my way and probably a fire hazard. (A lesson I learned the hard way after being screamed at in a hostel.) But the bartender is nowhere in sight, and I really do need the charger. I've already missed the last train to Cork, where the nearest hostel is located, and I have no idea how I'll get there without my phone.

"And you're sure the owner won't mind?"

"Positive." When the man holds out the charger, the cat takes a swipe at it with a paw. "Quit it, Bash." The cat meows but leaves the charger alone when the man hands it to me. "There's an outlet right there beneath the bar," he says.

"Thanks." I plug in the charger, and when the battery icon lights up on my phone, I feel both relief and dread. I can't put off calling my parents for much longer. Maybe the cat can conjure up my missing things if I ask nicely enough.

I'm searching for a hostel with vacancies when the man shrugs off his coat and hangs it on a hook beneath the bar. He pushes up the sleeves of his black button-down, and I'm distracted by the colorful tattoos that cover his forearms. He must be heavily tattooed beyond his arms too, because when I look him over again, I notice the hilt of a dagger peeking out from the collar of his shirt.

I set my phone on the bar and turn toward him. "Do they all mean something?"

The man looks at me as if he has no idea what I'm talking about. Which, of course, he doesn't.

"Your tattoos," I explain.

"Oh." He holds his arms in front of himself as if he's never seen them before. "They do." He stretches a forearm out on the bar. "This one," he says, pointing to a portrait of a ginger cat with flowers around it, "is because I like cats."

I scan his arm. There are so many tattoos that it's hard to know where to start. A three-headed dragon. A pint glass. The structural formula of a chemical compound I can't recall the name of at the moment because my brain has obviously stopped working. "I can't tell if you're joking or not."

He scratches behind one of Sebastian's ears. "I'd never joke about my tattoos," he says. "I really do like cats."

I want to ask him more about the cats and if this tattoo is of a particular cat, but then Sebastian yawns and leaps from the stool. He crosses the pub and turns his green eyes back on us for a moment before disappearing into another room and out of sight.

"I think I bored him," I say.

"Nah," the man replies. "There must be something interesting about you. Sebastian doesn't sit beside just anyone."

Something about the way he looks at me makes my brain short-circuit. "Are you flirting with me?"

When the man laughs, it makes me want to laugh too. "I wasn't, but I can if you'd like."

I'm sure it's a joke, but after everything that's happened today,

I'm feeling like a mess and not a hot one. Besides, it isn't every day a gorgeous tattooed Irishman offers to flirt with me, joke or not. Who am I to reject the universe when it sends something good my way?

"You know what? That would be nice. I'm having a bad day." I adjust myself on the stool to tuck one leg beneath my butt. "That's if you're serious about the offer."

A smile twitches at his lips when he looks me over. "I'm serious," he says.

I turn to face him. "Well then, let's see what you've got."

When he moves to the stool beside me, my heart ticks away like a metronome that's set a bit too fast.

"If you'll give me your hand, please," he says.

"Why?" I drop my eyes to his extended hand and find that even the underside of his arm is filled with color. His tattoos are of things that shouldn't go together but somehow do—two candy hearts, a pair of scissors, the ghosts from Pac-Man.

"Can't say. It's for the flirting."

Half of my brain says this is a bad idea. The other half doesn't particularly care. When he smiles, I decide to go with the latter half and tell the first half to shut it.

I place my hand in his, and the contact makes my skin sing. I know this is just for some pretend flirting, but human touch is not in high supply when you travel the world all by yourself. Except for on the Paris Metro, but that's an entirely different experience. If my skin is singing anything there, it's "Don't Stand So Close to Me."

The man flips my hand so that it rests palm-up on top of his. "Let's see . . ." His index finger drifts lightly along the center of my palm. "Interesting. Says here that you are very beautiful."

It's a cheesy line, but I smile anyway. "How lovely of my hand to say so."

The man lifts his gaze to mine. "I also think you're very beautiful, by the way."

"I'm glad everyone is in agreement, then," I say, trying to play it cool when, really, I'm melting more than a protein bar that's worked its way to the bottom of my backpack.

He laughs, then looks at my hand again. "You've got a big life-changing adventure coming up. That sounds fun."

"Or ominous."

He shakes his head. "It very clearly says the adventure is going to be fun." He tilts my palm beneath the light of the bare bulb that hangs above us. "You're a creative soul. An artist of some sort . . ." He squints at me. "Are you a musician?"

If I thought my heart was racing before, it's nothing compared to now. "How did you know that?"

"It's all here in your hand."

I stare at my hand. "I'm not sure if it's what you were going for, but I'm a little freaked out."

"Don't freak out." His touch is gentle when it skims across my fingertips. "I've tattooed a lot of musicians. The calluses gave you away. You've also got a tambourine poking out of your pocket. It jingles every time you move."

I look down at my pocket where, sure enough, my foot tambourine is in plain view. "You're a tattoo artist?"

"Sort of." Before I can ask how someone can *sort of* be a tattoo artist he says, "Shall I continue? Or are we still freaked out?"

"We're no longer freaked out," I say, though I am *very much* freaked out . . . by the intensity and immediacy of my attraction to this man.

"Good." He drops his gaze to my palm again. "Now that's nice. Says here you're going to meet a stranger. A charming one with blue eyes. A colorful character, one might say." His expression is playful when he looks up at me. "You could interpret that one in a variety of ways, I suppose."

I eye his tattoos. "If you say so."

"Apparently, this charming stranger is about one hundred and eighty centimeters tall, excellent at flirting, and really likes bagels. Not raisin, though. He's more of a poppyseed bagel kind of fella. He's also incredibly good-looking. Your hand says he's the best-looking fella in all of Ireland, but that seems a bit over-the-top, so let's play it safe and say he's the best-looking fella in County Cork."

"He sounds amazing. I hope he gets here soon."

The man gives me a wounded look, then glances at my palm once more. "Oh, and in the near future, a seagull will eat your lunch."

I snort out a laugh. "What sort of retaliation is that?"

He straightens on his stool but keeps my hand in his. "Who said anything about retaliation? I just say what I see. Don't shoot the messenger."

There's a beat of silence as we look at each other, and then he lets go of my hand and leans away. "How was that?" he asks.

"Perfect," I say. "I'll be sure to give you a great review on Tripadvisor. Ten out of ten."

"I appreciate the sentiment, but Tripadvisor ratings are only out of five."

"Ten out of five, then." Great, I'm talking nonsense now. I grab a napkin from the bar and run my fingers along its edges. I need to keep my hands busy because I am feeling . . . a lot. Not a lot of different feelings, but a lot of one, something like excitement or elation. Only a few minutes ago I was exhausted. Now I'm practically vibrating with energy. If it were socially acceptable, I'd sprint a lap or two around the room.

"Thanks for cheering me up . . . Gosh, I don't even know your name."

"Jack," he says.

"Well, thank you, Jack. I owe you a bagel. Poppyseed. Not raisin."

"I thought *I* was supposed to be doing the flirting." He fiddles with the coaster in front of him, spins it one, two, three, four times. "What's your name?"

"Raine."

"As in the weather?"

"As in *Lorraine* but cooler."

"Lorraine is a nice enough name."

"Raine is better."

He grins at me. "If you say so, *Lorraine.*"

"I say so."

"Well, it's lovely to meet you, Raine." He stills the coaster, then looks over at me. "Would you be opposed to me continuing to flirt with you by buying you a drink?"

My day has been spectacularly shitty, but at least it's taken a positive turn. "With a job like mine, it's unthinkable to turn down free drinks," I say. "Free *anything*, really. Except drugs, of course. It's surprising how often I'm offered free drugs." Jack raises his eyebrows. "That's not to say I *buy* drugs. I don't. What I mean is I don't *do* drugs, free or otherwise." I pause to take a quick breath. "What I'm trying to say is, yes, you can buy me a drink, though you might not want to now."

His eyes linger on mine for a moment before he responds. "I still want to," he says.

"Oh, well, that's good news."

He props an elbow on the bar and rests his cheek against his hand. The word LAST is tattooed across his knuckles. I eye his left hand, which is still fiddling with the coaster in front of him. CALL, it says. LAST CALL. Guess the Irish really do love their pubs.

"What is your job exactly?" he asks. "Are you in a band?"

"Oh, no, I'm a solo artist. Well, a traveling musician." I'm never certain how to explain my job when it comes up. Most people—my parents included—don't consider it a job at all. "Actually, that makes it sound fancier than it is. I'm just a street performer."

"I bet you've got a lot of stories to tell," he says.

"More than I know what to do with, but I'm not sure they're any good."

"If they're half as interesting as you seem to be, I'm sure they are."

I don't know where this guy came from, but I'm glad he's here. I'm about to say as much when the bartender returns from the kitchen and stops in front of us with a scowl.

"What are you doing here, Jackie?" he says. "It's Friday night. I told you to go have fun."

Jack grins at him. "I am having fun, Ollie Wollie. I'm buying this here girl a drink."

The bartender glances at me. "It's just Ollie," he says. "And I meant have fun somewhere *else*," he adds to Jack. "Somewhere with people your age."

Jack turns to me. "I hope you don't mind me asking, Raine, but how old are you?"

"I don't mind." I've never understood why some people do. "I'm twenty-eight."

"Hear that, Ollie Wollie? Raine's only a year older than me."

Ollie ignores him. "If you're gonna let this gobshite buy you a drink, I recommend ordering the most expensive thing you can think of."

Whatever the dynamic is between Ollie and Jack, it's amusing to say the least. "Maybe next time. I think I'll have another Guinness for now, please."

Ollie grunts. He takes my empty glass from the bar and grabs a clean one from nearby.

"Aren't you going to ask what *I* want?" Jack says.

Ollie sets my pint aside. "I will, yeah," he says, then walks away.

I've only spent a week in Ireland, but I've been here long enough to know that when an Irish person says *I will, yeah,* they most definitely won't.

"Believe it or not, that man loves me like a brother," Jack says.

"I can see it. That's what my sister looked like the last time I talked to her."

Clara and I couldn't be more different, in looks or personality. Her brown hair is always neat, while I gave up trying to tame my ginger curls years ago. The only makeup I wear is tinted lip balm, but Clara won't leave the house without concealer to blot away her freckles, one of the few physical features we have in common. Despite being two years younger than me, Clara has always had oldest-child energy. She writes thank-you cards and actually sends them. When our grandmother sends us cash for Christmas, Clara puts it in her savings rather than immediately filling an online shopping cart with vinyl stickers. Clara gets so many invites—to parties, weekend getaways, weddings—that she actually has to check her planner to make sure she doesn't have any prior commitments before she RSVPs (which she also actually does).

She wasn't always so perfect. When we were kids, we'd get in trouble together all the time. It wasn't until we got older that things between us changed. Somehow Clara grew up, and I didn't. She's halfway through her first year of medical school and is doing *amazing* according to our parents, who are also doctors. Whereas I am the med-school-dropout-turned-street-performer. In a family of Dr. Harts, I am the odd one out. A *miss* in every way.

"You said you're having a bad day," Jack says. "Can I ask why?"

I look him over. He seems like he really wants to know. And why shouldn't I tell him? I've never been one to hold back or keep secrets of my own. I don't understand why people keep so much of themselves hidden. And besides, after the last year of traveling, I've gotten pretty good at spilling my guts to strangers. *You can't assume everyone is your friend*, my inner voice warns. But I can't help it. If I like someone, it doesn't matter if I've known them for five minutes or five years. They're a friend until proven otherwise.

And this Jack . . . I like him.

# Two

When Jack turns to face me, I become *very* aware that our knees are touching.

"It's kind of a funny story," I say.

In truth, I don't think it's funny. I also don't really want to talk about it, but it's been boiling away in my head for the last few hours, cycling over and over, and if I tell someone, I can turn this story into a joke. I can laugh at myself, and Jack can laugh too, and then we can focus on how *funny* the story is, instead of all the things I should have done but didn't.

"I was busking on Grafton Street in Dublin yesterday when I met this girl, Krista," I begin. "She's a hula-hooper, probably the best I've ever seen. She has these light-up hoops, and when she's got nine or ten of them going at a time it's just. . . . incredible." The way Krista's face lit up as she talked about falling in love with hooping reminded me of how I feel whenever I hold my guitar. As I listened to her, I wondered if *I* look that happy when I talk about music, and if so, why no one back home understands that I simply can't do anything else?

"Can you imagine that?" I say to Jack. "Loving something like hula-hooping so much that you make it your whole life? Something people think is silly or just for kids and turning it into a career. She gets to travel the world just hula-hooping. And people love it! She has a *huge* following, and . . ." I realize I've followed my thoughts down a detour. "Sorry. The point is, she told me the cruise terminal here in Cobh was a great busking spot. So I headed down here from Dublin this morning and set up my pitch—"

"Pitch?"

"Oh, a pitch is a busking spot—like where I was performing."

"Right. Go on." Jack watches me with rapt attention. He doesn't so much as look up when Ollie returns to finish pouring my pint and sets it in front of me.

"I waited all morning for a cruise ship to come in, but none did," I say.

"That's because it's January, and the cruises don't really start up until April."

"Oh. Well, that explains it, then." My cheeks warm in embarrassment. I stare down into my beer, hoping to hide my face behind my hair. I shouldn't care. Anyone could make a mistake like that. Though I'm sure most people do more research than skimming a message board or two before heading off to a new place.

If I'd done my due diligence before impulsively buying a train ticket to Cobh, I probably would've gone somewhere else and avoided the whole mess I'm in now. But that's the beauty of my nomadic existence. I can do whatever I want with no one to bear witness to my mishaps, other than the people I meet on the road and will never see again. But after twenty-eight years of living with ADHD, I'm so used to making these little mistakes, so used to frustrating the people in my life with them unintentionally, that even the tiny ones feel huge because they're a reminder that I fall so short of what is expected.

"So, what happened next?" Jack asks.

*Right.* I take a sip of my beer, then pick up the napkin again. "I decided to pack up at around one to see if I could find a better spot closer to the park. I have this travel case I use to carry all my gear— street amp, mic stand, stuff like that. Everything else I own, other than my guitar, I carry in this giant backpack I bring with me every- where. It's gotta weigh, like, forty pounds."

Jack shakes his head. "You Americans and your imperial mea- surements."

"The point is, it's really heavy."

"Got it."

"I was in a rush to get over there so I could make the most of lunchtime and almost had everything put away when someone said I dropped something. I turned around and, sure enough, there's this guy holding up one of my instrument cables. I was sure I'd already put it away but didn't think too much of it. I thanked him and held out my hand for the cable, but instead of giving it to me, he grabbed my arm and shoved me to the ground, then took off with all of my stuff."

"That happened here? In Cobh?"

I nod, then set the napkin in my hands on the bar and take an- other sip of my beer. If I continue before collecting myself, I might cry, and I hate crying in front of other people, though it happens all the time. I've been in some scary situations over the last year, but nothing like that. One minute I was standing there, holding out my hand to a stranger, and the next I was on the ground. But as pissed off as I am at the guy who stole my things, I'm even angrier with myself. I made one mistake after another. I should've done more research before coming to Cobh. I know not to turn my back on my things even for a second. I shouldn't have put myself in a position where I was alone and vulnerable. It was stupid and careless, and I'm lucky all the guy wanted was my stuff.

"Once I got my head straight, I chased after him," I say. "But he had too much of a head start, and I still had the tambourine stuck to my foot." I shove the tambourine onto one of my boots and shake it for comedic effect. "Not exactly conducive to speed. I lost sight of him, and now *this*," I say, giving my foot another shake, "is pretty much my only possession."

I wait for Jack to laugh or at least smile, but he doesn't. He scrunches his eyebrows. "What's the funny part?"

"Have you ever seen someone run with one of these?" I shake my foot again. "I haven't, but I imagine it looks absolutely ridiculous." I stuff the tambourine back into my pocket, wincing at the pain that shoots through my elbow.

Jack looks me over. "Are you hurt?"

"Just a couple of bruises. Elbow, tailbone, *ego*."

"Have you talked to the Garda?" He eyes my elbow. "Have you seen a doctor? Maybe you should get your arm checked out. What if it's broken?"

"Oh, it doesn't hurt so bad. And yeah, I already filed a police report, but . . . I don't know, they didn't seem very optimistic. I've spent the last few hours walking around trying to find any sign of my things, but no luck."

Jack drums his fingers against the bar in a precise rhythm. "And you're sure your arm's okay? If it's a small break you might not notice it. It's not swollen or anything?"

I push up the sleeve of my hoodie and stretch out my arm a few times. "See? All good."

Jack looks like he wants to say something more, but he only nods and taps out that rhythm on the bar again. "So what'll you do now?" he asks.

I take the napkin in my hands again and run my fingers along each of its sides as I speak. "I guess I'll head to Cork and catch a flight home. I can't afford to stay and hope my things will turn up. I wasn't planning on going home . . . ever, but I don't think I have a choice now. I'm sure my parents will let me stay with them, and really, I'm so lucky I have that option but . . ." I shake my head, eyes on the napkin as I turn it round and round and round.

"You don't want to stay with your parents?" Jack says.

"They just don't get me. They always hoped my sister and I would become doctors like them. My sister's actually doing it. She's in medical school. So me leaving home to become a street performer . . ." I laugh, and it makes Jack smile. "Yeah, that didn't exactly go over well. They told me I was making a mistake, wasting years of education, throwing away my potential. They told me I'd regret it. Maybe it is a mistake, but I don't regret it. If I stay with them, they'll just poke holes in all my plans to try and push me into theirs, and I'm worried that if I let them help me, I'll give in. And I'm just not ready to give up on music or traveling. Not yet, anyway."

Jack nods thoughtfully. "I can understand that. Can't say my parents were thrilled when I started my tattoo apprenticeship. Mum came around to it eventually, but Da . . . he never did."

"Is that why you're only *sort of* a tattoo artist?" I ask. "I'm still not sure what a sort-of tattoo artist is, by the way."

He laughs, then looks away to spin the coaster around and around again. "Will you be upset if my answer is another 'sort of'?"

"Yes." I try to look very serious about this, but when he shoots me a smile and says, "*Sort of, but not really,*" I can't help but smile back.

Jack sighs. There's a sadness that flits across his face, but as soon as his eyes meet mine, it disappears. "What sort of music do you play?"

At his question, my smile becomes a grin. There's nothing I love talking about more than music. "Oh, everything. Top-forty hits bring in the most money. I throw in a few classical pieces now and then. People really love to hear covers of stuff like that. Holiday music is a hit in December, of course. I can't tell you how glad I am that it's finally over. Don't get me wrong, I love the holidays as much as the next person, but I've had 'Carol of the Bells' stuck in my head for weeks."

Jack laughs. "So the masses like top-forty hits, classical covers, and Christmas music."

"Pretty much."

"So what's *your* favorite music to play?"

I lean closer, as if telling him a secret. "I really love disco music."

Jack leans in too. "Disco?"

I nod. "Disco. Funk. Anything a little groovy, something you can't help but move to. I love it when I'm playing and the people walking past fall into the rhythm. Or when the people watching start dancing and head-bobbing and don't even seem to realize it. Give me a good bass line, and I'm in heaven."

"And do you play your own music?"

"Sometimes."

"What's that look about?"

"What look?"

"You've got this . . . pinched look about you."

I scrunch my eyebrows a few times. "Better?"

"Do you not like your own music or something?"

"It's not that," I say. "I just . . . well, it's not for everyone."

Jack squints at me. "And how's that different from any other type of music?"

I blink at him. I'd never really thought of it that way. "I guess it's not."

He smiles. "So tell me about your music, Raine, disco enthusiast."

"Well, like I said, I really like anything with a great bass line, so I always start there—"

"Do you play the bass too?"

"Oh, well, sort of. I mean, I *can*, but I can't carry around that many instruments, so I typically use a MIDI controller." At the look on Jack's face, I add, "It's sort of like a keyboard, but you hook it up to a computer so you can play software instruments. The one I have . . . *had* . . . was great live." I'm not sure I'm making any sense or really answering his question, but my mouth keeps moving anyway. "I don't play my own music when I perform, though, just cover songs."

There's the hint of a smile at the corner of Jack's mouth. "Because it's not for everyone?"

For a moment I'm not sure what to say. The thought of playing my own music is both thrilling and terrifying. The few times I've tried, I bailed halfway through the song, letting the chord progression take me into something else. Something more familiar. Something I'm sure people know and love. I'm not typically a shy person, but when it comes to my own music . . . well, I'm afraid of what might happen. My music is my heart out there in the world. What if I put my heart out there, only for it to be rejected?

Which is ridiculous. Of course my music will be rejected. Even the best artists have those moments of failure. But for whatever reason, I just can't get over it. What if rejection ruins my love for music? What if I can't get over the failure? I've got enough failure in my life already. Music is my one sure thing. If I lose my love for it, what do I have? It's why I've never finished recording a song before. I have a few snippets. A chorus here. A hook there. Maybe a verse or two. But nothing longer than a minute or so. If I don't finish a recording, I don't have to think about what to do with it.

"I just don't have anything polished enough for public consumption," I say.

Jack has a skeptical look on his face, so I start talking again before he can ask me any more questions about my music. "Sometimes I prefer to keep my performances simple, though. No foot tambourine. No MIDI controller. Just me, my guitar, and a looper pedal. I start with the bass line, like I said, and lay down riffs one at a time . . .

You'd be surprised what you can do with just a guitar and looper pedal."

*My guitar.* It hits me just how much I've lost this afternoon, and even though I can feel myself getting emotional, even though I know I need to slow down and shut up, I can't. My thoughts are unspooling too fast, flying out of my mouth as soon as I think them.

"It was my grandfather's guitar. An electric-acoustic Gibson from the sixties in this sunburst finish that is absolutely gorgeous. You can't just replace something like that. When I was a kid, I stuck this Irish flag sticker on the back of it and thought for sure he'd kill me, but he just laughed and thanked me for customizing it—though he did ask me not to customize any more of his stuff without asking. He grew up here, you know. Not *here* here. He was from Dublin. I even have Irish citizenship through him. My sister and I always said we'd come here together, but she's just so busy with medical school, and . . ." I clap a hand over my mouth, and Jack's eyes widen. "Sorry. Sorry. I'm oversharing, aren't I?"

Jack shrugs. "I asked you a question. You answered it. Maybe it's just the right amount of sharing."

"Depends on the person I'm talking to."

"Or maybe it depends on you and how much you want to say. Maybe you're the only one who knows if it's oversharing or just . . . sharing."

"Maybe." I look away from Jack and find a pile of bits of napkin on the bar in front of me. At some point during my monologue, I must've gone from fidgeting with it to tearing it apart. I hope Jack hasn't noticed. I'm not sure where to put them without having to ask, so I sweep the bits of napkin into my palm and shove them into the kangaroo pocket of my hoodie.

What Jack said unnerved me a bit. Not in a bad way. It just wasn't what I expected. Usually when I apologize for going on like that, people laugh it off or say it's okay. No one has ever suggested that I *wasn't* oversharing.

"Is there anything I can do to help?" Jack asks.

When Jack leans toward me, his knee bumps against mine again. The way he looks at me makes me think he's really asking, like the question isn't just a hollow gesture to be nice. I want to scoot my stool closer and suggest a few ways he can help take my mind off of things. But I've already made enough bad decisions today, and sleeping with a stranger I met in a bar would surely be another. "You're very kind, but I don't think so. You've already helped enough by getting me that phone charger and the beer."

"Happy to help," he says. "And for what it's worth, I really am sorry you lost all your things, especially that guitar. If you want to give me your number, I'll keep an eye out for it and let you know if anything comes up."

This is definitely flirting, right? I reconsider whether sleeping with this stranger I met in a bar would really be that bad of a decision. I *am* in need of a place to stay tonight. And wouldn't it be *more* dangerous to travel all the way to Cork this late? Who knows what sort of people I might run into? Or who I'd end up bunking with at the hostel, *if* it even has room.

If my worldwide tour is coming to an early demise, I might as well go out with a bang.

"That would be great," I say, and try not to seem too eager when he pulls out his phone. "Raine Hart. Raine with an E, Hart without it."

"Raine Hart," he says, gaze flicking to mine as he types. "You were destined to be a musician with a name like that. I can already hear them saying it on the radio. *Topping the charts, we have Raine Hart with her sensational single, 'That Fella from Cobh.'*"

I snort. "'That Fella from Cobh'? That's an awful title."

"Maybe, but the song itself is fierce. The anthem of a generation, some say." When I laugh, he grins at me. "Your number, Raine Hart."

I recite my number, and he slips his phone into his pocket again. "If I hear about any Gibson guitars with Ireland stickers, I'll let you know."

I lean toward him. "You should keep me updated either way, so I don't have to wonder. The uncertainty might kill me."

"There's nothing worse than uncertainty," he says. "So I suppose I'll have to update you regularly."

"Very regularly." The voice of reason tells me to take it down a notch, but I tell the voice of reason to suck it.

There's a beat of silence, as if neither of us knows where to go from here. There are too many options. I could be direct, I suppose. *Say, any interest in taking me back to your place tonight?* Or I could dance around the topic. *Do you have any plans for the rest of your evening? Because I don't, but I wouldn't mind finding some.* I take a sip from my pint and decide on neither.

"Enough about me," I say. "Tell me something about you."

Jack laughs. "I'll be boring to you."

I have a hard time believing that. It can be a challenge for me to give anyone my full and undivided attention. It's not personal. My brain is just a shitty computer. The browser is perpetually frozen on a tab for music. The error message *This webpage is using significant memory* is ever present. No matter what I do, thoughts of music are as persistent as pop-up ads. It's caused me real problems. It's hard to force-quit my thoughts, and, unlike an actual computer, I can't reboot my brain, or replace my faulty frontal lobe, or upgrade to a new one.

Most of the time, I feel as if I'm running a different operating system than everyone else. But sometimes, like right now, I meet someone who manages to minimize the music tab. Someone I can tune in to with such ease that I want to abandon the small talk and jump right into the good stuff. Hopes, fears, all the things that make someone who they really are. It can be too much. I know that. *I* can be too much. But hopefully, when I click with someone like that, they feel it too. They might even be a little too much themselves.

"What makes you so boring?" I ask.

Jack sighs. "Oh, lots of things. I've never been outside of Ireland, for one."

I'm about to ask him why he's never left Ireland and where he would go if he did, but he changes the subject before I get the chance. "Speaking of traveling, with all the traveling you've done, I'm guessing you've seen a lot of pubs."

"I've played in pubs, danced in pubs, had pints in pubs all the way from Boston to . . . well, here."

"And you seem like a woman who says whatever she's thinking."

"Most of the time." *Whether I want to or not.*

Jack eyes me thoughtfully. "So what do you think of this place, then?"

"What do you mean?"

"How does this pub compare to the other pubs you've been to?"

His voice is light, almost teasing, but there's something else there too, an earnestness. "Are you really asking?"

"I'm really asking."

I scan the pub. It isn't huge, but there are plenty of seating options. A few wooden tables gleam in the light of bare bulbs strung overhead. I can't see too far into the two smaller rooms that flank the main room, but one has a few secluded areas, while the other has at least one long table for larger gatherings. The liquor shelves behind the bar are organized and uncluttered. The music is good. But you don't go to a pub to listen to the music unless it's live. You go for conversation. And while I'm enjoying my conversation with Jack, I can't say it's inspired by the atmosphere of this pub, which feels a bit sterile. If anything, our conversation is lively *despite* it.

"It's . . . nice," I say, glancing at Jack to gauge his reaction.

"Care to elaborate?"

If there's one thing I know, it's that when someone asks for your opinion, they usually want you to say whatever it is they want to hear.

I shrug. "You seem to be a regular. It must be good if you keep coming back, right?"

"Sure, but . . ." Jack sighs and leans closer. "If you're worried about offending me, don't. I'm not exactly a regular customer here."

"Are you, like, the owner of a competing pub? Or a health inspector? You don't look like a health inspector." I pause, realizing he might think I'm suggesting he looks unclean. "That's a good thing, by the way. You look much cooler than a health inspector." But what if he really *is* a health inspector, and now I've insulted his profession? "Not that there's anything wrong with being a health inspector."

Jack's eyes dart to a nearby menu. He grabs it and pushes it into my hands. "If you tell me what you really think, I'll get you dinner. Whatever you want. You've got to have the truffle chips before you go. They're really good."

I look over the menu. "They do sound good. And I can't really turn down free food in my circumstances . . ."

"So is that a yes?"

I figure there's no harm in giving the man what he wants, especially if it results in free food. "Okay, fine." I snap the menu shut, then look around the pub again. "The beer is good. The bartender seems . . . intense, but in a likable way. The cat is cute," I say, catching sight of Sebastian crossing the room. "The place is beautiful . . ."

"But . . ."

"But it's a little . . . lifeless."

"Lifeless," he repeats.

"It feels like something's missing."

His gaze is sharp when it lands on me. "If you ran this place, what would you do?"

I laugh. "I could never run a pub. I can hardly run my own life, as evidenced by everything that's happened to me today."

"Let's say, hypothetically, you were *consulting* the owner of this pub. What would you recommend?"

"Well . . ." I turn so that my back leans against the bar and I can take in as much of the pub as possible. It's clean and comfortable, but nothing about it feels personal. "A good pub is less about the look and more about the feel. So the first thing I'd do is figure out what kind of vibe the owner is going for and start there."

"What do you mean?"

"My favorite pubs feel like . . . a home away from home, even if I've never been there before." I pause, trying to find the right words to explain what I mean. "I guess it's sort of like the feeling you get when you see an old friend after years of being apart, and somehow it's like no time has passed at all. Familiar, but exciting too." Jack watches me intently, and suddenly I'm unsure of myself. "I'm not making sense, am I?"

"You're making sense." He holds my gaze, then scans the pub again. "Say that's exactly what the owner wants to go with. How could they make that happen?"

"Well, it's Friday night and hardly anyone is here. A pub is only as good as its regulars, so they've got to find a way to bring people in and get them talking. I don't see anything about upcoming events, so if there aren't any, they should plan some. Nothing wild. Maybe a pub quiz. Winners get a free round or something. Everyone loves those."

"Pub quizzes, yeah."

"Maybe they could get some musicians in once a week. Any kind—traditional, contemporary, both."

"That could be nice."

"And I'd probably suggest updating the photos on the walls. Really, the whole place needs a bit of a makeover."

"What's wrong with the photos?"

"Nothing's *wrong* with them, but . . . I don't know. These feel like they belong in a textbook. It could be fun to hang some local art, candid photos of the owners or, when there are more of them, the patrons. Even the cat," I say, smiling down at Sebastian when he flops onto the floor beside Jack. "The coziest pubs are a little messy. Not *dirty*, but messy. I'm talking cluttered walls, photos, mementos, art. You want folks to have something new and interesting to discover everywhere they look. There's not much to discover here. And the things that *are* in here aren't interesting."

He looks around the pub as if trying to picture it. "Okay. Okay, yeah, I can see that."

"And, oh!" I'm practically bouncing in my seat at the idea. "There could be some board games in that room with the long tables. I've seen bars that have giant games of Jenga and stuff. Those are really fun." I look over the pub again. "There's a lot of potential here," I say, and mean it. Perhaps it's just the present company and beer, but I have a good feeling about this pub. "It's lifeless now, but it could really be something. It just needs a way to draw people in, to make them feel excited and at home at the same time."

"Excited and at home at the same time," he repeats.

"This bastard still bothering you?" a voice says.

I turn to find Ollie scowling at Jack again from behind the bar.

"Oh, yes," I say.

"It's true," Jack says. "I've made Raine here give me her expert opinion on this pub of yours, the one that's been in the family for generations, the Dunne legacy, that is, and I regret to inform you that, according to her, it's—"

"Wonderful!" I say, nearly choking on my beer.

"That's not what you said before." His expression is serious, but his eyes are bright with mischief.

I look between Jack and Ollie but can't think of anything to say. I take another swig of my beer, but I overdo it and some ends up dribbling down my chin.

Ollie gives me a strange look, and I'm positive I'm about to die of embarrassment, but before I get the chance, Jack lifts himself from his stool, startling me when he swings his legs over the bar.

"Get off the fecking bar, Jack!" Ollie says, but he doesn't do a thing to stop him from jumping to the other side.

I stare at Jack. "What are you doing?!"

"Getting you those truffle chips, of course." He grins, then pushes through the kitchen door before I can form a single coherent thought.

Ollie sighs. He shakes his head and wipes down the bar in front of where Jack was sitting.

"Shouldn't you do something about that?" I ask.

Ollie lifts an eyebrow. "About what?"

I gesture to the still swinging door Jack has just disappeared through. "About him waltzing right into your kitchen like he owns the place!"

Ollie shrugs. "He does."

"He does . . . what?"

"Own the place."

"But you . . . Jack said *you* own it."

"We both do. Jack's my smartass younger brother."

"Oh." I watch the kitchen door as it stills. "Oh!" I say again, remembering the less-than-positive things I just said about the pub. *I'm not exactly a regular customer here.* How did I not realize I wasn't *hypothetically* consulting the owner of the bar? But Jack is so young. A year younger than me. How can he be responsible for something as big as this, when I can hardly run a business that consists of just me and my guitar?

Ollie tosses the bar towel over his shoulder. "You all right?"

I shake my head. "I have no idea, Ollie Wollie."

He gives me another strange look, and I take the biggest swig of beer I can fit into my mouth, hoping it will keep me from sticking my foot in it again.

# Three

―――――

## JACK

"Does Jack happen to be short for Jackass?" Raine asks when I set a plate of truffle chips before her on the bar.

*She's the one.* It's the only thought that's run through my head for the last five minutes. *She's the one. She's the one. She's the one.* And I would know, seeing as I spent most of today bored out of my mind interviewing all the wrong people. People who were definitely not *the one.*

She'll make the perfect entertainment coordinator.

I swipe a chip from her plate. "You're not the first person to ask me that, you know." *She's the one*, I think again, then mentally shush myself. If I'm going to get her to agree to work at this pub, I can't be distracted. If I'm going to convince her that she should take a chance on me, I need a clear mind.

Easier said than done.

Raine gives me a withering look, but there's amusement in her eyes. The girl is good craic. She's also . . . beautiful. I wasn't lying when I told her that. Pale green eyes. Wavy red hair. And that mouth . . . I have no idea what she'll say next, and I like that. I like that a lot.

Ollie snaps my shoulder with a bar towel. "Quit being such a fecking langer, Jackie. We'll be lucky to have any customers at all if you keep fucking with them."

Before I can respond, someone calls to Ollie for another pint, and my brother leaves with a shake of his head. He's annoyed at me, but he'll get over it. Half the things I do annoy him. Half the things I do annoy *me*. I think he likes having something to be annoyed about, to tell you the truth, and I am more than happy to oblige. But I don't necessarily want to annoy the pretty redhead seated across from me.

Have I annoyed her? She has her bottom lip tucked between her teeth, so perhaps she *is* upset, though . . . *shite*, I shouldn't be looking at her mouth. I lift my eyes to hers. "Are you angry?" Better just to ask these sorts of things.

Raine looks away from me. Her hair tumbles from behind one ear, hiding her face from view. "I never would've said those things about the pub if I'd known *you* were the owner. I'd never insult someone. Not on purpose, anyway."

"You didn't insult me."

She tucks her hair back behind her ear and gives me a skeptical look.

"I didn't tell you I own the pub because I wanted an honest answer. I don't think there's a thing you could say about me or this pub that would insult me, so long as you really mean it."

She hums to herself as she looks me over, then says, "I think you actually mean that."

"I very rarely say things I don't mean." *I think them all the time, though.*

"Well, in that case, you're welcome for the honesty." She smiles and picks up a truffle chip from the plate. When she pops it into her mouth, a moan escapes her, and I have to work very hard to not react to that sound in any way. Fortunately, I am behind the bar. And fortunately, the moan turns into a weird little cough that I'm *pretty* sure is fake. But then I'm not so sure, because she starts coughing harder, and tears shine in the corners of her eyes.

Raine must sense my anxiety, because she holds up a hand and wheezes, "I'm fine."

"You sure? I've never had to do mouth-to-mouth, but I am up to date on my CPR training."

She spits out a laugh that's a little hoarse after all the coughing, then grabs another truffle chip and sways to the rhythm of the music as she examines it. She hasn't stopped moving since I walked in here. Sometimes it's subtle, like the swaying. And sometimes it's not, like when she was massacring that poor bar napkin. All the moving means the tambourine in her pocket keeps on jingling. It's like she's got her own personal soundtrack.

She points the truffle chip at me. "Are you flirting with me again?"

*Am I?* Fuck if I know. I really am up to date on my CPR training. I'd never get any sleep if I weren't. If I *had* to do mouth-to-mouth on anyone in this pub right now, I'd obviously prefer it to be her.

As soon as I think it, I'm horrified. I wouldn't actually wish for her to choke on something just so I could have an excuse to kiss her, right? But she *could* choke. I can see it now. She'll choke on one of those truffle chips, and I'll forget everything I know about CPR. I'll just stand there doing absolutely nothing. She'll topple off of that stool and die, and it'll be my fault. The end.

It's an unlikely scenario, but it's not impossible. The image is too vivid for me to push away, so I cross my arms on the bar to keep my hands out of sight as I press each of my fingertips to the wood and think, *undo, undo, undo, undo.* Each word at the same mental volume. Each word at the same pace.

The last *undo* is too loud. Or maybe too fast. I'm not sure. All I know is it doesn't feel right. Raine reaches for another chip, and before I can remind myself that thoughts are just thoughts and I can't make something happen just by thinking it, I call out, "Wait!"

Raine pauses with her hand in midair.

"There's a fly," I say, though it's January, and cold as fuck, and I haven't seen a fly for months. I wave a hand to shoo this imaginary fly, then snatch the plate away. "I heard they shite every time they land." Some truffle chips slide off the side of the plate, and I grab those too. I dart over to the nearest bin and dump the chips into it, giving the plate a good shake. I scan the floor around me to make sure I've gotten rid of every single one before setting the empty plate beside the cash register.

I avoid looking at Raine when I turn back around and grab a menu from nearby, flipping past the page with truffle chips before sliding it over to her. "You can't call a plate of truffle chips dinner," I say. "Where's the protein? The vegetables? That is not a balanced meal."

If Raine thinks anything that's happened in the last thirty seconds is strange, she doesn't show it. She looks down at the menu, then back up at me. "I couldn't possibly—"

"A meal was the deal." I push the open menu closer to her. "You give me your opinion of the pub. I get you dinner."

Raine narrows her eyes as if she's preparing to give me a good tongue-lashing.

*Tongue-lashing*, now that's an interesting word. *No, nope. Stop it, Jack.*

"Fine," she says. She hums to herself as she goes over the menu. When she looks up again, I pretend I haven't been staring at her for the last two minutes. "I'll have the stew, please," she says, and snaps the menu shut. "Just know that when someone offers me free stuff, I only turn it down once. To be polite. So don't go offering me anything you don't actually want to give."

"It wasn't free. You worked for this." I prop my elbows on the bar and lean forward so that my eyes are level with hers. Really, her eyes are lovely. *Focus, Jack!* I try to look elsewhere, but my gaze automatically goes to her mouth again. Nose? That should be safe. But I notice she's got a constellation of freckles across the bridge of her nose, and though I have never consciously thought about freckles before, I discover that I am a man who really likes freckles. Forehead? Yes. Nothing arousing about that. Nothing to admire but her eyebrows, red, which make me think of her hair, which looks very soft. I wonder what it would feel like to run my fingers through it and . . . *for fuck's sake.* I decide looking into her eyes wasn't so bad after all.

"Speaking of offers and work," I say. "How would you like to work here?"

Raine stares at me for a moment. "Here? In the pub?"

"Well I don't see how you could do it from anywhere else."

"Do what?"

"Revamp the pub, of course! Do all those things you were telling me about. The board games and pub quizzes and all that. Hell, get rid of these fecking pictures." That will certainly cause trouble, but there's no need to mention it.

Raine's brow furrows as she looks me over, and, *shite*, I discover that I am a brow-furrowing man too.

"I'm not following," she says, looking at me as if trying to figure out whether or not this is a joke. I am almost always joking about something. But I'm not joking about this.

"We need an entertainment coordinator," I say. "Someone to put some life into this place. And I want you to be that someone. What's not to get?"

Raine laughs. "Uh . . . there are a lot of things not to get."

"Like?"

"Like the fact that I have absolutely zero experience entertainment coordinating. Is that a thing? See? I don't even know if that's a thing."

I sigh. She's really making this more complicated than it has to be. "Forget the logistics for a moment. Does it sound like a job you'd enjoy?"

"I mean, yeah. It sounds better than whatever job I'll be stuck doing back home, but I don't think I'm qualified. I'm just a busker. I don't know a thing about business."

"You don't have to. I'm the business. You're the party."

She laughs, and that gives me hope that I can actually pull this off, so I keep talking. "You've been to loads of pubs, right?"

"Yes, but—"

"So you've got plenty of experience with pubs. You know what's out there. And you're a musician, one who has played all over, so you know how to entertain people."

"I guess, but I don't know how to run a pub quiz."

"You can google it."

She laughs. "This seems a very haphazard way of hiring someone."

When I lean toward her, I lower my voice so that no one else can hear me. "Look, I've been interviewing people for this job all day. Sure, they came up with a few ideas, but not a single one had vision. No one but you. You painted a picture. One I happen to like. You told me how this place could *feel*. This pub has been in my family for four generations, and you know what I feel when I come in here?" She shakes her head. "Nothing. Well, a little disdain, to tell you the truth. But I've never thought about what I *want* to feel. Or what I want other people to feel." I pat the bar with a hand. "An old friend . . . that's exactly what I want this place to feel like. And I like what you said about pub quiz nights and board games and all that. So sure, this is a bit sudden, but that doesn't mean it's haphazard."

Raine doesn't say anything at first. She shifts in her seat, freeing the leg she has tucked beneath her to pull it against her chest and rest her chin against her knee. She starts swaying back and forth again, eyes on the pint glass in front of her. The tambourine in her pocket jingles softly, and for a moment, I forget what we're talking about.

"They're just ideas," she finally says. "You can have them free of charge. You don't want my help. I'm a mess. Like, in every way."

*A mess in every way.* Someone must have made her see herself that way, and whoever it is, I hate them. "Then you're perfect for the job. I need someone who isn't afraid of a little mess." *Or a lot.*

"This is . . . very generous of you, and it sounds wonderful, but . . ." She looks up at me again. "You don't even know me."

"Well, Raine, you seem like an easy person to know."

And that's the thing, isn't it? She doesn't feel like a stranger at all. It's as if all of her is right there on the surface. Like if you wanted to know something about her, all you'd have to do is ask.

Or maybe I'm losing it. It wouldn't be the first time I've wondered. Maybe I'm letting a pretty face and a little flirting cloud my judgment. To my credit, I have flirted with plenty of pretty faces, and this is the first time I've offered one a job. This is purely a business decision.

I think.

I lean away from her. "Fine, let's say that, hypothetically, you are in no way qualified for this job."

"It's . . . not hypothetical," she says.

"You said it sounds like a great job. Did you mean that?"

"Yes, but like I said, I'm not—" I arch a brow, and she lets out an exasperated sigh. "Okay, fine. Go on."

"Here are the facts: You don't want to go home. In order to avoid doing that, you need an income. But in order to make an income, you need your instruments back. The only way that's happening is if they turn up or you replace them. But you don't have time to wait for them to show up, and you don't have a way of making money to replace them. I'm offering you a solution, one that keeps all your options open. You work for the pub, help us implement some of your ideas, and hopefully your instruments turn up, and you leave with some extra money. But if your instruments don't turn up, you can replace them with the money you make here. It won't be long-term. You can help us get everything up and running while you get back on your feet."

She opens her mouth to respond, but I continue before she can. "Twelve weeks," I say. "Just give me twelve weeks. From now until April. That should be enough time to replace your guitar and amp and all that, yeah?"

"Probably. But . . . don't take this as me not wanting the job, but there's got to be someone better qualified than me."

Jesus, this girl is definitely a musician. She sounds like a broken record. "If you don't want the job because you're not interested in it, that's fine. But if doubting yourself is the only thing holding you back, then take the job. Everything else we can figure out together."

She tugs the sleeves of her hoodie over her hands. "Let's say I do want the job. I don't see how I could take it. I don't even have a place to stay in Cobh *tonight*, let alone until April."

*Logistics.* Fortunately, I know practically everyone in Cobh. "Give me until noon tomorrow to find you a place for the next few months." No idea *how* I'll manage that, but I'm already turning over options in my mind. "As for tonight, I know just the place."

# Four

## RAINE

I'm slightly disappointed when I discover the place I can stay tonight isn't Jack's but Ollie's.

"You look like a highlighter," Jack says to Ollie's wife when she joins us at the pub a half hour after he calls her.

She replies without hesitation. "Someone's got to be the bright one in this family."

I look her over. If I thought Ollie was intense, it's nothing compared to her. The woman is tiny but terrifying. Everything about her radiates intensity, from the look in her eye to her outfit—a turtleneck paired with a knee-length skirt, tights, dangling unicorn earrings, and heels, all of them hot pink. She'd look like a walking glow stick if not for her dark hair, which is pulled up in a sleek high ponytail I could never manage with my frizzy ginger waves.

She shrugs off her coat (also pink) and hangs it along with her giant purse beneath the bar before taking the stool beside Jack. "You're lucky I already had a babysitter. Now, who is this friend of yours that needs a place to stay tonight? You having a new friend is certainly unprecedented." Her gaze is sharp but not unfriendly when she looks me over.

I give her a hesitant wave. "Raine Hart."

"Nina Lejeune-Dunne." Her eyes linger on me, and I realize I'm swaying back and forth on my stool. I will myself to still and wiggle my toes in my boots instead. When she finally looks away, she says to Jack, "How long did you say you've been *friends* for?"

"I didn't say, but I'd guess about an hour and a half or so." He turns to me. "Does that sound right to you?"

"Give or take a few minutes."

"*An hour and a half or so*," Nina says. She looks at me again. "You're American."

"I'm from Boston."

"South Florida," she replies.

"Lucky, you have all the nice beaches."

"We also have the strangest criminals."

I'm unsure what to say to that, but Nina doesn't seem to expect a response. She rummages through her purse and pulls out a tiny mirror and tube of lipstick. When she applies it, I'm unsurprised to find it is also hot pink. When she returns her purse to the hook beneath the bar, she eyes me again and says, "You're pretty."

The way she says it makes me unsure if this is a compliment or a statement or a question. "Thank you. You're . . . also pretty."

"Do you have a significant other?"

The question takes me off guard. "No . . ."

"Hmm." She searches my face, but I have no idea what she's looking for. "Are you drunk? You don't seem drunk."

I've only had two pints and am nowhere near drunk. "I . . . No?" My eyes dart to Jack, who looks mortified.

Ollie sighs from behind the bar and sets a margarita in front of Nina. "Between Jack messing with customers and you accusing them of being drunk, we'll be lucky if we don't run this place into the ground."

"Well, hello to you too, Mr. Delightful," she says.

The looks Nina and Ollie give each other make me feel like I'm intruding. I don't think anyone has ever looked at me like that, like I'm their favorite person. I'm not sure I've been anyone's favorite anything—daughter, friend, singer, student. I guess I'm Clara's favorite sister, but only by default.

"Sorry about Nina," Jack says. "She can be . . . direct."

I glance at Nina, who stirs her margarita absentmindedly as she listens to Ollie. "That's an understatement."

"Blunt, then."

"Better."

"She doesn't mean anything by it. She's just . . ."

"Intense?"

"Intense, yeah. Both of them are."

A customer waves Ollie over, and Nina turns to Jack again. "Don't think I forgot what we were talking about."

"What were we talking about?" he says.

"About why your pretty new friend is staying at *my* place and not yours."

He narrows his eyes. "Because my flat has one bedroom."

Nina lowers her voice but not enough that I don't hear what she says. "But it is a rather *large* bed, isn't it?"

"*Nina.*" Jack flicks his gaze my way, but I busy myself with my pint glass and pretend I haven't heard.

Perhaps this is a mistake. I would rather stay up all night than be an unwanted guest. "I'm sure I can find somewhere else to stay."

"Oh, you're more than welcome to use my guest room," Nina says.

"Uh . . . great. Thanks."

"I love playing hostess. I'm just confused."

*Me too*, I think.

"Raine here is going to be our new entertainment coordinator," Jack says.

"Ah." Nina turns to look at me. "Is that right?"

"I'm considering it," I say.

"Well, that makes much more sense. Jack has never been one to mix business with pleasure. He's surprisingly upright for someone who is always causing mischief. And you two clearly have something going on, so this must be an issue of morality, not desire."

Jack splutters on his beer.

"*Neen*," Ollie, who has returned for the tail end of this mortifying conversation, says.

Nina gives him an exasperated look. "What? I'm just trying to get to the bottom of things. He's asking us to host a pretty woman we don't know in our home, when he would obviously rather have her in his, and I would like to know *why*. I don't see the issue here."

I try not to laugh, but a giggle escapes me. These people, all of them, Jack included, are ridiculous, and . . . it's a little embarrassing, yes, but fun too. Jack doesn't look like he's having fun, though. He looks like he wishes he had a time machine so he could keep his past self from calling Nina.

"*Neen*," Ollie says.

She sighs. "Oh, all right." She turns to me. "Forget I said anything."

"I don't see how that's possible, but I'll try."

Nina smiles, and I feel as if I've passed a test I didn't know I was taking. "Jack says you've had quite the day." She props her chin in her hand and leans closer. "Tell me everything."

By the time the pub closes, I decide I like Nina, despite the incredibly awkward start. The woman has a million stories to tell. She was a professional gymnast until an injury ended her career, which was when she started working as a superyacht stewardess and met

Ollie. They moved to Ireland when Ollie and Jack inherited the pub, and she's been running her own party planning business ever since.

"Ready to head out?" Nina says after the last customer leaves. "The babysitter is probably bored out of her mind. The girls went to bed hours ago."

"I'll walk you two home," Jack says.

"Sure, yeah, I wouldn't like any help closing or anything," Ollie says.

Jack grins at him. "I'd help, but it doesn't sound very fun. And you *did* tell me to go have fun, Ollie Wollie."

Ollie mutters curses under his breath, and I try not to laugh as I slip on my coat. Instinctively, I reach for my guitar and travel case, only to remember how I've gotten myself into this mess. Jack must see something in my expression because he says, "Nina will make sure you're all right. It's not the same as having your own stuff, I know. But maybe it'll turn up in a day or two. Another reason to stay in Cobh a little longer."

"Yeah, you're probably right." I start toward the door and nearly trip over Sebastian when he darts between my legs.

"What's with that cat?"

"Maybe he thinks if he keeps following you around, you'll fall in love with him," Jack says.

I arch a brow. "Still flirting with me?"

"Maybe." He pauses, and his eyes are serious when they meet mine again. "Is that okay?"

I have a feeling that if I said I wasn't okay with it, he'd really never do it again. And the idea of that is . . . depressing. "It's okay," I say, busying myself with the buttons of my coat so he won't see me fighting off a grin.

"Good. Because it's loads of fun."

"Do you flirt with all the girls who wander in here? Or just the ones who are having bad days?"

"Only if they're cute and interesting to talk to," he says.

"How often do you offer *jobs* to girls having bad days who are cute and interesting to talk to?"

He halts just before we reach the door, and the alarm on his face surprises me. "None? Well, one. Just you. But the job offer . . . it isn't part of the flirting. Or because I think you're attractive. I guess it's partly because you're interesting to talk to. But I didn't offer you a job because of all those things. I really do think you'll be great for the pub. You don't even have to work for me. Ollie can be your boss. Think of me as a coworker. No . . . wait. That's still. . . ." He tips his head to the ceiling. "Shite, I'm making this weirder than it already is."

I stifle a laugh. "I don't think it's weird. I did say you could flirt with me."

"Yes, but I offered to flirt with you, and then I offered you a job. That's exactly something a creep would do."

"At least you didn't offer me your allegedly big bed."

He shakes his head. "If you take this job, I resolve to no longer flirt with you."

"You're doing a terrible job convincing me to work here."

He sighs. "I would love to continue flirting with you. And I would love for you to work here. But I don't think I can have both. And you not taking the job means you leave, which would give me a very limited window of time to flirt with you anyway. That, and I really need you to revamp this fecking pub. So starting as soon as we step outside, I will be the most professional future coworker you've ever had."

I groan. "Sounds boring."

"Listen, you, I am trying to be an upstanding citizen. Don't make it any harder than it already is."

"Oh, all right," I say, and step through the door when he pushes it open for me.

"There you are," Nina says once we're outside. "I thought you might've gotten lost in there."

The three of us set off down the street. I feel strange with my arms empty and no weight on my back as we trudge uphill.

Jack nods to a gray building as we pass a street that leads to the harbor. "There's the library. It's got a great view of the water." He turns to me. "Do you like to read?"

"Sometimes. Mostly audiobooks, though. That probably doesn't count."

"Why wouldn't it count?"

"Well, it's a lot easier, isn't it?"

"Why's that mean it doesn't count? Say you go to a book club and everyone read the paperback, and you listened to the audiobook. You could discuss it as good as anyone else, right? If you didn't say you'd listened to it, no one would know. Who cares if it's easier? Just because something's hard doesn't mean it's better."

"That's what she said."

As soon as I realize I've said it, I contemplate fleeing down some side street and disappearing into the night, never to be seen again. I'm emotionally exhausted, and a little buzzed, and the modicum of impulse control I sometimes have has fled the scene of the crime.

"Oh my God," I say.

But Jack's laugh cuts me off. "I walked right into that one, didn't I?"

I sigh in relief, tugging at the fingers of my gloves as we walk. "What about you?" I ask. "Do you read?"

Nina laughs. "Does he do anything else? That's the real question."

"What sort of books?"

"All kinds. Including audiobooks." He shoots me a grin. "I listen to them when I close the pub."

"He about killed Oliver when they closed together last week," Nina says.

"Nothing like hooking up my phone to the overhead speakers and a sex scene blasting out of nowhere at full volume to traumatize my big brother."

I spit out a laugh, because even though I've known Jack and Ollie for only a few hours, I can totally picture it. "You did it on purpose, didn't you?"

He sighs. "Am I that easy to read?"

"Not easy to read," Nina says. "Just predictable."

"I'm not predictable," he says.

"I wish he were *more* predictable to tell you the truth," I say.

"You only think that because you don't know him well enough yet," Nina says. "It's true," she adds at the dark look Jack gives her. "If you're not at the pub or our place, you're holed up in your apartment reading with that cat. You need to live a little, Jack."

"Sounds like a pretty good life to me," I say, and Jack sends me a grateful smile.

"Well, at the very least, you ought to start tattooing again." Nina slows her pace to fall in line with me and Jack. "He always says he'll look into it, but he never does."

"Why don't you?"

"Things changed," Jack says. "And I don't need to *live a little*. Work. Family. Cats. Books. What else do I need?"

"Dreams. Adventure. *Love*," Nina says.

"Not all of us can spend our twenties falling in love on super-yachts," he says, something like a warning in his tone.

Nina is quiet for a moment. "Fair enough."

There's an awkward silence as we continue down the road. I'm not sure what the context is here, and I don't plan on asking. But I hate silence, so when we pass a series of little houses all squashed beside each other, I say, "I've never seen so many colorful houses. It's like walking around in a candy store."

"Those are called the Deck of Cards," Jack says. "And they're the most Instagrammable landmark in Cobh. The secret to getting a good photo is to go around the block behind this park," he says, pointing to a small green area on the opposite side of the street. "Hold your phone above the wall, and you'll get a great shot of the houses and the cathedral too."

"Why're they called that?" I ask.

"Because if the bottom house fell down, so would all the rest. Like a house of cards," he says.

"I can't tell if you're joking or not."

"It's a joke, but I'm not joking. They're really called that. Haven't you heard? They say the people of County Cork are the cleverest in all of Ireland."

"By *they*," Nina says, "he means the people of County Cork."

When we arrive at a small but charming mid-terrace home a few minutes later, Nina unlocks the door, and I follow her inside. For the past year, I've slept mostly in hostels or on trains. It's been a long time since I've been in someone's home. Shoes are lined up at a small bench in the entryway. Candid family photos of Nina and Ollie and their two daughters (whose names escape me but both begin with the letter J) decorate the walls. In the living room, a basket of toys is tipped onto its side. Giant building blocks spill out onto the carpet.

When I see homes like this—imperfect but clearly loved—it makes my chest ache. I want to have a place like this. Somewhere to belong. A place that's mine, where I can be myself with people who understand me and like me just the way I am. People who don't wish I was someone else.

"Make yourself at home," Nina says once the babysitter leaves. "I'm going to check on the girls."

Nina disappears upstairs, leaving Jack and me alone in the living room. I take in as many details as I can. The décor is eclectic and sophisticated and cozy all at once. There are two slate-gray couches that look more comfortable than any bed I've slept in over the last year. Both have more couch pillows than seems necessary, and I want to laugh when I spot a few that have tumbled to the floor along with a chunky knit throw blanket in rainbow colors. On the coffee table are heavy books about fashion and cooking along with board books like *The Very Hungry Caterpillar* and *Goodnight Moon*.

I feel Jack watching me when I pick up a picture frame from a side table. The photo inside is of Ollie and Jack in front of the Local. The name of the pub is spelled out in gleaming gold letters, popping against the green facade of the building. In the photo, Jack and Ollie have their arms around each other's shoulders. They both wear wide grins as they squint into the sunlight. If I hadn't seen this photo, I would've never guessed Ollie was physically capable of a smile like that.

"That was one of the best days of my life," Jack says. It's the first thing he's said since Nina went upstairs.

"Why?"

He leans against the wall with a sigh. "I was twenty-two when Da died and we inherited the pub. I hadn't seen Ollie in about fifteen years, so I ran the place myself at first. It was . . . overwhelming. I never thought Ollie would come home, but then he did. That's the first day we ran the pub together."

*Fifteen years?* There are so many questions I want to ask that I don't know where to start. "I'm sorry about your dad."

"Don't be."

I want to know more, but then Nina appears on the bottom step. "Bed's all made up. I've left out a pair of pajamas and any toiletries you might need. There are some clothes in the drawer if there's anything you'd like to change into tomorrow. Nothing wild. T-shirts and jeans. Don't take this the wrong way, but you don't exactly strike me as a couture girl."

"Told you she's always prepared," Jack says. He pushes off from the wall. "Well, I better get going. It was nice to meet you, Raine. Think about that job, yeah? I hope you'll say yes, but I understand if you can't. Stop by the pub tomorrow and let me know. Either way, I'll be happy to see you. Just give me a heads-up before you come over."

"Okay, yeah. I'll stop by either way."

When our eyes meet, I feel like there's something more I want to say, but I'm not sure what. He clears his throat and looks away, then waves goodbye to me and Nina after he's tugged on his boots. Just as he reaches for the door, I call out, "Wait! You never gave me your number."

Jack pauses. He pulls out his phone and types a message. "Now I have," he says, shooting me one last smile before shutting the door behind him.

A second later, my phone buzzes.

**UNKNOWN NUMBER**
This is Jack ☺

I save his number as a contact. I feel Nina's eyes on me and realize I'm smiling to myself, so I pocket my phone without replying.

"Have you ever heard of the Drunken Joey?" she asks.

"The what?"

She waves a hand. "It's a cocktail. I'll make you one. You look like you could use another drink."

When I head upstairs two hours later, I'm more than a little tipsy. Halfway through our second drink, Ollie returned home, and listening to his and Nina's stories about life working on yachts was just the distraction I needed. Even so, all night my mind kept drifting to Jack.

I change into the pajamas Nina lent me, then flop onto the bed and reread his message, smiling to myself as I type out a reply.

> **RAINE**
> I don't think the most professional future
> coworker I'll ever have would use emojis.

I'm surprised when he replies right away.

> **JACK**
> So, I'm your future coworker?

Even though I'm not sure how it'll work, I don't feel ready to leave Cobh just yet. I want to find my things if I can. I like Nina and Ollie and Jack. And I really could use a bit of a break from the hostels and trekking to new cities. Not a long one. It would only be for a little while, like Jack said, and if I have to get stuck anywhere for a few months, I'd much rather be stuck here than at home.

I type a reply to Jack, then delete it, then type it again and hit send before I can change my mind.

> **RAINE**
> If I can find a place to live, then yes.

I stare at my phone, excited and a little worried I've just made another one of my impulsive mistakes. I watch the words **Jack is typing** . . . above our chat.

> **JACK**
> I've found the perfect place. Rent-free,
> and the commute is glorious.

**RAINE**

I'm afraid to ask.

**JACK**

Don't be. You'll love it. I'll show you tomorrow.

A moment later, he sends a photo of Sebastian fast asleep in his lap. Beyond the sleeping cat, I can see a bit of color on Jack's shins. More tattoos. I zoom in but can't make out what they are. I wonder how many he has and where else they might be.

Really, what was in those drinks? Because I have never been attracted to a man's partially obscured shins before.

**JACK**

See how relieved Sebastian is that you've agreed
to be my most professional coworker?

I laugh, then make a goofy face and snap a selfie. If this angle happens to highlight my cleavage, it's completely unintentional.

**RAINE**

You promised to be the most professional
coworker I've ever had. I promised nothing.
Look at me, I don't have a professional
bone in my body.

It takes only three seconds for me to regret sending the photo, and I panic. *What do you think you're doing sending a photo like that to your de facto boss?* the voice of reason says.

I'd delete it, but Jack has already seen it. I stare at the banner above the chat that switches between **Jack is typing . . .** and **Online** for what feels like forever. I'm halfway through typing an apology when his reply appears.

**JACK**

As if I haven't been looking at you all night.

Before I can even think about how to respond, another message comes in.

**JACK**

Is what I would say if I weren't the most
professional coworker you've ever had.

I roll my eyes.

**JACK**

But since I am the most professional coworker
you've ever had, I will just say good night.
Good night, Raine.

I clutch my phone to my chest, unable to stop myself from grinning. The voice of reason warns me that this is not what reasonable people do. They do not take random jobs they are not qualified for, or stay in a stranger's home, or flirt with their sort-of-boss they've known for all of four hours. But I have never been a reasonable person. Why start now?

# Five

## JACK

After I walk Nina and Raine home, I head back to the pub. As soon as I step inside, I feel Ollie's eyes on me, but I zip behind the bar and pretend not to notice when he follows me into the kitchen. I keep my eyes on the floor and hold my breath as I pass through it and to our office so I won't have to stop and make sure the knives are where they ought to be. It's only once I'm seated behind the desk that I look up at Ollie standing in the doorway. He's wearing a scowl, of course. It's only almost always present, but I like to joke that it's more permanent than my tattoos.

I nod to the door. "Mind shutting that? I've got paperwork to prepare."

"Mind telling me what the hell you think you're doing?"

Jesus, he seems even grumpier about all this than I expected. I pull open a filing cabinet, riffling through the folders until I find the forms Raine will need to fill out tomorrow if, no, *when* she takes the job.

I hold up the forms. "I think I'm doing paperwork, like I said."

I try to keep my expression serious, hoping to convey the part of *very logical business owner* convincingly. But it's no use. I'm awful at it. Nina says I have *resting imp face* because I always look like I'm planning mischief.

What can I say? Life is better when you don't take it too seriously.

For being brothers, Ollie and I aren't much alike. Perhaps it's all the time we spent apart, or maybe it's the ten years between us, but I'm convinced we would've turned out opposites no matter what. Ollie's intense. He takes almost everything seriously. Whereas I treat every interaction as if it's some sort of game. Probably because everything feels like a game to me. On bad days, it feels like a game with nonsensical rules. Rules I know don't actually have consequences, but rules I have to follow nonetheless. It's exhausting.

So on the good days, I have as much fun as I can.

Ollie crosses his arms over his chest. "Quit acting the maggot, Jackie, you know what I'm talking about."

I tip back in the office chair and prop my feet up on the desk.

"And for Christ's sake, keep your fecking feet on the floor. We have to share that, you know."

I sit upright again with a sigh. "Why so touchy today, Ollie Wollie?"

He gives me an incredulous look. "Because my smartass brother is hiring random people off the fecking street without so much as asking my opinion."

"I didn't hire her off the street. I hired her from within the pub."

Ollie drags his hands over his face. "All right, fun's over. Tell me what you think you're doing offering that girl a job."

"There's not much to say. She's perfect for the job. So I offered her the job."

He stares at me, then closes his eyes as if praying for patience, which is probably what he's doing. I'd guess he's running through the Serenity Prayer in his head. Mum was always muttering it when we were kids. I bet he's thinking the words so fast he doesn't register a single one. I could never pray it like that. I have to pay attention to every single word. I have to get them all right. Otherwise it might not count, or worse, something bad will happen. Even now, I feel my pulse pick up. I focus on *not* thinking the opening line to that prayer, because if I do, I'll have to say the whole thing, and I'll have to say it right, and I really have better things to do right now.

Ollie lets out a slow sigh and opens his eyes again. "How's that girl perfect for the job? She's a busker. She's not even from here. She doesn't know the first thing about us or the pub."

"Now, now. Don't go talking about your future employee like that."

"*My* employee? No, Jackie. You hired her. She's *your* employee. Does she even have a résumé? Did you run a background check? Call her references?"

"It's on my to-do list." I snatch a pen and a Post-it note from the desk and jot down a reminder to run a background check. I pause, then add, *Rare Gibson guitar, Ireland sticker on back.*

"You needn't bother adding anything to your to-do list. She's not working here. Hire someone else."

I toss the pen onto the desk. "Ollie. You sat through the interviews today. They were awful."

"I wouldn't go so far as to call them awful."

"They were *boring.*"

"So what? I don't see why we need someone in the first place. Why change the pub? Business is . . . fine."

He says the last word like he knows he's full of shite. Which he *does*, because he *is*. I spin a slow circle in the office chair, halting once I face him again. "You already know this isn't the life I wanted, but it's the one I have. It's killing me to be here every day, living right above this place, when it still feels like it's *his*, you know? It's been five years, and even though we've taken down most of his stuff, it's just . . ." How to explain? Our father is dead, but it doesn't always feel that way. I don't hate my life here in Cobh, even if it wasn't what I'd have chosen for myself. And yet . . . I still feel as if I am living the life *Da* wanted me to live. Running the pub *Da* wanted me to run. Living in the flat *Da* wanted me to live in. All I want is to feel calm and in control for once in my life. *My* life.

But it's impossible to feel any sort of peace when I'm still haunted by the ghost of a man who once sprained my wrist because I left the milk out overnight.

But if anyone can understand, it's Ollie. "I want this to be *our* pub. I want to change things, but . . . I don't know what else to do. And you, my dear big brother, as wonderful and, dare I say, cheerful, as you are, have enough on your plate. We've just got too much baggage to do this on our own. We need an outside perspective. Someone who doesn't have a connection to *him*, or this place, or you, or me. Now's the perfect time. It'll be easier for Mum if we do it while she's away on holiday with Ed. And Raine is perfect for the job, even if she doesn't look it on paper."

Ollie sighs, and I can tell I'm wearing him down. "You sure you and that girl don't have a connection?"

"Well, of course we've got *some* sort of connection, but not in the way you're thinking."

He gives me a skeptical look.

I do a slow spin in the office chair again. "Okay, so *maybe* in that way a little." I grab hold of the desk to stop myself and prop my chin in my hand. "She's . . . pretty. Funny too." My eyes are fixed on the schedule taped to the wall, but talking about Raine has me thinking about her mouth again. I glance at Ollie, who has a smug look on his face. "And look at me, I'm gorgeous. A few sparks are inevitable, but that's not why I offered her the job."

"Then why did you?"

"I had a good feeling about it."

"If you want me on board, I'm gonna need more than that."

I look away to gather my thoughts, and my attention snags on a corner of the desk. Jacqueline fell while she and Josie were running around in here the other day. What if she hit her head against the corner of this desk? She's got all that hair; it could be easy to miss a lump on her head. What if she developed a brain bleed? I didn't see her fall. She didn't say anything about her head, just her knees. But what if—

"Jackie."

I look up at Ollie. "How's Tiny Jack? That kid's got a ton of energy, doesn't she? She hasn't been taking longer naps, has she?"

"What the hell are you talking about?"

"Jacqueline. The little blond one with the Muppet hair. About yea high." I gesture to what I guess to be her height. "Surprisingly cute for someone who got half her genes from you."

"I know who my own daughter is, Jackie."

"Well, that's a relief." I drum my fingers against the desk. "That kid has a great vocabulary for a two-year-old. Have you noticed? Some toddlers, you can hardly understand what they're saying. It would be weird if she was suddenly slurring her speech, wouldn't it? She hasn't been acting weird, has she?"

"The only one acting weird around here is you."

"Which is hardly anything new," I say, relieved Ollie hasn't noticed anything, but only a little. It would be easy for him to miss something. He's not even home right now. Nina is, though. I pull my phone from my pocket and contemplate texting her. I'll just tell her Jacqueline hit her head, even though I'm not sure she really did, and then Nina will go make sure she's okay. I know I shouldn't do that. Martina, the therapist I used to see, would tell me that I'm just getting others to perform my compulsions for me.

*That's a rather pessimistic way of looking at it, Martina. Some might call it good delegating.*

"*You'll only make the thoughts worse.*"

*Fuck off, Martina, with your normal brain that only thinks normal thoughts.*

And then I think, *undo, undo, undo, undo* and press my fingertips to the desk, because actually, I like Martina, and she is a great therapist, and I should have called her weeks ago when I started arguing with the intrusive thoughts again.

But things aren't *that bad.* They were far worse before. This is just a small slip-up in my recovery, one I can come back from. And besides, the thought of calling Martina, of telling her that I've fucked up the progress I made and am scared I'll end up where I was three years ago . . . it's too much.

I shove my phone back into my pocket without texting Nina. *See, Martina? I'm fine, and I can feel you rolling your imaginary eyes from here.*

"And you *really* think this girl can do what you need her to?" Ollie asks.

"So Raine's never managed a project like this before! She's got insight. Vision. She's seen tons of pubs. She's . . . creative. Creativity— that's a transferable skill, you know."

"And where's she supposed to live? She doesn't have any money. I know you think you're a good judge of character, but I don't recommend forking over anything in advance before we know more about what we're dealing with here."

*More about what we're dealing with here.* I perk up at that. He's actually considering it. "Oh, I've got that all taken care of." I figured it out on my walk back from his and Nina's place. "She can stay in the flat."

"What flat?"

"The flat upstairs, of course."

Ollie looks at me as if I've said I have an appointment for laser tattoo removal. "Jack . . . *you* live in the flat. This whole situation is already questionable. You can't have the girl move in with you."

I shoot him a glare. "I know I seem crazy, but I'm not senseless. She can take the flat while she's working here. I'll stay with you and Nina."

"Now don't go putting words in my mouth. I've never called you crazy. Not once."

We call each other names all the time, but he's right. He's never called me that. "All I'm saying is I know I do things that don't always make sense to you. Hell, I do things that don't make sense to *me*. But this isn't one of them."

"What makes you think I want you moving in with me?"

I grin at him. "Why *wouldn't* you want me to move in with you?"

"I don't think we have enough time for me to list all the reasons."

"Oh, c'mon. We'll make up for lost time. It'll be fun. I can help out with Josie and Jacqueline. Nina'll be thrilled. She's always saying there aren't enough hours in the day. I'll be like a live-in nanny. Consider me your personal Mary Poppins."

He narrows his eyes. "Always thought Mary Poppins was fecking annoying. Singing all over the place. Dumping sugar down kids' throats."

"Think of the children. They love Uncle Jack."

Ollie pinches the bridge of his nose. "You realize you're bending over backward to make this work, right? Please tell me you know this makes absolutely no sense."

"If I say I agree with you, will you do it? Try it, at least?"

He looks as if he's praying for patience again. To hell with serenity, I think. *God, grant me the ability to actually change shite.*

"You're not bringing that fecking cat with you," he finally says. "It's bad enough him coming into the pub. You know I'm allergic."

I leap from the chair and give Ollie a slap on the shoulder.

"But don't get too attached to the idea of her working here. I want to reassess in a month, and if things aren't working out—"

"Done," I say, and goad him into a reluctant handshake.

"I'm not convinced this is really about the job," he says when I take my seat behind the desk again.

"It's about the job."

"If you say so."

When Ollie turns to go, I say, "There is just . . . one more thing." He looks at me with a wary expression.

I try to keep my voice light, as if this is a totally reasonable request. "If it wouldn't be too much trouble, could we perhaps, keep the sharp items . . . elsewhere . . ." At the look on his face I add, "Just temporarily!"

Ollie doesn't say anything at first. "You're asking me, a chef, to take all the knives out of my house, so you can move in with me for absolutely no reason?"

Just the thought of those knives has my heart beating faster. "Only the very sharp ones."

"Jackie . . ."

"How about this? You can keep the sharp things in the house but hide them. Don't tell me where they are. If I don't know where they are, I can't worry about them." *Or waste my entire morning checking and double-checking they're where they ought to be.*

Ollie just looks at me. I hate that I'm like this. There was a time not too long ago when I could walk through the kitchen to this office without holding my breath or pausing to check the knives. I could even hold a knife in my hands. I could sit at a table with my nieces and use a pair of scissors. The thoughts were still there, but I could let them float through without giving in to my compulsions.

*"Please,"* I say.

Ollie sighs. "Fine." He shakes his head. "I don't know how you talk me into this shite."

"It's because you love me."

"A lot of good it does me."

Once he's gone, I sit at my desk and try to look over invoices. I'm too wired to sleep, but too exhausted to actually work, so I end up doodling on Post-its. Sebastian on a stool. A girl with wavy hair and hiking boots and a smile that must have some sort of gravitational pull. And . . . fuck, I need to stop thinking about this girl. I toss the notes into the wastebasket, then check that the knives are where they ought to be before I lock up the pub and trudge upstairs. I settle onto the couch to read a book with Sebastian curled up in my lap.

It's after one in the morning when my phone pings. I glance at the screen, and the sight of Raine's name has me wide awake again.

**RAINE**
I don't think the most professional future
coworker I'll ever have would use emojis.

I set my book on the floor and read the message again, a million different replies flooding my mind all at once.

*Most professional coworker. Most professional coworker. Most professional coworker. Most professional coworker.*

Maybe if I say it enough times, I can keep Ollie from being right.

# Six

The next day, I lead Raine upstairs to show her the flat. As soon as we step inside, Sebastian leaps from the window overlooking the street and rubs up against her legs. It makes me wonder if someone has switched out my cat for another, because this is a cat who darts beneath my bed as soon as he hears I have company. A cat who loves exactly one person—me—and tolerates two others—my nieces, Josie and Jacqueline.

Raine mutters to herself and pulls a toy baguette from one of the shopping bags in her arms.

"Nina took me to the store this morning, and I just *had* to get this for him," she says. "I looked for a bagel one, but they only had baguettes and cinnamon rolls, so I went with the most bagel-like option."

"Why is the baguette the more bagel-like option?" I ask. "Cinnamon rolls have the more bagel-like shape."

"Please tell me you're joking."

I am, but I want to see where she'll go with this.

"It's all about the flavor, and a bagel tastes more like a baguette than a cinnamon roll." She rips off the price tag and sets the toy before Sebastian.

"All right, you win," I say.

Sebastian rubs his face against the toy baguette. "Look at that," she says. "Seems you and Sebastian both have a love of carbs."

"I'm starting to worry he's going to like you better than me."

"It's my natural charm." She grins, then clumsily takes off her boots without untying them and leaves them in a heap by the door. She doesn't wait for me to give her some grand tour. Just swans into the living room as if she's been here a thousand times.

I have to agree. The girl is charming.

I follow her into the living room, nearly bumping into her when she halts beside the couch and turns to face me. "Hold on," she says, and I take a step back. She looks at Sebastian on the floor, then scans the room. "I can't possibly stay here."

I look around the flat. The place is nice, especially this late in the morning. Natural light floods in through two large windows. Squares of sunlight scatter across the wood flooring. The decor isn't half-bad either. I think, anyway. I've brought in as much color as I can. The first piece of furniture I bought was a canary-yellow couch. Mum about killed me when I tried to get it up the stairs by myself. But I was so mixed up about coming home, about running the pub, about living up here in this flat, that I didn't know who or how to ask for help. In the end, Mum called Ed, one of the regulars, and he helped me get it up here. I was grateful to him for the help, but even more grateful he didn't try to talk to me. He helped me out a lot those first few months I was running the pub without Ollie. But then he had to go and start dating Mum, and while I like the man, I don't want to like him and make sure he knows it. Childish, I know.

It didn't matter how much I changed things in the flat, though, because I hate the place on principle. If I didn't, I'd never move out so some girl could take it over for a few months.

"Why can't you stay here?" I ask.

"*You* live here," Raine says. "When you said I could use the place above the pub, I didn't realize you meant *your* place. It is your place, right?"

"I won't be living here while you're living here, if that's what you're worried about."

"But where are *you* going to live?"

"I'll stay with Ollie and Nina. I've been meaning to spend more time with my nieces anyway."

Raine chews her lip and looks over the living room again. "You can't let me stay here for free, and I couldn't possibly afford to rent a place this nice."

"Ollie and I don't owe anything on the building," I say. "There's no need to charge you rent."

She hums to herself for a moment. "You have to let me pay *something*."

"If you must pay something, you can throw some money at the utilities."

"Utilities . . ." She shakes her head. "I don't know . . . it feels like too much."

"Consider it a benefit of the job."

She laughs. "This is the best freaking job I've ever had. I keep waiting for the catch."

Ah, I was wondering when would be a good time to bring this up. "There's no catch, but there is a . . . cat."

She eyes Sebastian. "Well, yeah."

"What I mean is . . . Ollie is allergic to cats. So Princess Ugly here would have to stay with you. He usually hangs around the pub during the day whenever I'm there, and I'm happy to do all the litter box changing and feeding, but he'll be around, is what I mean. I hope that won't be a bother."

Raine looks at me as if I've just said something offensive. "You're telling me this place is rent-free *and* comes with a cute roommate? Sounds like a dream. I'm happy to do the cat chores. It'll make me feel a teensy tiny bit better about mooching off of you."

Raine peers down at Sebastian, who has abandoned the baguette and is rubbing up against her legs again. *Suck-up*, I think. She scoops him into her arms, and I want to laugh, because he's so big he practically covers her entire torso.

"Jeez, he weighs a million pounds," Raine says. "Excuse me, a million *kilos*." She turns away, humming to herself as she wanders around the room. She pauses in front of the gallery I've hung on the wall separating the living room and the kitchen. "Did you do these?"

I move to stand beside her. "I did."

Most of the pieces are ink drawings from my tattooing days. Some of them I actually did tattoo; some of them I wanted to tattoo, but I quit before I got the chance.

Raine inspects a surrealist drawing of a man with a blender for a head. The blender is filled with various fruits and bits of rubbish. His expression is off-kilter, one blueberry eye lower than the other. Raine leans closer.

"Are those . . . cigarette butts for eyebrows?"

"Em . . . they are, yeah."

I know it's odd. Not all my stuff is so out there. I did a lot of traditionalism and realism too, but surrealism was always my favorite. It never fails to evoke an emotional response, whether it be good or bad. I once told Martina that I have so little control over my own mind that it's cathartic to put something nonsensical into the world on purpose.

Raine leans away and nods. "I feel you, blender dude. Half of my thoughts are garbage too."

I don't realize I'm waiting for her reaction until she says that, and my shoulders relax a bit.

She scans the wall, then slides her gaze to me. "Did you design your tattoos?"

"Some of them. But not any of these," I say, and nod to my arms.

"Where all do you have tattoos?"

"Oh . . . here and there. It would be quicker to tell you where I don't have them."

"Interesting . . ." The way she looks me over has me imagining situations in which she might find every single one.

*Most professional coworker.* I ask the first question that comes to mind. Anything to knock those scenarios out of my head before it becomes obvious what I'm thinking about. "Do you have any?"

"Tattoos?"

I nod.

"Not yet. But I've been wanting to get one." She turns away and drifts over to my bedroom door.

I trail after her. "What do you want to get?"

"Hmm . . . I don't know." She pauses before the door to my bedroom. "Do you mind?"

I shake my head. She sets Sebastian down, then opens the door to poke her head inside. After a moment she turns to me with a barely contained smile. "Nina was right, your bed is huge."

I roll my eyes.

She pulls the door shut again. "Oh, I know! Maybe you can give me my first tattoo before I go."

"I don't tattoo anymore," I say.

"Maybe you'll change your mind."

"I don't think so."

She walks over to the three bookcases that line the wall opposite the couch. "Jeez, you really do read everything." She squats in front of the first bookcase and drags a finger over the spines, slowing when she reaches the books I have about Obsessive Compulsive Disorder. Perhaps I should've tucked a few out of sight. One or two books about

OCD could be explained away, but seven? I tidied up this morning, but I didn't expect her to do such a thorough examination.

My OCD isn't a secret, but it's never an easy conversation. I usually hold off on telling people because it inevitably changes things. Not at first, but only because most people have no idea what OCD really is. They assume I'm obsessed with germs or lining up office supplies, but I'm not. And when people learn what my intrusive thoughts are really about, they look at me differently.

Jack is a clown. Jack is fun. Jack worries he'll kill someone on a weekly basis. Jack isn't one hundred percent sure he hasn't and will ask you about it a million times. It's all fun and games until my OCD flares up. Then people decide it's too much. The whole time my ex was breaking up with me, I wanted to say, *If you think it's too much for you, imagine being me!* But I didn't say it. There was no point.

But maybe I *should* tell Raine about it now. She'll only be here for twelve weeks, but the way things are going, she'll find out anyway. More importantly, I like her more than I should. If I'm not mistaken, she likes me too. Maybe if she'd shown up a year ago it would be different, but she's here now. I'm not at my best and don't need to drag anyone else into it, however temporarily. And sure, we've agreed for Ollie to be her boss, but it's just semantics. I own the pub; she works at the pub. Best to put that wedge between us now, just in case.

But Raine doesn't say anything about the books, and when she gets to her feet, I lose my nerve. I want a little more time to be Jack before I become Jack-who-has-OCD.

I show her the bathroom next.

"Wow," Raine says as soon as we step inside. "What a bathtub."

I've spent a lot of time updating things since moving home. It keeps me busy, and every improvement makes it feel a little more like it belongs to me and not *him*, especially the changes I know he'd hate.

Like this bathtub. Da would say it's a waste of space, too feminine for a man. I use it as often as possible. An excellent reading spot, actually.

When Raine leans over the edge of the tub, I try not to stare at her arse. She turns over her shoulder, and I flick my gaze up to hers, hoping it isn't obvious that I failed miserably at not staring at her arse.

"Well, I know where I'll be every night," she says with a grin. "I haven't taken a good bath in ages."

*Don't think about it. Don't think about it. Don't think about it. Don't think about it.* I'm not sure if she is doing this to me on purpose or not, but the problem with a brain like mine is that whenever I try not to think about something, the more it boomerangs back into my head, especially if it is something I shouldn't or don't want to think about. This is definitely in the first category.

I turn away from her and straighten the toothpaste tube beside the sink while discreetly pressing my fingertips to the counter and mentally undoing the thoughts I haven't even thought yet, because I'm unsure if thinking about *not* thinking about them counts as thinking about them, and even though I don't believe in hell, I am suddenly terrified I'm wrong, and it does exist, and I'm going to end up there.

"I have a washer farther down the hall," I say, desperate to change the subject. "I don't have a dryer, but I do have a clothes-drying rack."

"Great," she says. "I'm going to need it, seeing as I have exactly five outfits, and two of them are Nina's." She turns back around, thank God, and perches on the side of the tub. She tugs at the shirt she's wearing. It says *Straight out of patience #momlife.* "Would you believe me if I said this was the most normal one?"

"I would."

She sits with one leg crossed over the other. Something about her mismatched socks and the way she bounces her leg up and down makes me want to grab a pencil and a piece of paper, to capture her in a way a photograph never could.

I turn away from her to face the sink. "I know you went shopping this morning, but I have extra pads, tampons, all that sort of stuff in here," I say, nudging the cabinet beneath the sink with my toe. "I've also got some hair elastics and one or two little deodorants too, I think."

"Pads and tampons?"

I pull open the cabinet with my foot. "We keep the restrooms in the pub stocked with this stuff and have a ton extra, so I brought some up in case you'd need it."

Raine laughs. "Well, thanks for the supplies. They should definitely last until April." She gets to her feet with a sigh. "A man who considers menstrual needs? That's sexy as hell." As soon as the words are out of her mouth she freezes. "You didn't hear me say that."

I most definitely did and am adding it to the list of things about Raine Hart I will likely spend the rest of the day thinking about. "I've no idea what you're talking about," I say.

"Um, well . . ."

"Should we . . ."

"Go to another room?" She gets to her feet. "Yes, please. I think I've seen enough of the bathroom for now."

She pushes past me as if she can't leave the bathroom fast enough. I watch her go and, *shite*, now I'm staring at her arse again. In the hall, I step around her and lead the way into the kitchen, where we find Sebastian lounging on the floor with his toy baguette. When he takes notice of Raine, he picks up the baguette in his mouth and crosses the kitchen to drop it at her feet.

Raine looks down at him. "Oh! Let's get this string off for you, buddy. That's a choking hazard." She picks up the toy, and I notice the string from the price tag is still attached to it. "Sorry," she says, her eyes flicking to me as she winds her finger around the string. "I should've paid better attention." She tugs at the string but can't snap it off. "Can I borrow your scissors?"

The word *scissors* immediately has me on edge. "I don't have any up here," I say. "But there are some in the pub."

"Oh." Raine frowns at the string and . . . *shite*, I'm looking at her mouth again.

She probably thinks I'm an arse for not offering to run down and get the scissors myself. I would. I would love to get them for her and bring them up here, but just thinking about holding a pair of scissors and bringing them into the flat, the very idea of being around her with them and passing them into her hands . . .

Before I lose my nerve, I blurt out, "I have disturbing thoughts about scissors."

Raine pauses in another attempt to rip off the string and looks up at me.

"That's why I don't keep any up here," I explain. "They make me . . . anxious." An understatement if I've ever heard one. Scissors throw me into a full-on panic. Scissors put the most violent images into my head. Scissors make me question my very character.

The thought has me desperate to touch my fingers against something, but I don't want to seem too jumpy. Fortunately, the counter is just behind me. I try to look calm and casual as I lean against it to press my fingertips along its edge and think, *undo, undo, undo, undo.*

Raine looks down at the toy and yanks the string again. "Because of your OCD?"

It takes me a moment to register the question, but Raine must interpret my surprise as annoyance because she looks at me with wide eyes and says, "Sorry! That was a super invasive question. I didn't mean to—"

"It's all right—"

"I shouldn't assume. I didn't mean to diagnose you or anything—"

"But you're right."

Her gaze meets mine, expression hesitant. "Still . . . it's none of my business. It was rude of me to just blurt that out."

"Do you . . . know a lot about OCD?" I ask.

"Probably more than most people. I'm sure it's hard to believe, but I finished two and a half years of medical school before dropping out to play music. In an alternate universe, a different Raine is getting pimped during rotations."

It *is* hard to believe. Not because I don't think she's capable, but because I can't picture her in a pair of scrubs, that red hair tucked out of sight. "Pimped?"

She laughs at my expression. "Not pimped like, you know. Pimped stands for *put in my place.* It's when the attendings quiz you during rotations."

"Do they teach a lot about OCD in medical school?" I ask.

"Everyone gets a little training on it. Not enough, but some. I wanted to go into emergency psychiatry, though, so I know more than most people, I think." She tugs at the string again, and when it doesn't snap off, looks up at me. "Sorry you have the really shitty thoughts. Sounds rough."

"It is." I stare at her, unsure what else to say. I've never met someone outside of a therapist or doctor who actually understood OCD without my having to explain it. Hell, there are *doctors* I've had to explain it to.

"What about knives?" Raine asks.

"And razors, box cutters, even knitting needles," I say.

She looks at me as if she has no idea what I'm talking about, but then she laughs and pulls the string on the toy baguette taut. "I meant for this!"

"Oh . . . here." I pull my keys from my pocket and Raine tosses the toy baguette to me. I snap the string off with a key and pass the toy back to her.

"There we go," she says when she sets the toy in front of Sebastian again. "So, bad thoughts about sharp pointy things. Anything else you want me to know about your OCD?"

I watch her wander over to the fridge. She examines the photos and cards from friends I've stuck there while I tap out a nervous rhythm on the counter. "It might make your job difficult at times," I say. "There are a few triggers related to the pub, and some of the changes you'll be making are ones I've tried to do myself, but the intrusive thoughts are . . . a lot. Ollie and Nina have tried to help, but they always let me put things back to the way they were before. I know that's probably not what you signed up for, so if you've changed your mind about the job, I understand."

Raine takes one of the Christmas cards from the fridge and turns it over. It's from the tattoo shop I used to work at in Dublin. For the first two years after Da died and I came home to run the pub, I managed to head up to Dublin a few times a month to tattoo clients, but then my OCD got in the way, and it became too much. I haven't worked at the shop in three years, but Shauna, my mentor, sends me a card every year, and every year, she writes the same Pablo Picasso quote on the back of it: *The chief enemy of creativity is good sense.* Raine reads it and smiles.

"So just to recap," she says, "certain changes around the pub might trigger your OCD, and sometimes it's not pretty."

"Right."

"And you need someone who won't give up if your OCD makes things messy."

"Exactly."

Raine searches my face, then nods. "I can do that."

"You can?"

She returns the Christmas card to the refrigerator. "That's the only part of this job I'm confident I can do."

"And the flat?"

She leans against the counter with a sigh. "I did say I only turn down free stuff once, so I can't say no to a place like this, can I?" She looks down at Sebastian. "Or a roommate like you, huh, floofs?"

When she lifts her gaze to mine, the first thing I think is, *I've fucked up*, because it's at that exact moment I realize I'm going to be undone by this girl.

# Seven

## RAINE

When Jack leaves on my first night in his apartment, I shut the door behind me and try not to think about the many ways this can go wrong.

Yesterday I was wandering around Cobh, desperate to find my stolen things and positive I'd be booking a flight back to Boston. Yesterday Jack Dunne was a stranger. Now I'm living in his place. Now I'm in Cobh for twelve weeks. I can hear my mother's voice in my head. *You just don't think, Raine.*

It probably seems that way when I misplace my keys for the fifth time in a week or miss the bus because I lost track of time playing guitar or forget to charge my phone. (Or impulsively accept a job I am not qualified for and move into a strange man's apartment with his giant cat for a roommate.) But my problem isn't that I don't think. It's that my brain only has two modes: think everything all at once and make sense of none of it, or think about one thing obsessively at the expense of whatever actually needs my attention.

The point being, I am *always* thinking. Just never about the right things.

At the sound of Sebastian meowing, I look down and find him staring up at me with those huge green eyes.

"I don't speak cat," I say, then flop onto the couch.

Sebastian doesn't respond. He picks up his baguette and carries it to the cat perch in one corner of the living room.

"What should we binge-watch tonight, roomie?" I ask him. "Should we pretend to be intellectuals and watch a documentary?"

Sebastian licks himself, which I take to mean, *Don't kid yourself.*

I sigh. "You're right. Reality TV it is. What's popular these days?" I reach into the pocket of my hoodie for my phone, but it isn't there. I put it in the Ziploc bag holding my cash and passport, which I also thought was in the pocket of this hoodie but isn't.

I know I put it in a safe place. I remember putting it somewhere special, where I'd be sure to run into it. Given past experience, it probably is safe. Safe from *me*, because I never remember where these special memorable places are. After a few frantic minutes zipping through the flat, I sink onto the couch in frustration and catch sight of my boots by the door. *Of course.* I reach my boots in a few quick strides, and sure enough, the Ziploc bag is in my left boot.

I hold up the bag for Sebastian. "I can tell you're judging me, and I don't like it."

As soon as I slip the phone from the Ziploc bag, it buzzes in my hand with a video call from my sister. I'm not really in the mood to hear about her wonderful and successful life at medical school, but we've been playing phone tag all week, so I throw myself onto Jack's yellow couch and answer the call.

"Did you go running?" Clara asks as soon as her face pops up on the screen. "You look out of breath."

"Don't be ridiculous," I say, the wind knocked out of me from having landed a bit too hard on the couch. "You know I'd never willingly subject myself to structured cardio."

I smile at the familiar sight of my sister. Her dark hair is tied up into a bun. Perched on top of her head are the giant sunglasses I bought her two Christmases ago. An exact replica of the ones Audrey Hepburn—whom Clara is obsessed with—wore in *Breakfast at Tiffany's*. The year before that, I bought her a satin scarf just like the one in *Roman Holiday*, her favorite Hepburn movie.

Clara munches on a carrot stick and looks at me with that intense, clinical stare of hers. I roll onto my stomach and tuck a bright blue couch pillow beneath me. Really, Jack's apartment is ... wonderful. All the light. The colors. Interesting things to see everywhere. Clearly he has a great eye. Why hasn't this translated downstairs to the pub?

"What's up, doc?" I say.

Clara's mouth tips into a crooked smile. It's my favorite thing about her. It's not a beautiful smile, but it's a real one. "Lunch break," she says. "Where are you?"

"Ireland." I haven't told her or my parents anything that's happened in the last forty-eight hours. And thanks to Jack, I don't need to and never will.

"Well, yeah. That's obvious from your social media," Clara says. "Which is basically the only reason I know anything happening in your life, by the way."

"Sorry." We haven't talked much since she started medical school and I dropped out of it, which, like everything else, is my fault. It isn't that we don't get along. It's just hard to talk to her sometimes. She's more like our parents than I am. She's driven and focused. She knows exactly what she wants and how to get it. Whereas I'm usually not sure where I'm going to be from week to week.

Long story short: I may be traveling, but Clara is the one going places.

"But *where* are you exactly? That doesn't look like a hostel."

"This is my new place," I say, and flip the camera around so she can see the bookcases, the large windows, the gallery wall.

"Your new place?" Clara looks as if she's waiting for the punch-line to a joke.

"I'm taking a break from traveling for a bit," I say, and flip the camera back around to my face.

Clara is silent. And when there's silence, I can't help but fill it. Blame the faulty frontal lobe.

"I'm in a town called Cobh," I say. "It was the last port of call for the *Titanic* before it sank," I add, which is still the only fact I know about this place.

Clara frowns. "Why do you have a place in Cobh?"

"I got a job at a pub."

Clara munches another carrot, waiting until she's chewed and swallowed before continuing, because, unlike me, my sister has manners. "I thought music was your job," she says.

"The pub job is temporary. Where are *you*?" I ask, though I know she's sitting on one of the benches outside Harvard Medical School because I used to eat my lunch there too.

Clara doesn't take the bait to change the subject. "Why are you taking a break in Cobh? Come home. Then you wouldn't be wasting money on rent, and besides, you didn't come home for Thanksgiving, Christmas, or New Year's." She ticks off each holiday on her fingers. One, two, three strikes for Raine.

"I'm not wasting money on rent. Free lodging. Comes with the job."

"Free lodging comes with a bartending job?"

"I'm not bartending. I'm an entertainment coordinator. Just for twelve weeks. Then I'll be back on the road. Why take a break in Boston when I can take a break in *Ireland*."

Clara looks as if she's about to say something, but she shoves a carrot into her mouth instead.

"Want to meet my roommate?" I point the camera at Sebastian, who dozes on the cat perch, before Clara can answer.

"Cute," she says, though I really don't think she cares as much as she should. This cat is adorable.

"His name is Sebastian but—"

"Are you ever going to come home?" Clara interrupts.

"Home is where the Wi-Fi automatically connects," I say. "So *home* is a lot of places."

"Including Boston."

"Actually, I don't think my phone automatically connects to the Wi-Fi anywhere in the US now. I got a new one after I dropped my phone off Tower Bridge and it disappeared into the Thames. RIP."

Clara rolls her eyes but doesn't respond. I flip the camera to selfie mode again. "You could come visit *me*, you know. Now is the perfect time, since I'm staying put for a bit and have a nice place for once. You could probably use a vacation anyway. I should still be here during your spring recess. End of March, right?"

"Right."

I take a closer look at Clara and discover that she isn't as put together as she usually is. There are dark circles under her eyes. Wisps of frizzy hair stick out from her usually neat bun. There's a mysterious stain on her coat, normal for someone like me, but Clara once asked for a tiny iron and ironing board for Christmas so she could bring it with her to college and was genuinely excited to get Tide to Go pens in her stocking. "You look like shit."

Clara rolls her eyes. "Thanks, Lorraine."

"I mean you look like you *feel* like shit."

She sighs. "I don't see how that's any better."

"You can be beautiful while looking like you feel like a turd. It's a fact. Look it up."

Clara shakes her head, eyes darting away for a moment, and I start to actually worry. If I'm not mistaken, there are tears shining in her eyes. Before I can get a good look, she flips her sunglasses over her face, blocking me out.

I sit up on the couch. "Are you okay? Did something happen?"

Clara faces the camera again, but I can't tell what she's thinking with those sunglasses on. "I'm fine, but I've got to go. Can't be late for Essentials." She gives me a grin that is absolutely one hundred percent fake.

"But didn't that class already—" Clara's face disappears before I can say "end."

I stare at my phone. "That was weird, right?" I say to Sebastian.

He licks a paw, as if to say, *What would I know about it?*

"Trust me, that was weird."

Sebastian continues licking himself. If Clara wanted to tell me something, she would. It's probably just med school stress, but I don't want to leave things like that. I pull up our chat on my phone and type out a message.

> **RAINE**
> Seriously, come to Cobh. I'll take you to
> the Titanic museum and buy you a beer.
> Also, do you have any Raine-proof
> dinner recipes?

I wait for her to respond, but she doesn't. I toss my phone onto the couch and stare up at the ceiling, suddenly uninterested in reality TV after talking with Clara. I'm unsure how to fill my time without my guitar. Maybe I'll be mindful. I'll stare at the ceiling and meditate. I don't even last a minute before I'm bored out of my mind.

I sit up and spot Jack's bookcases across the room. I've never seen so many books in such a small home before. I choose a random book from the top shelf. "See?" I tell Sebastian. "I can be an intellectual too." I scan the title of the book in my hands. *The Shock of the New: The Hundred-Year History of Modern Art.* I hold it up for Sebastian. "Any good?"

Sebastian ignores me and keeps licking himself.

I flip to a random page and scan a paragraph. Something about art and how it uses emotion to connect us to the world. When Sebastian meows, I look up, unsure how long I've been standing there reading.

I tuck the book beneath my arm. Jack's shower has a glorious bathtub, and I haven't taken a good bath in ages. In the bathroom, I set my phone and the book on the sink. Something yellow catches my eye, and when I look at the mirror, I find a Post-it stuck there.

Jack's handwriting is neat and clear. My handwriting is practically illegible, even to me.

> *Turn the hot water tap at least halfway,*
> *but no more than a quarter-turn*
> *above that or you'll burn yourself. —J*

Beneath the words is a diagram of the hot water tap. There's a shaded area Jack has labeled *the safe zone*. To the left of the safe zone he's written *cryogenic therapy*. To the right, *literal Hell on Earth*. I laugh, then take the Post-it from the mirror and stick it into the book.

I turn on the tap as instructed and grab my phone.

> **RAINE**
> Thanks for the shower instructions.
> I'm not yet ready to leave the mortal
> plane. I've heard cryotherapy is great
> for anti-aging though.

I sit on the edge of the bathtub as it fills and continue to read the book. After a few minutes, my phone pings with a message from Jack.

**JACK**
It's excellent. I'm actually 67, not 27.

I chew on my lip and type out I've always been into older men but have better sense than to send it. As the tub fills, I walk out to the living room and snap a photo of Sebastian asleep on the cat perch.

                                        **RAINE**
                                You didn't tell me he was
                                    such a party animal.

**JACK**
Looks like you wore him out.

                                        **RAINE**
                            Nah, I think I bored him to sleep.
                            I'm a very underwhelming human.

**JACK**
I doubt it.

Something about the sound within the flat catches my attention, and I remember I've left the tap running. I make it to the bathroom and turn off the water just in time to keep the tub from overflowing. I let a bit of the water out, my heart racing at the near miss. I've hardly had the place to myself for an hour, and I'm already courting disaster.

Crisis averted, I undress and slip into the water. After setting my phone on the edge of the tub, I take the book in my hands. The note from Jack peeks out at the top. *The Shock of the New*, I think, tipping my head back to rest against the edge of the tub. That would be a good title for a song. Too bad I don't have my guitar.

And speaking of *new*, if I am going to be in this new place for a while, it's the perfect opportunity to be New Raine. New Raine reads every evening instead of scrolling on her phone for hours. New Raine does yoga in the morning and eats a balanced breakfast at a table instead of a half-frozen waffle as she's rushing out the door. New Raine always puts her keys and phone in the same place. New Raine doesn't have to say *I'm sorry* so much.

A reset is exactly what I need. A fresh start. My time here will be a trial run of this new and improved version of myself. All I need is a plan. I'll type one out right now and start tomorrow.

When I pick up my phone, I find a text from my sister. I hope she'll say something about coming to visit, but it's just a link to a one-pan chicken-and-veggies recipe. Perfect. I give the message a thumbs-up. New Raine will go to the grocery store and actually make this recipe before the veggies rot in the fridge, because New Raine not only cooks, but cooks meals with *vegetables*. New Raine eats however many servings of them you're supposed to have in a day. (Something New Raine needs to look up.)

I open my notes app. **New Raine's Morning Routine**, I type. To-morrow, I'll be a better version of myself. Someone who doesn't lose important documents inside of shoes, or leave the bathtub running, or talk to cats when other people are around.

I'll show Jack that he isn't wrong to believe in me. I'll show *myself.*

# *Eight*

New Raine manages to stick around for two whole days. And then, despite living directly above the pub, New Raine manages to be fifteen minutes late to work. Because believe it or not, simply *writing* a morning routine is not enough to make me a new person. Believe it or not, I have to actually *follow* it. And not just once, every day. Which wasn't so bad at first.

But today, when I went to find a ten-minute yoga routine, I somehow ended up watching cat videos with Sebastian and stumbled upon a T-shirt cat tent tutorial. It looked easy and like a much better use of my time than yoga. But of course it was not easy, and by the time I realized it was going to take up my entire morning before work, it was too late. I was *in it*. I kept glancing at my phone, telling myself I could finish this later. I needed to get in the shower. I needed to organize the note on my phone with all my ideas for the pub before my meeting with Jack. But I just couldn't move. I kept mentally revising how long it would take me to do things. I didn't really need five whole minutes for a shower if I was just washing my body, right?

(Wrong.) It wouldn't take more than sixty seconds to toss on a shirt, cardigan, and jeans, right? (Wrong.)

"I'm sorry I'm late," I say when I rush into the office. "I was making a cat tent for Sebastian out of a T-shirt and totally miscalculated how long it would take."

When I finally look at Jack, my heart leaps in my chest. He's seated at his desk with a mug of coffee in his hands. Today he's in a gray Henley that, with the sleeves pushed up to his elbows, shows off his forearm tattoos. Paired with dark jeans and pristine white sneakers, he looks like someone who has his shit together. While I, on the other hand, look like someone who got ready in under five minutes, which is accurate.

*I need to find a cardiologist*, I think.

He leans back in the chair. "Did you finish it?"

"The cat tent?"

Jack nods.

"Yes."

He swivels from side-to-side in the chair. "Did he like it?"

"The cat tent?"

Jack nods.

This conversation is ridiculous, and ridiculous is not the plan. I am trying to be New Raine, and New Raine is not ridiculous. But Sebastian really did love the cat tent, and I have the cutest photo of him lounging inside it. I decide to accept being ridiculous, just for the moment.

"He loved it." I cross the space between us to show Jack the photo. "He's a king."

"Sounds like a good enough reason to be late to me." When Jack looks up, our faces are so close that I'm suddenly self-conscious that my breath smells bad. Thank God brushing my teeth is one thing I *definitely* did this morning.

But I'm not sure if I remembered to put on deodorant, so I straighten and step back.

Jack picks up the mug from the desk and looks me over. He takes a sip, and the corner of his mouth tilts into a smile. "You ready to get to work?"

"Yup."

"You sure about that?"

"I think so. But the look on your face is making me doubt myself."

Jack squints at my feet. "Are those avocados on the one sock?"

As soon as he says it, I know why he's asking. "I'm not wearing my boots, am I?"

Jack simply raises his eyebrows, and I peer down to find that I am, in fact, wearing one avocado sock. The other sock is neon pink with dancing bananas on it and says, *Weekend Vibes.* "The store had an impressive selection of anthropomorphic foods to choose from," I say.

"I rather like avocados."

"Then you'd love the underwear I'm wearing. At least *that* matches one of my socks."

Jack chokes on his coffee mid-sip, and I realize that I have just described my underwear to my *most professional coworker.*

"Oh my God, I'm going to put on my boots," I say, already headed for the door. "If I'm not back in five minutes, it's because I've died of embarrassment."

I flee the office as quickly as I can. It was nice to be New Raine while it lasted, I suppose. But I shouldn't be surprised she didn't stick around long. This isn't the first time I've tried to be her. It always starts out great, but I inevitably lose steam once the novelty wears off. Even New Raine gets tired of my shit. I feel her pack up her motivation and disappear. *See ya, wouldn't wanna be ya.*

When I return to Jack's office a few minutes later, my mismatched socks are tucked safely out of sight inside my boots. "That happens more often than I'd like to admit," I say.

Jack picks up a pen from the desk and twirls it between his fingers. "Which part of what just happened are you talking about?"

I shoot him a glare. "I was talking about the shoe thing, of course." I sink into the chair opposite the desk with a sigh. "Though the sharing of personal details no one asked for happens a lot too."

When our eyes meet, Jack can't keep a straight face, and the pen slips from his fingers. "I don't mean to laugh," he says, but the last word is mangled as the laughter he tries to hold back fights its way out. "But, Raine, it's January. Weren't your feet cold?"

"I was in a hurry! And I'm sorry for being late, by the way. And for being even more late because I forgot my boots. And I didn't mean to tell you about my underwear, really. It won't happen again. Well, I can't promise that. It might happen again. Actually, it probably will. But I'll *try* not to do it again. It's just I have a hard time with these sorts of things because I . . ." Jack raises an eyebrow, waiting for me to continue. "I have ADHD," I say. "When I told you that I am kind of a mess . . . that's what I meant."

As soon as the words are out of my mouth, I'm on edge. I never know what sort of reaction I'm going to get when I tell people about my ADHD. Some people shrug it off like it's no big deal, when to *me* it is a very big deal. It impacts almost everything in my life. Then there are the people who don't even think it exists. And we can't forget the classic, *Don't we all have a little ADHD?* (No, we don't.)

He pauses in his pen twirling and sits up straighter. "Can I be honest with you?"

When I say yes, it comes out more like a question than a statement.

Jack smiles. "I sort of wondered."

"See? I'm a mess."

Jack is quiet for a moment, but then he starts twirling his pen again and says, "Aithníonn ciaróg, ciaróg eile."

I know I'm not always the best at paying attention, but I'm fairly certain that wasn't English. "I didn't catch that last part," I say.

"Aithníonn ciaróg, ciaróg eile," he says. "It's an Irish proverb. Roughly translated, it means, *One beetle recognizes another.*"

I don't say anything. Jack laughs and sets the pen on his desk. "What I'm trying to say is that I wondered if you have ADHD because I have it too."

"You do?"

He nods. "The OCD sort of overshadows it, but yeah. It takes one to know one. Like attracts like."

"You did jump over the bar and offer me a job after knowing me for all of thirty minutes," I say.

"An excellent decision, if I do say so myself."

I laugh. "I haven't even worked here an entire week, and I've already shown up to work late and without shoes. If anything, you saying that makes me question your judgment."

Jack shrugs. "Most fun I've had at work in a long time, though."

"I'm not sure fun is the objective."

Jack picks up the pen again and twirls it between his fingers before tucking it behind his ear. "So you were a few minutes late and forgot your boots. This isn't a time-sensitive job. You live upstairs and can grab your boots. No harm done. You're sort of working independently anyway, so if these hours don't work for you, we'll figure out something better. We should probably discuss workplace accommodations while we're on the topic."

"Accommodations?"

"If there's anything I can do to make sure you have the best chance of succeeding here, I want to do it."

I shake my head. "I don't need special treatment. I'll do better, I promise."

Jack stares thoughtfully at the pen in his hand. "If you don't need any, that's fine. But it wouldn't be special treatment. If I didn't own the place, I'd have to ask for them too."

"You would?"

He laughs. "Oh, yeah. You're not the only one who shows up late to places. Making a cat tent sounds a lot more fun than getting stuck flicking light switches. *Sorry I'm late, Mr. So-and-so, I had to flick this light switch over and over until it felt right while only holding good thoughts in my head so my cat won't accidentally catch the place on fire while I'm gone.*"

I try not to laugh, but a giggle escapes me, and I widen my eyes. "I'm not laughing at you," I say.

Jack shrugs. "I know you're not laughing at me. I made a joke. OCD isn't funny, but I'm okay with laughing at some of the weird shite my brain tells me to do."

"Noted."

"The point is, it isn't a burden." He leans forward on his desk. "So, what's helped you to succeed at other jobs?"

It's as if I've forgotten every work experience I've ever had. "I . . . don't know. I've never really thought about it. I was only diagnosed with ADHD three years ago, and I was in school the whole time, so it's all pretty new to me."

"Three years ago?"

"I know it's hard to believe—"

"That's not what I mean," Jack says. "It's just . . ." He laughs. "I didn't know I had OCD until three years ago."

"Really?"

He swivels this way and that in his chair, and it's so obvious to me now the ways we are alike. I should've realized it when we clicked right away.

"I always knew the things I worried about weren't normal," he says. "But I never thought it was OCD because I'm not a neat freak." He gestures to his desk, which has papers spilling out of folders and

Post-its stuck in random places. "I don't usually have contamination themes, and hand-washing was pretty much all I knew about OCD. I never saw or heard anyone talk about . . ." He lets the words trail off, but then he clears his throat and continues. "I never saw anything about OCD that looked like *me*. But I finally had a friend who put two and two together."

"I'm glad you have such good friends," I say.

"Me too."

There's a beat of silence. "About accommodations . . . While I really appreciate the offer, I don't think I'll need any. It's just been a while since I've had a routine. I actually did pretty great in school, until med school, anyway. Then I got lazy and left everything until the last minute and didn't study enough. But I can get my act together. I'm just adjusting."

Jack looks as if there's more he wants to say, but then he sighs and drums his fingers against the desk. "Well, if you change your mind, let me know. There's no expiration date." He tucks the pen behind his ear. "Why don't we move on to something more fun? What do you think?"

"Yes, please. I can only take so much serious conversation at a time."

"That makes two of us," he says.

"One beetle recognizes another," I say.

"Now you've got it." He looks down at his desk and flicks at a sticky note. "So, what are you planning to work on first? More cat tents? Maybe we could rebrand as one of those cat cafés."

"You want to turn this place into a pussy pub?" I say, and at the look Jack gives me add, "I didn't mean it like that."

"I imagine we'd get plenty of customers if we started calling it that," he says. "But perhaps that's not the direction we ought to go."

"Yeah, probably shouldn't do any false advertising." I pick at the corner of one of the many Post-its haphazardly stuck to the edge of the desk. On it is a sketch of a girl beneath a string of random letters and numbers.

I hold up the Post-it for Jack to see. "This is cute," I say.

A strange look passes over his face. "Oh, that's just . . . that's nothing. Just a password for something."

"Speaking of passwords," I say. "I need the usernames and passwords to the pub's social media accounts."

Jack doesn't look at me when he plucks the Post-it from my hand and tucks it away into a drawer. "We don't have any," he says.

"You don't have any . . ."

"Social media accounts."

I stare at him. "How have you been advertising to potential customers?"

He winces. "We haven't?"

"Well, then," I say. "I know *exactly* what I'll be working on next." I pull my phone from my pocket and shake my head. "No social media accounts . . . You're lucky you found me. And speaking of lucky, *TheLocalCobh* is free for the taking. How's that sound?"

After we finish going over my ideas for the pub, I'm buzzing with enthusiasm. Normally, I'd be overwhelmed after brain-dumping a bunch of half-baked ideas. I'm really great at coming up with them. But actually *doing* things? Well, let's just say that my lost laptop contains at least fifty half-finished songs I hyper-focused on making for a day or two before giving up and moving on to the next sparkly song idea.

Fortunately for me, Jack took notes during our conversation, and when I answered his question about what I wanted to post about first with a shrug, he suggested one of my ideas for a video series about the pub.

But as soon as I leave Jack's office and take a seat at the bar, a little bit of that overwhelmed sensation finds me. It's lunchtime and the pub is pretty much dead. The only customers are the Old Codgers, three white-haired old men who sit at the same corner of the bar every day. One of the Old Codgers—Dave, or maybe it's Drew (I'm not sure which Old Codger is which yet)—hollers something about a horse race to Aoife, the bartender.

I've only been here a few days, but I already like my coworkers. Other than Jack and Ollie, there are two. Aoife, a gossipy middle-aged woman who started bartending to support her three teenage sons after her husband died, and Róisín, a quiet young chef with chin-length black hair and almost as many tattoos as Jack.

"There's our Raine," Aoife says when she looks up from the newspaper that's open in front of her and catches sight of me. "You need a drink, love?"

"I'm . . . working right now."

Aoife winks. "I won't tell if you won't."

I can't tell if she's joking and decide I'd rather not know. "Actually, I was hoping you could help me with something. I'm making a Meet the Locals video series for our new social media accounts. Do you mind if I interview you real quick?"

Aoife rests a hand over her heart. "I've only been waiting for my time in the limelight for the last fifty-five years."

"Great." I pull out my phone. "Ready?" When she nods, I start recording and say, "This is Aoife, one of the bartenders here at the Local. Aoife, why don't you tell us a bit about yourself."

"Name's Aoife," she begins. "Now, you may have been told that the Dunne boys own this place, and while that's true, I'm the real one in charge around here. Isn't that right, Róisín?"

"Dunno what you're talking about," Róisín, who has stepped out from the kitchen to deliver food to the Old Codgers, says.

"Oh, you know, Ro, you do."

Róisín tries to step around Aoife and disappear into the kitchen again, but Aoife slings an arm around Róisín's shoulders and turns them toward the camera. "And this is Róisín, most talented chef in Cobh, if you ask me."

Róisín blushes. "Oh, I don't know . . ."

"Don't be humble, Ro," Aoife says. "And if you're watching this, Ollie Dunne, I meant exactly what I said."

"That's not true. He taught me everything I know."

Aoife elbows Róisín in the side. "Don't get all worked up, now, I'm just acting the maggot. Don't think it'll be long before you really are better than him, though."

Róisín fumbles for something to say and settles on, "Oh, I give up."

"And cut!" I say, ending the recording. "Thanks, you two. That's perfect."

Aoife grins. Róisín looks skeptical. Sure, I'll need to do a bit of editing, but this is exactly what I wanted to convey—camaraderie, family. Not some clean and perfect aesthetic. Something *real*.

Aoife returns her attention to the newspaper in front of her. She drags a finger down a page of race listings, then eyes me. "You like horse racing?"

"I don't know a thing about it," I reply.

"Neither do I. Doesn't keep her from talking my ear off about it," Róisín mutters.

Aoife attempts to swat Róisín with the newspaper but Róisín dodges it.

"That's right!" Aoife calls after them. "You ought to quit messing around or I'll tell Jack you're slacking off."

Róisín only laughs and disappears into the kitchen.

"They know he wouldn't give a damn," Aoife says. "Jackie's as goofy as the rest of us." With a sigh, she unfolds the newspaper on the bar again. "Now, Moneyball or Typhoon? Odds are 7-2, and 5-1 respectively. What do you think?"

I know so little about horse racing that those numbers mean absolutely nothing to me. "Typhoon sounds faster, but I'd place my bet on Moneyball."

"Why's that?" Aoife asks.

I shrug. "I like the name."

"Moneyball it is." She snaps the newspaper shut. "You'll do good here. You go with your gut. That's what Jackie's problem is. I tell him that, but he just shakes his head."

"I think maybe he should go with his head more. Then maybe he'd have hired someone who is actually qualified for this job."

"Oh hush," she says. "And stop worrying, will you? Jackie can't make up his mind about hardly anything, but he seemed very certain about you. I haven't seen him so upbeat about this place in a long time."

I feel my cheeks flush. "I have no idea why."

"Let me tell you something about that boy," Aoife says. "He and Ollie spent weeks trying to find someone for this job, but Jack couldn't decide on anyone. You shoulda seen Ollie, thought he'd start pulling out that beautiful hair of his if Jack didn't pick someone soon. I'm always telling that man to mind his mouth, but he just shakes his head and tells me I'm not his mum. *And thank God for that*, I always say. I've got enough on my hands with my own three boys. I don't need another, especially one with a mouth like that."

She sighs, then folds the newspaper up and tucks it out of sight beneath the bar. "Point is, Jack's picky about who he hires. He grew up in this pub. It's been his whole life since his da died, and he doesn't trust just anyone. So if he thinks you're capable of the job, it's probably true."

"I don't know . . ." I think about the chatty, open guy I met at the bar and don't know how to fit this new information in with the picture I have of Jack Dunne. I'd thought he was like me, overly trusting to a fault, someone who would make friends with anyone. There's so much I don't know about him.

Aoife watches me, and I get the uneasy feeling that she can know things about a person just by looking at them. I'm unsure how to exit this conversation, but then I catch sight of Sebastian crossing the pub. "Should probably get a good video of him too, right?"

"If you say so, dear."

I follow Sebastian to the side room with the long table. "Are you ready for your thirty seconds of stardom?"

It doesn't take long to get some great footage. Afterward, he flops onto the floor beside the fireplace. "You've got the right idea," I say, and sit down beside him. I tug off my boots so I can warm my feet, and at the sight of my avocado sock, remember my incident with Jack earlier in the day and laugh.

"You just don't think, Raine," I mutter to myself.

Sebastian meows and nudges my hand with his face, so I pet him with one hand and edit the video with the other.

"You're a superstar, floofs. Want to see?" I say, and turn the phone toward him.

"I want to see it."

Jack's voice startles me. I turn and find him settling onto the floor beside me.

"It's probably not that great," I say, and pass him the phone.

"It's a cat video, Raine. How can it not be great?"

I watch him watching the video, more nervous than I should be, because he's right, it's just a cat video, but I really, really want him to like it anyway.

"Award-winning," he says once he's finished it. Before I can ask what he really thinks, he holds up my phone. "Your turn."

"For what?" I say.

"For a video, of course!"

"I don't think so . . ."

"Aw, c'mon now. Shouldn't the people know who's behind all the cat videos?"

"I can't get out of this, can I?"

Jack grins.

"Fine. Fine." I glare at him, then tug on my boots and get to my feet. "Where do you want me?"

"You're perfect right there." He stands and steps back a few feet, then holds up the phone and says, "Action!"

I stare at him awkwardly for a moment, unsure of what to do. Jack peers at me from over the phone.

"I'm not sure what to say."

"This is Raine Hart," Jack says. "Traveling musician, disco enthusiast, and our intrepid entertainment coordinator." As he talks, I pose like a model at a photoshoot. "She comes to us all the way from the US. Maybe if we're lucky, she'll play some of her music for us before she leaves. What do you think, Raine?"

"I think I still don't have any instruments," I say.

"You have a tambourine."

I roll my eyes. "Oh yes, come on down for Tambourine Tuesdays here at the Local!" As soon as I say it, I catch Jack's eye. The look on his face makes me wonder if he's thinking the same thing I am.

"Actually, that could be sort of fun," I say, at the same time Jack says, "That's not a bad idea."

"Not me standing there playing tambourine for everyone," I say. "But what if we had a weekly jam session? People could bring whatever they have and just make music together. What do you think?"

"I think we should do it."

"Really?" The idea of playing music again, even if it's just following along to others with a tambourine, has me so excited I start dancing in place.

Jack smiles. "Can't hurt, can it? Might as well try it and see what happens."

"Oh, this will be fun. I'm going to go grab my tambourine." I spin on my heel, but Jack laughs and calls out after me.

"Your phone, Raine Hart!"

I spin back around to face him. "I was just letting you hold on to it for me."

I hold out my hand for my phone, but Jack doesn't give it to me.

"You've only got three percent battery left. How's that possible? It's hardly past noon. Do you not charge your phone at night?"

I narrow my eyes at him. "Maybe *some* of us don't feel the need to adhere to strict phone charging schedules. I'm spontaneous. I'm fun. I live on the *edge.*"

"I had no idea you were so dangerous. I'm a bit intimidated."

I narrow my eyes at Jack, but when he grins at me, a smile forces its way onto my face. "Oh, you should talk, Jack Dunne."

I reach for my phone, nearly bumping into his chest when he holds it out of reach. "What's that supposed to mean?" he says.

*You're standing too close*, the voice of reason suggests. At least I *think* that's what it's saying. I'm not exactly listening. "You're basically a Bad-Boy Aesthetic Pinterest board come to life, but the truth is you're as fluffy as that cat," I say, and nod to Sebastian.

"What I'm hearing," Jack says, "is that you have a Bad-Boy Aesthetic board on Pinterest."

"I don't!" Jack raises an eyebrow at me, and I add, "Not technically."

Jack grins. "What do you mean by *not technically?*"

"I don't have a Pinterest board called Bad-Boy Aesthetic," I say.

"Then what's it called?"

"Moody Broody-Boy Vibes," I mutter.

"You called it what, now?"

I don't answer. Instead, I pluck my phone from his hand. "You heard me. Now if you'll excuse me, I have a tambourine video to make."

# Nine

———

## JACK

A week after Raine starts working at the pub, I find myself at a table with my laptop and a pad of Post-its, pretending to update our expenses while I'm actually watching Raine flit around with her phone as she takes photos for the pub's social media accounts. I *should* be in my office. I never do paperwork out here. But as soon as she came downstairs for the day, Sebastian at her heels, I set up in this corner to make sure no one gave her a hard time.

But as it turns out, I didn't need to. I've known most of the people who have walked in here today my entire life, but somehow Raine manages to pull stories from them I've never heard before. When she asks if she can take their picture, they agree willingly. And by the time they leave, it's as if *she's* known them her entire life.

So I've got no reason to sit here other than I like watching her. Which seems a good enough reason to me, even if going over the pub's finances is taking twice as long as it usually does.

Just before lunchtime, Raine peers over my shoulder, then slides into the seat across from me. "I had no idea running a pub involved so much paperwork," she says. "The only paperwork I have to worry about are permits and visas."

I set the pen down, pleased to have an excuse to talk with her. "I think the paperwork is the worst part. When I was tattooing, all I had to worry about were consent forms."

"I hope you have some on hand. I'm ready for my tattoo whenever you are."

"I'll happily take you to a tattoo shop if you really want one that bad."

"I'm really only interested in a Jack Dunne original."

Me giving Raine her first tattoo has become a running joke over the last week. At least, I think it's a joke. I'd hate for her to expect something that is never going to happen.

"How're the pictures turning out?" I ask. "Anything usable?"

Raine doesn't answer me. Instead, she reaches into her pocket and pulls out a crinkled receipt, then smooths it on the table and eyes the pen in front of me. "Can I borrow that?" She snatches it up before I can answer and starts scribbling away on the receipt. The way her hair spills over her face makes it so that I can't see what she's writing.

"Raine?"

She continues writing, humming something under her breath. When I say her name again, she shushes me without so much as a pause in whatever she's doing.

I have no idea what is going on but decide it's better to stay quiet and wait it out. Every few seconds she pauses, then hums something to herself before putting pen to paper again. After a minute or two, she straightens and pushes the hair from her face. She squints at the receipt, eyes flicking back and forth over it. Her brow furrows, but only for a moment. She scratches something out before scanning the receipt once more, expression smoothing when she turns whatever she's written face down on the table.

"The pictures are going great," she says, as if the last two minutes never happened. "The one I posted today already has a dozen likes. It's not much, but it's a start. I credit Sebastian. He's irresistible."

I'm not sure what look I have on my face, but it must be something like confusion, because Raine pauses. "That's what we were talking about, right?" She raises her eyebrows. "Did I . . . shush you?"

"Only a little."

She presses a hand to her forehead. "Oh, God. I'm sorry. I can be a butthead when I'm interrupted . . . even though I interrupted you . . . Sorry, sorry."

"What were you doing?"

She draws one knee up to her chest and wraps her arms around it, swaying slightly from side to side as she talks. "I had this idea for a chorus, and I always think I'll remember it and write it down later, but I never do. I usually have a notebook for song ideas, but it was in my backpack when it got stolen." Her gaze drops to the table. "There go all my song ideas."

I've spent more time than I'd like to admit looking for Raine's things over the last week. I shouldn't care so much about this girl I hardly know, and yet I do. Perhaps it's because, in some way, I know what she's feeling. I've actively avoided thinking about tattooing for the past three years, but whenever Raine brings up her lost guitar and how much she misses making music, I can't help but think about tattooing. How much I loved it. How much I miss it. Even though I still have my tattoo machines, tattooing feels like it was stolen from me. *I* stole it from myself. Though Martina would tell me that my OCD and *me* are not the same thing.

When Raine takes the receipt from the table and shoves it into her pocket, another receipt slips out and onto the floor. She groans and disappears beneath the table to grab it. When she rights herself again, she glances at the receipt.

"Oh! Hey. I didn't lose all my song ideas." She grins and waves the receipt at me, then looks at it again and frowns. "Mm . . . not sure how good this one is."

The things this woman keeps in her pockets never cease to surprise me. Receipts with song lyrics, that Ziploc bag she uses as a wallet. The tambourine, of course. Just the other day she pulled a sock from her pocket and a cat treat came tumbling out. *I was wondering where I put that*, she said. I didn't ask if she meant the sock or the cat treat. Neither would surprise me. The only time I've been up to the flat since Raine moved in—to help her work the washer—I found socks in random places. Between the couch cushions. Beneath the kitchen table. On a windowsill.

I don't mind the mess. With Raine in the flat, it doesn't feel so much like Da's. He hated nothing more than a mess. I can only imagine what he'd say if he saw a sock beside the refrigerator. He's probably rolling in his grave.

Let him. Who knows, once Raine leaves, I might start leaving socks around myself.

And besides, who am I to judge what someone keeps in their pockets? I've had stranger things in mine. One of the things I had to do for exposure response therapy to treat my OCD was carry a knife on me at all times. Driving into Cork? Knife on the passenger seat. Taking a nap? Knife on the nightstand. Grocery shopping? Knife in my pocket. A sock and a cat treat seem normal in comparison.

When Raine stuffs the receipt into her pocket again, I get to my feet.

"Where are you going?"

"Stay here," I say. "Be back in a sec."

She gives me a confused look, and I head to my office, where I pull open desk drawers until I find a little zippered pouch. I turn it upside down, and some stray paper clips clatter onto the desk.

When I return to the table, I pass the pouch to Raine.

She takes it, but looks at me as if she isn't sure what to do with it.

"For the receipts," I say. "Your pockets are always full of stuff, and I'm worried you'll throw them away by accident."

"Oh!" She drops her gaze to the pouch in her hands and runs the zipper back and forth. When she lifts her eyes to mine again, she's wearing a smile. "That happens to me all the time. I always tell myself I'll keep my song ideas in one place, so I have that notebook I was telling you about. But I don't like it to be messy, and the ideas come faster than I can write neatly, especially when I have to write out the guitar part. So I end up writing early drafts on receipts and napkins and tell myself I'll transfer them to the notebook later, but sometimes I lose them before I can. It's a real pain. So, thanks." She unzips the pouch and sets it on the table before her, then reaches into the pockets of her cardigan and pulls out a pile of receipts.

"Wanna make a bet?" she says.

"That depends on the bet."

"What percentage of these do you think is garbage and what percentage is actually something important? Loser has to eat a raisin bagel."

I narrow my eyes at her. "Don't you like raisin bagels?"

She shrugs, a smile twitching at her lips, and before I know it, I've agreed to this ridiculous bet. "You believe in me way too much," she says when I guess that only twenty percent of the receipts are rubbish. A few minutes later, she has half of the receipts tucked safely inside the pouch, and I have a date with a raisin bagel.

Raine leaves the pub. When she returns a half hour later, she's carrying a brown paper bag from the coffee shop down the street and a stack of tin signs she's managed to scrounge up from . . . I don't even know where. The woman makes friends faster than a tattoo machine pierces skin. She's talking a mile a minute, something about a girl she met in the bakery yesterday and a box in a storage container.

"Must my punishment come so soon?" I ask when she tosses the bag onto the table.

She grins, but when I open the bag, instead of a raisin bagel, like I expect, I find a poppyseed bagel.

I raise an eyebrow at her. She shrugs, then spreads the signs out on the table. "I didn't have it in me. These are for the pub," she says. "Do you like them?"

Each sign features a different Irish brand—Beamish, Murphy's, Guinness. I touch each corner of the one closest to me. "They're great," I say, though the thoughts are already there, telling me that changing the pub will only lead to awful things. "When are you planning to redecorate?"

"Oh, I don't know. Once I collect enough stuff, I think."

I pretend I'm inspecting the signs, but really, I'm trying to resist mentally counting the corners of the photos we currently have on the walls. I don't *need* to count them. I already know there are sixty-four. Four corners for each of the sixteen pictures. There are ten bigger pictures and six smaller ones. Only two of the frames match. Ten photographs are of boats, four are of buildings, two are landscapes.

They're just walls. They're just photographs. I don't need to count them. Nothing bad will happen if we change things up.

*Are you sure?*

I'm sure.

*What if you're wrong?*

I'm not.

But it doesn't matter that I *know* I don't need to count them, because I *feel* like I do. It doesn't matter that I'm pretty sure I'm right, when there is a tiny part of me that worries I could be wrong. It doesn't matter that I know I have to sit with the anxiety to feel better in the long run, when all I want is to feel better right now. I don't want to spiral over some photographs with Raine sitting across from me.

I don't want to count them. I don't need to count them.

But I do it anyway.

# Ten

———

Until Raine started working here, I knew exactly what to expect whenever I stepped inside this pub. But by the last week of January, I find myself pausing at the door to make sure I've got only good thoughts in my head before stepping inside, because now I never know what I'll find, and for whatever reason, my brain has decided that if I walk inside with only good thoughts in my head, then whatever I find will be good.

It doesn't make sense. I know that. But it doesn't stop me from telling myself the compulsion is just a moment of *mindfulness* and not a big deal anyway.

Today, I find Dave, one of the Old Codgers, seated at the bar with an acoustic guitar in his lap. I've known the man since I was a boy, but I had no idea he spent his twenties as a touring musician. Not until he showed up to our first Tambourine Tuesday with his guitar and some of the wildest stories I've ever heard.

Today Raine sits beside Dave at the bar. The two of them are turned toward each other. She has Sebastian in her lap and is absent-mindedly stroking his fur as she watches Dave play.

I linger at the other end of the bar for a moment and watch Raine as she listens. When the song ends, Raine leans closer to him and says, "Can you show me that second chord you played in the bridge?"

"Our Raine here is going to be a world-famous musician, you know," I say, giving Dave a clap on the shoulder before sinking onto the empty barstool beside him.

Raine laughs. "I might need more than a foot tambourine to become a world-famous musician."

I shoot her a grin. "Dunno about that. You're at least the second-best foot-tambourine player I've ever heard. I think if you practiced a bit more, you could eventually be first."

"And who's first?"

"It's a tie between Josie and Tiny Jack," I say, thinking of the other day when Nina brought the girls to the pub for dinner. Somehow Raine ended up sitting cross-legged beneath one of the tables with Josie and Jacqueline. I sat at a nearby table with Nina and Ollie, watching Raine and the girls pass the tambourine around for a game I didn't quite understand. Both of my nieces sat as close to Raine as they could, their faces eager as they waited for their turn to shake the tambourine. I watched for a few minutes, trying not to laugh at how serious the girls looked—faces red, brows scrunched—whenever they had the tambourine in hand. Raine seemed to take the game as seriously as they did, but then I noticed the slight twitch of a smile at the corner of her lips. After a particularly enthusiastic turn from Josie, Raine caught me watching and her control slipped. I couldn't help but laugh at how she had to cover her mouth with her hands to keep the girls from seeing.

"I can't argue with you there," Raine says. "Those girls have raw talent." She drops her gaze to Dave's guitar and sighs. "I really miss playing."

"Well, here you go, girl," Dave says. He holds out the guitar to her. "Play us something."

When Raine takes the guitar from Dave and settles it on her lap, her hands are in motion right away, plucking out a pattern as if it's second nature. She sits a bit taller. Her shoulders seem more relaxed than they were moments before. She doesn't look like a different person, exactly, but she looks more like herself. Not that I know anything about it, seeing as I haven't even known her for a month.

When Raine tries to give Dave his guitar back, he refuses to take it. "Borrow it if you like."

"I couldn't . . ." she says, though I notice her grip on the instrument tightens.

"Just for while you're here. It's no fancy Gibson, but it should hold you over. I've got another at home."

Before Raine can respond, I nudge her shoulder with mine. "You only turn down free stuff once, remember?"

Raine looks at me, then at Dave, and then down at the guitar in her hands. I think there are tears in her eyes, but she blinks them away before I can be certain. "Thank you," she says. "Really, you have no idea what this means to me."

"Ah, but I do, darling," Dave says. "You have that look."

"What look?"

"The look of a musician."

Raine doesn't say anything, but her fingers are still moving, playing a soft melody I don't recognize. When she looks at Dave and me again, she's got a gentle smile on her face. "Any requests?"

"Something that's yours," Dave says.

"I don't have anything of my own," she says. When the color rises in her cheeks, she looks away, gaze on the strings vibrating beneath her fingers.

Dave laughs. "You're an awful liar, darling."

Raine sighs. Her fingers still, and I miss the music as soon as it stops. When she crosses her arms over the top of the guitar, she seems so much smaller than she did moments before. I want to poke her in the side where I know she's just a bit ticklish and keep her from folding in on herself.

"I don't have anything good," she says.

Dave takes a long pull from his pint. "You're gonna have to get over that, darling. There's no room for that sort of doubt in the creative life. You've gotta believe in what you make, otherwise why would anyone else?"

Raine opens her mouth to say something, but no words come out. Dave raises his eyebrows, and after a moment in which the two of them stare at each other, Raine says, "How about some Niall Horan? Irish singer. Irish song."

"Oh, all right," Dave says. "But don't think I don't see what you're doing. Expect me to ask for an original song every time I come in here from now until you leave. I'll wear you down eventually."

I wonder if I should tell Dave not to push, but then she sits up and starts strumming. The rhythm is so different from the soft melody she was playing before. She seems to sink into the song as she plays. She closes her eyes, as if to shut out everything else, and when she does, the uncertainty written across her face eases.

I think of the night we met and how Raine told me she loves anything that gets people moving. I glance at Dave, and there it is, a head bob, a sway. When she begins to sing, I want to look around and see who else is listening and what they think of it, but Raine has me enchanted. The music slips from her fingers. It spills from her mouth. It lights her up and works its way into the room, breathing a soft glow into the air around her, like the aura of a candle flame.

Watching her reminds me of how tattooing felt before OCD ruined it for me. Before things got bad, there were so many ways I could slip into that state of mind where time ceased to exist. Drawing up a flash sheet. Working on a custom design for a client. The best, though, was whenever I tattooed a client who could sit well. I'd get to work, and after a few minutes I'd find myself in this headspace where nothing existed but skin and ink and the machine in my hands. I could always tell when the client was there too. The endorphins take over, the conversation goes quiet beneath the buzz of the machine, and yet . . . there's more connection for me in that moment than any other.

Watching her play makes me realize I so rarely feel that way anymore.

The song ends. Scattered applause sounds from around the pub, but Raine doesn't open her eyes right away. I can tell when she's brought herself back to the real world, because the soft dreamy look on her face is shaded by tension. She blinks her eyes open and smiles, as if she can tuck away the feeling for later.

"Bravo, darling. Bravo," Dave says.

Raine catches my eye, and her brow furrows. "What's so funny?"

I have no idea what she's talking about. "Nothing," I say.

"Then why do you have that look on your face?"

"Like what?"

Dave laughs. "You're grinning like a fool, Jackie."

"That's one of my favorite songs," I say. Somehow it feels true, even though I've never heard it before in my life.

Raine gives me a skeptical look. "I had no idea you were such a big Niall Horan fan."

I shrug. "There are a lot of things you don't know about me, Raine Hart."

She shakes her head. I pretend I don't see the amused look Dave gives me.

I'm starting to think this *most professional coworker* thing is going to be even more challenging than I expected.

After Dave leaves, Raine asks if she can work in my office, and I don't see or hear from her for hours. I make drinks and do inventory and spend a half hour searching resale sites for Raine's guitar but find nothing. When five o'clock rolls around and I haven't heard a peep from her, I go into the kitchen and, after making sure all the knives are in the right place, put some of the brown soda bread and chicken schnitzel Róisín made on a plate.

I hear music as I approach my office. The door is slightly ajar, so I pause for a moment to listen. When I finally step inside, I find her with her back to me. She sits in my chair, singing along softly to whatever song she's playing on Dave's guitar. On the floor is a giant corkboard. Polaroids and newspaper clippings and postcards are artfully arranged on half of it, but the other half is bare. Messy piles of papers and photographs cover most of the office floor. I'm sure Raine's got a method to this madness, but I have no idea what it is.

"Have you eaten?" I ask.

Raine takes no notice of me. I step carefully over the piles on the floor until I'm standing behind her.

"Raine."

Still, nothing, so I rest my free hand on her shoulder and lean closer. "You're stuck in your head, ciaróg."

Raine looks up from the guitar. She turns her head and tilts her face up to mine. "Did you just call me a beetle?"

I did, and I shouldn't have. I shouldn't be giving her nicknames. Or touching her, for that matter. I pull my hand from her shoulder. "Have you eaten at all today? It's after five."

"Already?" She looks around the room in a daze, wincing when she catches sight of her piles on the floor. "Sorry for making a mess of your office." She looks down at the guitar, then back up at me, and her cheeks flush pink. "I lost track of time. Sorry." She bolts from the chair and sets the guitar gently back in its case.

"How long were you standing there?" she asks, not meeting my gaze when she plops back into the office chair and starts poking around at something on the computer.

"Long enough to like what I heard," I say. "What song were you playing?"

Raine shrugs, her blush deepening in the soft glow of the computer monitor.

"Was that one of your songs?"

Raine doesn't answer, though I'm sure she's heard me. When she glances over at me, her gaze snags on the plate in my hands. "That smells amazing."

"Róisín's latest," I say, and set the plate on the desk beside her.

"For me?" I nod, and Raine pulls the plate to her. "We haven't known each other for very long, Jack Dunne, but I have to say, you are quickly becoming one of my favorite people."

"You must only know terrible people, then."

"Oh, please." She takes a bite of the brown soda bread. "Don't pretend to be humble now." When I take the seat on the other side of the desk, she grabs the plate and starts to get to her feet. "Crap, I'm in your seat."

"Don't get up."

"I don't mind moving, really."

I prop my feet up on the desk and lean back in the chair with my hands laced behind my head. "Ah, but I've already made myself comfortable here."

Raine slowly sinks back into the office chair. "Don't make me eat by myself, at least."

She nudges the plate toward me, so I sit up and grab some of the bread. She shoots me a smile, then flicks her gaze back to the computer screen.

"What are you working on?" I ask.

"Oh, this and that. When I get sick of looking at the corkboard, I play a few minutes of guitar, then work on the flier for the pub quiz."

"What do you have left to do?" I ask.

"I'm almost done. And speaking of the flier, I think you would really enjoy helping me pass them out." She flutters her eyelashes at me.

"I'll think about it," I say, though I already know I will.

"Anyway, once I finish the flier, I'm going to go through those," she says, nodding to the messy piles on the floor. "I've gotten photos of everyone who works here except for *you*." She points her bread at me. "Don't think you can get away with not having your photo on here."

"I'd never dream of it. I'm the number one attraction this place has to offer."

She laughs. "There's that ego of yours. I was starting to worry something was wrong with you. Anyway, if I really focus I think I can get it all done in half an hour or so."

I look at the mess on the floor. "How do you figure?"

"I'm thinking it'll take me ten minutes to finish the flier and print it, ten to go through those papers, no time at all to take your photo as long as you cooperate, and only a couple of minutes to pin everything in place."

"Does that include arranging everything on the corkboard?"

"Oh," she says. "No, it doesn't."

"Are you at a good stopping point? You've already worked eight hours. You should've stopped working twenty minutes ago."

"I took a few guitar breaks," she says sheepishly.

"As is your right."

Raine shrugs. She takes a bite of her bread and scans the corkboard. "Maybe I ought to pin everything I have arranged and save the rest for tomorrow. That shouldn't take long. What do you think? I can print the fliers in the morning."

"Sounds like a good plan to me."

She glances over at me. "Thank you. For the food and the gentle nudge. I probably would've been here until the pub closed if you hadn't."

I push the plate in her direction. "Bugging people is one of my favorite activities, ciaróg."

"Seeing as *you're* the one bugging me, you're the . . . ciaróg," she says, pronouncing *ciaróg* like *Keurig*.

"Close, but not quite. It's cure-*oh-g*, not Keurig."

"*Maybe* I wasn't calling you a beetle. Maybe I was calling you a mediocre coffee maker."

"Whatever you say, ciaróg." I sigh and get to my feet. "I'll be back in fifteen minutes, and if you aren't done here, you're only getting Keurig coffee from now on."

She groans. "Fine! Fine. I'll be done in fifteen minutes."

I give her my sternest look, but it only makes her laugh.

Fifteen minutes later, I return to the office and find all the photos pinned into place on the corkboard and Raine still squinting at the computer.

I clear my throat, and she looks up at me guiltily.

"What are you doing?" I ask.

"Nothing."

I give her a skeptical look.

"I just wanted to make a few more tweaks to the flier. It'll only be five more minutes tops!"

I shake my head and step around the desk. Raine squeals when I spin the office chair away from the computer to face me.

"Are you kicking me out?" she says.

"I am. You're off the clock."

"But I'm almost done!"

"You'll finish tomorrow."

Raine grins. "That's what she said."

"Now you're really in trouble. No more work for you today."

Raine groans and covers her face in her hands. "You're the worst boss ever."

"I'm not your boss, I'm your—"

"*Most professional coworker.* Yeah, I know." She drops her hands and squints up at me. "If you're just my coworker, then why are you bossing me around?"

"I'm not bossing you around!"

"Then what's all this about?"

"I'm . . ." I scan the office for inspiration and spot Raine's boots in a corner of the room. When I look at her again, I notice her socks, mismatched as usual. A Monday sock and a Tuesday sock.

It's Thursday.

"Get your boots on. We're having a walking meeting."

"A walking meeting?" Raine says. I know I've caught her interest, because she saves her document and closes the alarming number of tabs she has open.

"You've never heard of one?" I say.

She shakes her head.

"The concept is simple. Walk while you have a meeting. Very popular in Silicon Valley, I hear."

"Well, if it's popular in Silicon Valley, then we've got to do it."

I have to take a step back when Raine gets to her feet. I don't remember my office feeling so small before.

Raine steps around me with a grin. She sits on the floor beside her boots and tugs one on, then pauses halfway through tying the laces. "Wait. What are we meeting about? I thought I was off the clock."

"You're back on the clock," I say. "We're meeting about this flier, since you insist on working on it beyond reasonable working hours."

She gives me a skeptical look. "Why do I feel like this is a trick to get me away from work, and once we get outside, you'll say one word about the flier and then change the topic to a non-work subject?"

I nudge her boot with my toe. "Because that's exactly what's going to happen."



"Guess what I did today?" Raine says as we leave the pub and head in the direction of the harbor.

"You played guitar, designed most of a flier for the pub quiz, and put together half of a lovely collage," I say.

She rolls her eyes.

"What did you do today, then?" I say.

"Do you remember those musicians we met on Oliver Plunkett Street when we went to Cork last week?"

I do remember. Raine made friends within a few minutes of our arrival in Cork. She visibly perked up as soon as she heard the music. She walked a little faster, with a little more bounce in her step. I watched her mind drift away as we drew closer to Oliver Plunkett Street. She took longer to respond in conversation, and by the time we could see where the music was coming from, she was so absorbed in it that she didn't respond at all.

The musicians were two women. One with a guitar, the other with a laptop and small keyboard. Both had microphones before them and an array of pedals at their feet. Raine halted right in front of them as if someone had glued her to the spot. I watched her watching them, her attention fully on the music.

She must have sensed I was watching her, because she turned to me then. "Do you mind if we hear the rest of the song?"

I shook my head and turned to watch the musicians too, but really, my attention was on Raine, who head-bobbed along to the music, a smile on her face. Around us people passed by as if they took no notice of the music at all, and yet Raine seemed all wrapped up in it, and I couldn't help but watch her watching them again. Her gaze traveled from one musician to the other, as if examining their technique.

As soon as they finished the song, Raine fished a few coins from the Ziploc bag she keeps all her money in and dropped them in the guitar case. Within moments, she was in conversation with the musicians, and by the time Raine said goodbye, they'd traded social media accounts and made a promise to grab drinks the next time Raine was in Cork.

"What about them?" I ask.

"I was messaging with Tara—the one who plays the guitar—and guess which pub they're adding to their rotation next month?"

My eyes land on the nearest pub. "Kelley's," I say with a nod.

Raine elbows me in the side. "Not Kelley's! The Local, of course!"

I look at her. "Really?"

"As long as you're okay with it."

I stop in the middle of the pavement. "Of course I'm okay with it. How'd you convince them to come all the way out here?"

Raine waltzes ahead of me. "With charisma and grace," she says, and turns in a little spin. As soon as the word *grace* leaves her mouth she catches her foot on the pavement and stumbles. I lurch forward and catch her by the arm, pulling her upright before she can fall.

"With what, now?"

She grins at me. "All right, there was no grace involved. Just charisma."

"I believe it," I say, and reluctantly let go of her sleeve.

"Don't tease me."

"I'm not teasing! I'm serious. I think you're very charming."

Raine smiles down at her boots as she walks beside me. I love how easy it is to make her smile. I want to do it again, but I have to be careful. I can't forget that this is supposed to be a very professional work relationship, the *most* professional.

"I just asked if they'd like to play now and then for free beer."

"Nothing like the bartering economy," I say.

She shakes her head with a laugh. "They said they could come twice a month, at least for now. They might be able to come more often in the future."

"Nail down the dates and let me know what you need from me. And to think you told me you had no idea how to do this job."

"Well, don't get too confident in me. I could still screw it up."

Her voice is light, but I think she really means that. "I have a hard time seeing how you could screw up something like that."

"You'd be surprised at the many ways I can screw things up." Before I can respond, she looks out at Cork Harbour and sighs. "I can't believe I'm still here."

"Say your things didn't get stolen. Where would you be now?"

"Oh, I don't know. I try not to plan too far ahead. I was only supposed to be in Cobh that one afternoon. I was going to stay the night in Cork, busk Oliver Plunkett street for a few days, then move on to the next place." She pauses. "Galway, probably." She stops walking and leans against the railing. I stand beside her, following her gaze across the water to the windmills that spin in the distance. It reminds me of the thoughts I can't seem to shake, how they burrow into my head and just keep circling.

"If you could go anywhere, where would you go?" Raine asks.

I look her over. "You're from Boston, right?"

"Yup."

I shoot her a grin. "Then I'd go to Boston."

"Come on. Really, where would you go?"

"Boston," I say again. "I need to see the hometown of my favorite musician."

She bumps her shoulder against mine. "How can I be your favorite musician? You've only heard me play one song."

"It was a really good song."

She rolls her eyes. "Come on."

"I mean it! And that's not the only song I've heard you play." At the look on her face, I have to laugh. "Do you really think I've never looked you up?"

"You have?"

"Of course I have. You smile when you sing. Even for the sad songs."

"You . . . watched my videos?"

Rather than answer, I sing a few lines from one of her cover songs. When I watched her video the first time, it took me a minute to recognize the song because her interpretation of it was so . . . different. The original song is dreadfully sad, but Raine's version was upbeat, fun, something to move to. It made the lyrics take on a totally different meaning without changing a single word. I *could* sing the whole thing, but the surprise on her face has me laughing too hard to continue.

Raine stares at me open-mouthed, turns away for a moment, then looks back at me again. I prod the center of her forehead with a finger. "You okay in there, ciaróg?"

She blinks. "What did you think? Really?"

The wind picks up and blows her hair across her face. I have to put my hands in my coat pockets to keep from tucking her hair back behind her ear. "I said you're my favorite musician, didn't I?"

"It's okay if you don't like them. I know it's not everyone's thing. It comes down to personal taste, you know. For example, I can appreciate house music, but I don't particularly enjoy it."

I raise my eyebrows at her. "I told you I very rarely say things I don't mean. You're really good, Raine. I'm not just saying that because . . ." *Shite.* She looks up at me, waiting for me to finish my sentence. "Because I'm your most professional coworker."

"You're the silliest person I've ever met."

"A role I take very seriously."

Raine shoves me playfully. "Fine, don't tell me where you'd really go."

"Can I ask you something?" I say, hoping to change the subject.

"Sure."

"Would you ever want to play your own music?"

She stares down at her hands for a moment and tugs at the fingers of her gloves. Her hair hides her face from view, and I feel that urge to sweep it out of the way again.

When she lifts her head and looks out over the water, I realize I'm holding my breath. "I want to," she says. "If I had the courage, I'd find somewhere to stay for a while and put together an album. Really dedicate some time to it. But . . ." She lets the words trail off, then turns to me. "I don't know. I'm not ready. I wish I was. But I'm not."

Before I can find the words to respond, she smiles at me and says, "Want to make a bet?"

"I'm not sure. It didn't go so well for me last time."

"Race me to the Annie Moore statue. If you win, I'll buy you a bagel every day this week. If *I* win, you have to tell me where you'd really go, and your answer can't be Boston."

"And you think *I'm* the silliest person you've ever met? Look in a mirror, ciaróg."

"One beetle recognizes another," she says.

"Don't go using the proverbs of my own people against me, now."

She grins up at me, waiting expectantly.

"Oh, all right," I say.

Her face lights up, and I'm so caught up in thinking about how beautiful she is that it startles me when she shouts "Go!" and takes off running.

As soon as my brain catches up, I bolt after her. "That's cheating!"

Raine's laugh echoes back to me. For someone who says she would never willingly subject herself to cardio, she's surprisingly fast. Likely all the traveling with that giant backpack of hers. She doesn't so much as look over her shoulder as she runs, red hair streaming behind her.

Raine is fast, but I'm faster. Just as she's about to reach the statue, I lurch forward and grab her around the waist, picking her up and spinning away from it. She laughs wildly as I hold her out of reach of the statue and touch it with my boot.

"There," I say, out of breath when I set her on her feet again. "I win."

"You cheated!" Raine cries, false indignation in her voice.

"Oh, no," I say. "Don't even start with that. You cheated first."

Raine's chest rises and falls as she tries to catch her breath. Her cheeks are flushed. She looks so very alive.

Lately, I feel as if I'm on autopilot. The intrusive thoughts come more frequently, taking up so much of my time and attention that I feel like an observer of my life. This moment with Raine is a brief reprieve, one I don't want to waste. I have so little time with her. No one, not even Raine, can keep me safe from my own head. But today, being around her is like sitting in the sunshine on a cold day. It makes the winter tolerable, almost nice.

She leans against the sign beside the statue and groans. "I don't think I can take another step. You'll have to carry me back to the pub."

She looks at me as if this is a challenge. She's poking at the boundaries of my professionalism, and I am too weak to hold the line. I mentally nudge the boundaries an inch further. "Oh, all right," I say, and turn my back to her.

"Really?"

"Come on," I say, "before I change my mind."

She jumps onto my back and wraps her arms loosely around my neck. I start in the direction of the pub. When I heft her higher onto my back, her laugh warms my cheek, and I tighten my grip on her. This is the closest we've ever been. The most we've touched.

I try not to think about it.

"Not sure how you conned me into this," I say. "Can't say this is very professional."

"I told you I didn't have a professional bone in my body." She rests her chin on my shoulder, and her hair presses against my cheek. The smell of her shampoo, something light and floral, wafts over me.

I must be a masochist. There's no other explanation for why I would torture myself like this. Why else would I have her so close? Why else would I willingly drown myself in her when I know I won't—can't—do anything about it?

Raine is quiet as we cross the street. It's a quiet evening in the town center too, but the few people who are milling about cast us odd glances. I don't care. A lifetime of ridiculous thoughts dulled my capacity for embarrassment years ago.

We pass by the Cobh Tourist Office, and it reminds me of Raine's question. Where would I go if I could go anywhere? I don't like to think about things like that. I'd love to see new places. Have adventures. New experiences. Meet all sorts of people. But traveling means uncertainty. It means unfamiliar places and situations, new triggers, no routine to rely on. It's easier to pretend I don't like traveling than to admit that this is one more thing OCD has taken from me.

"Tokyo," I say.

"Hmm?"

"That's where I'd go."

I can hear the smile in her voice. "Why Tokyo?"

I turn right, taking the shortcut to the pub so I don't have to carry her uphill the entire way. "There are some great tattoo artists there I'd love to work with. Before I left Dublin, I was thinking about seeing if I could get a guest spot at a tattoo shop somewhere. Not Tokyo. I was thinking closer to home, maybe London. But I hoped that one day I could work my way up to something like that."

"A traveling musician and a traveling tattoo artist walk into a bar," Raine says.

I wait for the punchline.

"That's all I've got, but it sounds like the start of a great joke."

"The joke is the idea of me ever becoming a traveling tattoo artist."

"Why?"

"Because I don't travel, and I don't tattoo anymore."

"I bet you could find a few clients here if you wanted."

"I didn't quit because I moved here. For a while, I'd head up to Dublin now and then to do bookings."

"What happened? Oh, you don't have to answer that, sorry."

"I don't mind telling you." Part of me even *wants* to tell her, but I'm also nervous. What if it makes her pity me? Or worse, what if she thinks I'm crazy?

She wouldn't think that. At least, I don't think she would.

"My OCD got in the way," I say. "I started getting new intrusive thoughts. What if I didn't sterilize my equipment well enough and someone went septic? I went through gloves like you wouldn't believe. I was on edge constantly because I was convinced that if I had a bad thought while tattooing someone, the tattoo would be unlucky. If I had a bad thought when I was drawing, I could just throw it away and start over, but with tattooing, that wasn't possible."

I don't tell her about the other thoughts. The ones that bothered me the most. What if instead of tattooing a picture of a client's dog, I tattooed a dick or *Fuck your mum*, or some other awful thing? I knew I wouldn't *really* do those things, but . . . what if I was wrong? What if I just lost it one day and did it? Why else would I have those thoughts? I developed a compulsion to confess to my clients the awful thoughts I had. I'd try to pass it off as a joke, but it was awkward.

"I started being late to appointments, and then missing them completely. So one day I just . . . quit. Canceled all my bookings. Deleted my social media accounts. Recommended other artists to my clients. My mentor, Shauna—that's Róisín's mum—was the one who suspected I had OCD and suggested I see a psychiatrist. The girl I was seeing at the time tried to be supportive and stuck around for a while, but it was too much for her. Can't say I fault her. I was in a really bad place."

"And therapy helped?"

"It changed my life."

"But you still don't want to go back to tattooing?"

"It would be a lot to take on with the pub."

It isn't the real reason, but Raine doesn't question it. I don't want to tell her the truth—that I'm scared. I'm scared that not even therapy can help me get to a place where I enjoy tattooing again. Somehow it feels easier not to try.

Raine's arms tighten around my shoulders. "Do you miss it?"

"I do."

It feels strange to talk about that time. It feels so long ago, but also too close for comfort.

"Well," Raine says. "If you ever change your mind about traveling, will you promise not to go to Tokyo without me?"

I laugh. That's an easy promise to make, because I can't see that happening. Not anytime soon, anyway. "Sure. If you go to Tokyo without me, do you promise to send me pictures?"

"I'll do better than that. I'll take a million videos. I'll get a tattoo, just so you can live vicariously through me."

"I can't tell if you're teasing me or not," I say.

"I'm not teasing. I really will. Before I leave Cobh, you'll have to give me the names of some tattoo artists there."

*Before I leave Cobh.* How is it that only a few weeks ago I didn't even know Raine Hart existed, and now I hardly go a few minutes without thinking about her?

"If you go as soon as you leave here, you might make it in time to see the cherry blossoms," I say. "I've always wanted to see that."

Raine hums to herself for a moment. "Maybe next year. Just in case you change your mind."

The image comes to me so clearly. Raine in Tokyo. Her face tilted up to the trees. Cherry blossoms in her hair.

It hurts to think about. Because when I try to imagine myself there too, I can't.

# FEBRUARY

# Eleven

## RAINE

Before I know it, more than half my time at the Local is over.

The pub might not look all that different than it did a few weeks ago, but I have managed to make some changes. Tambourine Tuesday and our pub quiz nights have more and more participants each week, but my favorite visible change by far has been the corkboard. It's filled with photos I took on Nina's Polaroid. Photos of Ollie, who looked grumpy even as he smiled at me from behind the bar. Of Nina and the girls. Aoife and Róisín. Of the Old Codgers and our other regular patrons, new and old alike.

My favorite photo is one I took of Jack. I found him on the steps out behind the pub with Sebastian at his side. Jack had propped his chin in his hand and turned his face to Sebastian, who, at the exact moment I took the photo, turned to look at him too. In it, the two of them look deep in thought-provoking conversation. Whenever I walk past the corkboard, my eyes find that photo first, and it never fails to make me smile.

Today is my day off. Jack isn't working today either, but we didn't hang out like we normally do when our schedules line up. He had a mysterious errand to run. I was a bit bummed he didn't invite me. It wouldn't be the first time I've tagged along for some mundane task. But seeing as he didn't invite me, I've spent most of the day playing Dave's guitar or mindlessly scrolling on my phone, all while pretending the various piles of dirty clothes around the flat do not exist.

The minutes drag on, but the day passes in a flash, and before I know it, I find myself on the floor of the flat, texting Jack with useless updates about Sebastian like I do every night.

**RAINE**

8:05pm Cat loafed on top of couch.

8:08pm Gave me a very nasty look when I sneezed, but did not move.

8:15pm Had an unidentified object in his mouth but swallowed it as soon as I tried to see what it was.

Breaking news—I'm pretty sure the unidentified object Sebastian ate was a piece of lint.

I toss my phone onto the couch and close my eyes. A minute later, my phone dings with a message from Jack.

**JACK**

I have a surprise for you. Ditch the cat and come downstairs. Better yet, bring him along.

I'm off the couch and tugging on my boots before I can type out a reply.

"There's our Raine," Aoife says when I enter the pub and approach the bar.

"There's our Aoife," I reply. I scan the room. It's busier than usual, but I don't see any sign of him.

"Looking for Jack?"

I try to ignore the knowing smile she gives me. "Maybe."

She nods to the room with the fireplace and pulls me a pint. "He's in there."

As soon as I have my drink in hand, I spin away from Aoife, trying not to seem too eager as I cross the pub.

When I first arrived in Cobh, this room was nothing but a fireplace and a few tables. I've been wanting to transform it into a game room, but have spent most of my energy focused on getting our regular events up and running. When I step into the room now, I don't take any notice of Jack. Instead, my eyes are drawn to the tables. There are at least a dozen board games spread around the room. Chess and checkers and Scrabble and Monopoly. Almost any board game I can think of, it's here.

When I do finally spot Jack, I find him standing beside the fireplace, frowning down at something in front of him. It takes me a moment to realize what it is, but when I do, I can't help but squeal in excitement.

The sound startles him, but when Jack sees me, his expression relaxes into a smile. I speed over, narrowly avoiding sloshing beer all over myself. When I reach him, I set my glass on the nearest table, too excited to stand still as I stare at the giant game of Jenga in front of me.

"A game room! Was this what you were up to today?"

Jack grins. "Do you like it?"

"Do I like it?" I look around the room, then walk around the giant Jenga to take it in from all sides. "I love it! Oh, everyone is going to have so much fun with this. Maybe even Ollie will join in."

Jack laughs. "I think that's hoping for too much."

I look closer at the blocks of the giant Jenga set. Each one is stamped with the name of the pub. "Where in the world did you get this?"

Jack rubs at the back of his neck. "I had it made."

"You . . ." I can't even finish my sentence. I'm so excited, I'm practically jumping in place. "We have to play right now. Oh! We can make it a game!"

Jack laughs. "I don't know how to tell you this, but it already is a game."

"I mean we'll add another layer to it."

"It's Jenga. Layers are sort of the point."

I swat him on the shoulder. "Oh, stop."

Jack leans against the wall beside the fireplace and crosses his arms over his chest. "What's the layer, then?"

"For every block successfully removed, you get to ask the other person a question."

Jack presses his lips together as if thinking it over. "What if it's a question I don't want to answer?"

"Uh . . ." I look around the room for inspiration, and my eyes land on my beer. "You drink. It's a drinking game, of course."

"Ah."

"So? What do you think?"

Jack sighs. "I think I'm about to learn all your secrets, Raine Hart."

We rope a few of the regulars who are already here into our game. Róisín comes into the room not long after we start playing and wipes down tables. They hover nearby, and I'm fairly certain I've never seen someone wipe a table so slowly. Or wipe each table twice. Jack says hello to Róisín when they pass by us, then does a double-take.

"You don't need to bus tables, Ro. You only have to worry about the kitchen," he says.

"I don't mind," they say.

Jack furrows his brow as he looks them over. "Isn't it your night off?"

Róisín shrugs.

"We've got room if you want to play, Róisín," I say, and pat the spot on the floor beside me. "Grab a pint and come on over."

As it turns out, the Jenga Drinking Game is an awful drinking game when most of the players are open books anyway. I answer every question I'm asked: My grandfather taught me to play the guitar. I left Boston because I hated med school and wanted to avoid my parents' feelings about it. I don't have a favorite flower because I like them all.

Jack only passes on one question (*What's your greatest fear?* asked by yours truly), and by the end of a few rounds, I know more about these people than I do my own sister.

When last call comes and the others go home, Jack and I rebuild the tower, then sit across from each other at the long table at the center of the room to drink one more pint.

"So, Lorraine Susan Hart," Jack, who is very clearly delighted to have asked me my full name, says, "are you excited for the band to play tomorrow?"

I tap my fingers along the side of the glass. "No, Jack Stephen Dunne, I wouldn't say I'm excited."

Jack gives me a look that I have come to learn means, *Go on.*

I keep my eyes on my beer. "I'm nervous."

"Musical sensation and intrepid world traveler Raine Hart is nervous about hosting some musicians at our wee little pub?"

"Ha." I take a sip of my beer, then set it back onto the table with a sigh. "It's just . . . what if no one comes?"

"I'll be there," Jack says.

"You own the pub, Jack."

"But I'm technically off tomorrow. So really, I could do other things."

I have to laugh at the absurd thought. I don't think there's been a day I *haven't* seen Jack since we met, whether or not he was working. "I'm starting to suspect you don't have anything better to do."

He runs his hand along his pint glass and flicks the condensation at me. "Listen, you, I have plenty of things to do."

"Like what?"

"Like . . ." He turns to look at the fire. The light slants over his face, making him even more colorful than usual. "Okay, I've got nothing."

"I think you hang around the pub so much because you want to see me."

Jack raises his eyebrows but doesn't say anything. He spins the coaster in front of him. "Tomorrow will be great."

He looks at me as if he really believes that, as if it's impossible I could do something that *wasn't* great, and I decide that I'm at least a quarter in love with him already, if not halfway there.

After the pub closes and Jack leaves, I wander around downstairs, spinning a coaster in my hands and thinking of Jack and the way he didn't answer when I said he only hangs around to be with me.

I look down at Sebastian, who's been a quiet shadow at my side for the last ten minutes. "Do you think it's time to redecorate this place?"

Sebastian doesn't answer, of course. He rubs up against my legs, then leaps onto a nearby chair and yawns.

I've been collecting things for weeks, but other than the corkboard, I haven't even begun redecorating. I think through the items I've collected—artwork from Jack, old photos of celebrities, framed jerseys, memorabilia from various Irish brands. I should have enough, right? When I close my eyes and imagine the Local, I don't see it like it is in this moment—empty, dark, sparse. I see the image I had in my head the night I met Jack. In it, every table is occupied. There is laughter and conversation. Music fills the room. Some people stand around the musicians, swaying to the music or singing along. Others wander quietly around the perimeter of the room, taking in all the little details. Everywhere you look, there's something to catch your eye, something worth seeing.

Tomorrow night, I'll have the music. I'm not sure if I'll have the people. That's out of my control.

I think again of how Jack surprised me with Jenga for the pub, and I want to surprise him back. I want him to walk in tomorrow and be blown away, to finally see this place the way I see it.

Energized, I set the coaster down and head to the closet where I've been keeping the artwork we've collected in tubs. I haul the tubs out to the main room. Some are so heavy that I have to drag them through the kitchen and behind the bar. Once I have all the tubs in front of me, I connect my phone to the speakers. It's past midnight, but the music and excitement have me so energized that I don't feel tired in the least.

I push the tables aside, clearing space in the center of the room where I can lay out everything we've collected and see it all at once. I take down all the dreadful photos hanging on the wall and sort through the new stuff, placing things in piles in front of the wall I think they should go on. I realize I've forgotten a hammer and nails and ladder. It takes me half an hour to find the hammer and nails. I have no idea where the ladder is, so I decide to use a chair stacked on top of a table in place of a ladder for the places I can't reach.

It isn't until I'm halfway through the second wall that I realize I've majorly fucked up. I've been using the frames from the old photos for Jack's artwork, replacing them as I go along. The first wall looks as wonderful as I'd hoped. But I only eyeballed the measurements for the frames. I was sure I had enough frames in the right sizes for Jack's art, but as it turns out, I've got a grand total of five.

"This is . . . not good," I say, surveying the mess I've made. "Oh, don't give me that look," I add to Sebastian, who stares at me with what I imagine to be a smug expression.

"It's all right. I can figure this out," I say, but my panic only increases. It's three in the morning, and this is taking much longer than I expected, and I'm starting to realize I can't finish what I've started. I think through my options. I suppose I could abandon the art idea and hang up everything else. But I'd have to figure out what to put in it. I could leave everything as it is now, but the pub looks a bit ridiculous with one and a half walls decorated.

The energy I felt when I began has faded, and I realize I'm exhausted. I'm so tired, I feel delirious. Suddenly, I'm on the verge of tears, unsure I can take a single step, let alone spend the next few hours figuring out what to do about this mess.

I can't do it anymore. I need to sleep. Just an hour or two, and then I can come down here and figure out what to do before Ollie comes to open the pub.

"It's going to be okay," I tell Sebastian. He doesn't look concerned about it. He yawns, which makes me yawn, and I take it as a sign that sleep is a good idea.

"Come on, you lazy cat."

Sebastian follows me up to the flat. I set an alarm for five a.m. and fling myself onto the couch, too tired to make it to the bed.

I'm woken up by sunlight. It streams in through the windows, practically blinding me. For a moment, I have no idea where I am. But as soon as I realize I'm on the couch, I remember *why* I'm on the couch and bolt upright. I fumble for my phone, but it's dead of course. The clock on the stove in the kitchen informs me it is nine a.m.

After a moment in which I am frozen in panic, I spring into action. I'm still wearing the same outfit I had on last night, but I don't care. I only pause to grab my key before I race downstairs, startling Ollie when I appear beside him just as he's unlocking the pub.

"For feck's sake, you nearly gave me a heart attack, Raine," he says, and turns the key in the lock. Ollie arches a brow at me. "What's gotten into you? You look like you've been through hell and back."

"About that."

He shakes his head. "About what?"

"About being through hell and back. It might look a little ... hellish in there." I nod to the door.

"What do you mean?"

"It's a mess."

Ollie narrows his eyes. "What kind of mess are we talking about?" He glances at the door as if he might be able to see through it into the pub.

"Just know that I have it under control. The pub doesn't open for awhile yet, right? And really, not many people come in right when it opens, so it'll give me time to clean up."

"Clean *what* up, Raine?"

"The mess."

"What— Oh, just fecking forget it." He shakes his head, and I brace myself as he opens the door.

I step inside behind Ollie, tense as he scans the pub.

"Raine," he says, not even bothering to turn and look at me. "What the hell happened here?"

"I've got it under control!" I say, though I am not at all sure that's true. "I wanted to surprise everyone by redecorating the pub in time for the music tonight."

When Ollie finally turns to face me, he looks as if he's about to have a stroke. "You thought you could spontaneously redecorate this entire pub overnight by yourself?"

A nervous laugh escapes me. "Well, when you put it that way it sounds ridiculous."

Ollie curses under his breath. "I dunno who is gonna kill me first, you or Jack."

"I'm sorry, I just ... overestimated what I could get done."

"I'll say," Ollie mutters.

"I'm so, so sorry," I say. "I didn't mean to make today more stressful. Really, it's stressful enough with the band playing for the first time tonight. Believe me, I know. And you've got enough on your plate with cooking. Pun not intended, really, I'm not trying to make this a joke, and—"

"Raine," Ollie says, his voice stern enough that I snap my mouth shut.

I'm sure I'm about to be fired. I'll lose this job, and after all this I'll have to go back home to Boston anyway because I haven't even replaced my guitar yet.

He looks at me for a moment, then sighs. "Let me make a few calls. See if anyone can come by and help."

"Oh." I'm unable to say anything else because I don't know what I feel. Ashamed. And relieved. And I feel like an absolute turd. I drop my eyes to the floor and almost start crying when I realize I've shown up to work without shoes again. *You just don't think, Raine.*

"I'm sorry," I finally manage. "I didn't mean to make everything more difficult."

"I know you didn't," he says. He pulls out his phone with a sigh. "Why don't you get started fixing this fecking mess, while I go and call for backup."

"Okay." My emotional state goes from *Oh crap, this was embarrassing* to *This was the worst idea I've ever had and now everyone will secretly hate me.*

Nina is the first to arrive. As soon as she walks through the door, she turns to me and says, "Well, you're certainly ambitious, I'll give you that."

Róisín shows up next, closely followed by Aoife and one of her sons. Ollie disappears into the kitchen, while the rest of us dart around the pub at Nina's bidding. Nina put on her "Cleaning like a Bad Bitch" playlist, and despite the screwup, everyone seems to be having fun, even Aoife's son, who looks like someone who never willingly wakes up before noon.

Fifteen minutes before we're supposed to open, Ollie emerges from the kitchen and scans the room. He crosses the pub to where I've been attempting to hang one of Jack's larger paintings for the last five minutes. I thought it looked straight three minutes ago, but Nina insists it isn't. Finally, when I'm sure I can't hold on to it any longer, Nina shouts, "There! Don't move!" and I step back before I can accidentally nudge it the wrong way.

Ollie slings his arm around Nina's shoulders. "Nice work, kitten. How much longer do you think you'll need?"

Nina looks around the pub and winces. Róisín has most of their side of the pub decorated. Aoife and her son are across the room, hanging string lights over the entryway to the game room, which we haven't even touched and is currently littered with books, because what is better than a game room that is also a library? Especially when the owner is such a bibliophile.

"We need another hour or two," she says. "At least."

Ollie sighs. "Well, we ought to delay opening, then, yeah?"

Nina shrugs. "At least until we get the main room put together. We can work on the side rooms while customers are here."

Ollie turns to me. "Why don't you make a post to let everyone know we'll be opening late today?" he says.

It takes everything in me not to cry in frustration in front of Nina and Ollie. I nod and take a seat at the nearest table, grateful for an excuse to keep my head down.

I stare at my phone, but the tears blur my vision so that I can't even do this small task Ollie has asked of me. I'm over it. All the little costs of having ADHD that add up in the long run. Lost customers. Overdue bills. Replacement phone chargers. Time spent looking for things. The way it makes me feel, like a child. As if everyone else is a real adult and I'm just pretending. The frustration that I can't do the simple, everyday things that most people can. Like laundry, and making phone calls, and remembering to take out something from the freezer for dinner. It's the missed deadlines for opportunities I could've had. The broken relationships. How people think I'm lazy and selfish. How they think I don't care. How *I* think I'm lazy and selfish, even though I *know* I care.

I hear someone take the seat across from me.

"What's wrong?" Nina says.

"Nothing," I say, refusing to look up at her.

"Clearly not nothing," Nina says. "You look like you're being cyberbullied by your phone or something."

I wipe at my tears with the sleeve of my hoodie before looking up at Nina.

"Oh, hon," she says when she sees my face. "*Are* you being cyberbullied?"

I laugh despite myself. I hate how much I love this place. How much I love these ridiculous people. I hate that my mistakes have lost the pub business and disrupted everyone's day.

"No, I'm . . ." I look up at the ceiling to try and blink back tears. When I finally find my voice again, it's just above a whisper. "I'm just really, really sorry. I didn't mean to . . . I wanted to help." I sigh down at my hands. "I told Jack I was a mess. He didn't listen to me."

"Yeah, you're a mess," Nina says. The words surprise me. I glance up at her and her usually severe expression softens into a smile. "And so am I. And so is Oliver, for that matter. I swear the man can't take off a pair of shoes without leaving them in a heap. The point is, everyone's a mess. Your messes just happen to be quite literal. Those are the best kind, believe me."

I fiddle with my phone. "I don't know."

"Well, I do know. I'm the queen of figurative mess-making. Surprise, I know."

Sebastian startles us both when he leaps onto the table. He looks at Nina, then at me, and steps from the table and into my lap. I give him a scratch between the ears.

Nina eyes Sebastian. "See? That cat knows. And for what it's worth, I think Jack will like the pub's new look when he sees it, but . . . if he doesn't . . . don't take it personally, okay? It wouldn't be about you."

I meet her gaze. She wears a sincere look of concern. It's tinged with a sadness I haven't seen from her before.

"Now," Nina says, making both me and Sebastian jump when she slaps the tabletop with both hands. "Back to work. We've got plenty of mess left to clean up."

Nina leaves, muttering under her breath about the string lights. I finish making my posts about the pub's delayed opening and think about Jack. All night I'd been imagining how excited and surprised he'd be to see the pub's transformation. I hadn't really considered it could go any other way, though, of course it could. Jack told me himself he doesn't do well with changes at the pub.

Well, he'll definitely be surprised.

Sebastian purrs beside me, as if to reassure me, but it doesn't help.

I've got the uneasy feeling that my great idea might be even more of a disaster than it is already.

# Twelve

## JACK

When I finally arrive at the Local, I wonder if I've somehow stepped into the wrong place. The pub is almost unrecognizable. All the black-and-white photos are gone. In their place are paintings—many of them mine, but some that aren't. Photographs. Framed newspaper clippings. Guinness and Murphy's and Beamish paraphernalia. And dozens of items I can't yet identify.

For weeks, Raine has been collecting things. Every Saturday, she goes thrifting with Nina. Even the customers are in on it. They dig things out of storage or buy them at estate sales. As soon as they step inside the pub, they look for Raine. And every day it seems we have more customers, many of whom come in just because they met her out and about and she invited them.

So I've had plenty of time to prepare for this. But I didn't expect to walk in this evening and find a completely different pub. She had to have been up all night to pull this off. Or perhaps she had help. I don't know a single person in Cobh who wouldn't help her if she asked.

The walls are filled with things, but all I feel is the absence of those pictures. I scan the pub for Raine but don't see her. The pub is packed. There haven't been this many people in here at one time since Da's funeral.

A couple sits together at a nearby table. Beside one of their half-empty plates is a knife.

*You could pick that up and stab someone and no one would see it coming. No one would be able to stop you in time.*

I don't want to do that. I wouldn't do that.

My pulse picks up. I've been dealing with intrusive thoughts about harm for weeks, but this is the first intrusive thought I've had during this flare-up about hurting someone on purpose.

I look away from the table, but all I see is everything I could use to hurt someone. A pint glass. A bottle. A chair. I could carry a napkin over to the fireplace and use it to burn the place down. If there are a thousand ways to kill someone, my brain must know all of them.

Of all my themes, the violent ones scare me the most. The first violent intrusive thought I had was of strangling my cat. I was fourteen and had just started working at the pub. We used the flat upstairs for storage then, but I liked to go up there on my break to read, and Cleo, an orange tabby who lived in the pub, always came with me. One afternoon, I looked up from the book I was reading and caught sight of Cleo, when I thought, *I could kill this cat with my bare hands.*

I was so alarmed, I went back downstairs well before my break ended. Cleo followed me around the pub like she always did, and the thoughts kept coming. I tried to shoo the cat away, but it didn't work. I tried to distract myself as I cleaned tables by looking at those black-and-white photos on the wall and counting every corner of every one. One, two, three, four. One, two, three, four. And it worked. It helped me to forget. By the time I'd gotten through all of them, Cleo had disappeared to some other place in the pub. Magic.

After that first violent intrusive thought in the flat, I never went up there during my lunch break again. Instead, I'd leave the pub and walk. I hardly ever sat down, because it was easier to distract myself if I was moving. Even so, the thoughts only got worse. I was fourteen and terrified. I thought I was crazy. My brain had been hijacked by some other version of myself, a version I feared was the real Jack Dunne. Someone who wanted to hurt others. Someone like Da.

And now those violent thoughts are back in my head again telling me I'm not safe to be around.

*Are you sure?*

I'd never hurt anyone.

*Are you sure?*

I'm sure.

*Then why do you think such awful things?*

Because I have OCD. They're just thoughts. They're not real. They don't mean anything.

But . . . what if they do? What if I don't really have OCD? What if I'm a psychopath? Real psychopaths don't worry about others, and worry is as automatic to me as breathing. Real psychopaths don't worry about being psychopaths. I want to disappear and reread the article I have bookmarked on my phone about the differences between psychopathy and OCD, even though I have it memorized and have come to the conclusion that I am not a psychopath countless times. *A classic case of Obsessive Compulsive Disorder,* Martina, my psychiatrist, said when she diagnosed me. Surely she'd be able to tell if I was a psychopath.

*But what if she missed something?*

She wouldn't. It's been a while since I've seen her, but she treated me for years. There's no way she'd miss something like that.

*But psychopaths are charming and manipulative, aren't they? What if you purposefully said just the right thing to convince her you have OCD?*

I didn't. I'm not a psychopath. I have OCD and this is just an in-trusive thought.

*But what if it's not?*

*What if what if what if what if?*

The anxiety is overwhelming. I can't stay out here. I keep my head down and make my way behind the bar.

"Took you long enough to get here," Ollie says.

I don't bother responding. It's loud in here, and I'm exhausted. I suppose I could've stayed home, but I promised Raine I'd be here, and if I didn't show, she'd want to know why, and I don't want to tell her.

At our best during off-season, we manage to fill about a fourth of our seats. Right now, at least half of them are occupied. I know most of the people here, but some I don't. Groups of people are huddled around tables, heads together as they wait for the music.

"Jesus," I say.

"I know," Ollie says. "Your girl did good, yeah?"

"She's not my girl," I mumble.

"Whatever you say, Jackie."

"Piss off." I push through the door to the kitchen and head straight for the office, not daring to look around the kitchen in case I see a knife.

As soon as I shut myself inside the office, I press my fingers against the door, each one four times, each one with the same pressure, trying to cancel out every *what if* with as many *undo*s as I can. I should've told Raine that anything involving those photos would be particularly challenging for me. Then she could have warned me, and I could've prepared myself and planned the exposure. But I didn't want to get in her way. I didn't want her to hesitate with any of the changes she planned to make.

The last time I panicked about taking down those photos, Ollie put them back, saying it wasn't worth making myself sick over.

I scan the office, but don't see any of the photographs. I need to find them. I want to put them back. No, that's not true. What I really want is for the thoughts to go away.

But they never go away. Not completely. Not for long, anyway.

A knock on the door startles me. I need to get myself under control, because if Ollie sees me like this, he'll put everything back, and things will never change, and everything Raine has done will be for nothing.

"Jack? Are you in there?"

*Raine.* I'd really rather it was anyone else.

I take another deep breath, then turn and open the door.

"You hate it," she says.

I drum my fingers against the doorframe. Raine's got her hands on her hips and this look on her face that I *shouldn't* like but definitely do.

"Have you ever heard of Grumpy Cat?" I ask.

She narrows her eyes. "Yes. Why?"

"You look like Grumpy Cat right now. It's very charming."

She stares back at me, unamused. "It's your pub. If you hate it, I'll change it. You can tell me the truth."

"I don't hate it," I say. She raises an eyebrow, and I add, "I ... don't know what I think about it."

She searches my face. She's got her bottom lip between her teeth again, and for Christ's sake, why am I always looking at her mouth?

"You look like you don't feel great," she finally says.

"I don't feel great," I say. I don't know if we're talking about the same thing. I don't know if she understands this is an OCD thing. Part of me hopes she does. The other part hopes she thinks I have a headache or something. What would she think if she knew what my intrusive thoughts were really about? I've only been vague with her about it. Would it scare her? Or would there be a part of her that wonders if I'm really capable of the things my brain tells me I want to do?

I look away from Raine, unsure what to say. I feel wound up and weighed down at the same time, as if the fear is sitting right there on my chest. And of course, there are the thoughts. Circling and circling and circling.

After a few moments, Raine says, "Would you like to go out there and sit at a table with me for a while? I could use some help brainstorming ideas for the pub quiz next week."

*No. Not really,* I think. It's actually the very last thing I want to do right now. But sitting with the discomfort is what I'm *supposed* to do, which Raine must know. I'm thankful she's not making a big deal out of it. It makes it easier.

"Okay," I say. "Yeah, sure."

"Great."

When she starts walking, I follow. I avoid looking in the direction of any knives as we make our way through the kitchen and behind the bar. Raine grabs a pen and pad of Post-its from beside the cash register. The thoughts keep coming, but I tell myself they're just thoughts. They're not true. They don't mean anything.

Raine stops at a small, somewhat hidden table in a corner of the main room. I sit opposite her, and she sets the Post-its and pen in front of me.

"What's this for?" I ask.

"I want a Jack Dunne original sketch, of course. I'm thinking of getting a tattoo, you know."

"Oh, really?" I pick up the pen and twirl it between my fingers, ignoring my OCD when it suggests a variety of ways I could hurt myself with it. "What are you going to do? Walk into a tattoo shop, hand some poor tattoo artist a Post-it, and say, *I'll have exactly this, please.*"

"No," she says. "I'm going to hand *you* the Post-it, and say, *I'll have exactly this, please.*"

"I don't think so," I say, but I've already started doodling a beetle.

We fall quiet then. I doodle on the note, and Raine taps away at her phone, asking my opinion about pub quiz topics every now and then. I glance up every few minutes and make myself look at the walls, at the people around us. When the thoughts come, I try not to argue with them. *Yes, you're right, I'm a violent murderer*, I tell them. I keep my hands busy drawing so I can resist tapping my fingers against the table. Whenever I want to think the word *undo*, I ask Raine a question instead. The anxiety doesn't lessen, but after about half an hour, I get used to it. I decide I don't hate the changes Raine has made. In fact, I really like them. It's cluttered, but not chaotic. It's colorful, and interesting, and the opposite of lifeless.

When I finish the beetle drawing, I stick it between us on the table. She picks it up and examines it. "It's perfect."

She sticks it on the table beside her phone, and we fall quiet again. On the Post-it pad I draw a picture of Sebastian with his toy baguette. Once I finish the top Post-it, I flip to the next, and then the next. I glance at Raine. She's looking at the beetle I drew for her. I keep doodling, but I watch from the corner of my eye as she looks around the pub and then back at the drawing in her hands.

"Your work is really beautiful, Jack. It makes people stop and look," she says.

I laugh. "Who says they're stopping because it's beautiful? Maybe they're shocked by how bad it is."

"You don't really think that."

She's right. I don't. I like my work. Otherwise, I wouldn't have tattooed it onto a person to carry around for the rest of their life. But it is easier to pretend my work sucks than to think about how it was taken away from me.

"Beauty's subjective anyway," I say.

"Yes. But that doesn't mean it isn't real."

"Why aren't you a doctor or something?" I say. "I've been wanting to ask, but I don't want you thinking I think less of your career or anything. It's really fucking cool you travel all over playing music. I was just wondering—"

"Why did I get half of a medical school degree if I was just going to quit and become a street performer?"

"That's exactly what I didn't want you to think."

"Relax, Jack," she says. "I know you wouldn't think that."

"Good. Because I don't."

She sighs. "I guess I just preferred making beauty to saving lives. I'm selfish like that." She smiles, but there's a trace of sadness in it.

"You're not," I say.

She worries her bottom lip. "I . . . well, I really did like emergency psychiatry. I liked the people and the science, but I never really wanted to be a doctor. Long story short, I realized that while I liked medicine, I loved music. Maybe it's a silly reason—"

"It's not silly. It makes sense to me. I did make a living jabbing ink into people's skin. Now I do it selling alcohol. Imagine the world without art or music?" I look up at her. "Imagine *Ireland* without alcohol."

She laughs.

"And weren't you just telling me how important beauty is? Take your own advice, ciaróg."

She sighs. "I suppose you're right."

I make the last stroke of the drawing I'm working on. "Speaking of important things, want to see something incredibly useless?"

"Always."

I hold up the Post-it pad for her and flip through it. Raine's face lights up as the drawing of Sebastian comes to life. He picks up the toy baguette and flops onto the ground.

"Useless and silly and important," she says. "My favorite kind of beautiful."

The musicians arrive then, and Ollie calls to Raine. "Will you still be here for a few minutes?" she asks when she stands up from the table.

I nod.

"Perfect," she says. "I'll be right back."

I watch her race across the pub to greet the musicians. I don't hear what she tells them, but they both laugh. I look around. Almost every table has someone sitting at it. The pub is exactly what I always hoped it would be—a place filled with laughter and excitement.

But I can't enjoy it, because the thoughts won't leave me alone, and I'm too exhausted to fight them. My fingers are restless, so I try to keep myself occupied doodling on Post-its, but not even that can dim the noise of my thoughts.

I feel something brush against my legs and look down to find Sebastian. I set my pen on the table and crouch down to pet him.

"Hey, Bash." Sebastian rubs his face against my hand. Living at Nina and Ollie's has been great, but I do miss having him around. He's usually glued to my side at work and at home.

"Have you been good, bud?" I ask, giving him a scratch behind his ears. The best thing about Sebastian is that he always knows when I'm upset. He knows, and yet he can comfort me without worrying, or trying to help, or judging me. He doesn't wonder if he did something that caused me to be this way, like Mum and Ollie do. He just lets me know that he sees what I'm dealing with. He's just . . . there. Which is really all I want. Dealing with OCD is hard enough on its own. Dealing with everyone's feelings about *my* OCD is why I keep it to myself most of the time, even when I'd really like to talk about it with the people in my life.

"Hey, Keurig. Hey, floofs."

I look up and find Raine standing beside the table. She searches my face. "Think you're up for a walking meeting?"

I look across the pub to where the musicians are setting up. "You'll miss the beginning of the music."

She shrugs. "I'll catch it next time. I've been here all day, so I could use some fresh air. It won't be long. We can just do a loop around the block or something."

"Okay, yeah." I give Sebastian one last scratch, then tuck the pen and Post-it pad in my pocket, relieved to have an excuse to escape for a while. "Let's go."

The musicians have just started playing when we step outside.

"You sure you don't want to stay?" I ask.

"I'm sure."

Raine walks beside me as we make our way down the block. Her hands are tucked into the pockets of her coat, and thank God for that, because we're walking so close our shoulders keep bumping, and if her hand were free, I would probably take it in mine without thinking.

When we turn a corner, Raine halts in the middle of the pavement. I slow to a stop and follow her gaze to St. Colman's Cathedral. It glows above the town, a gentle giant, a figure of light to break up the monotony of the dark sky.

"Isn't it pretty?" she says.

I look at her. "It's beautiful."

Raine turns to me then. She tilts her face up to mine, and I'm certain I've never seen someone look so beautiful in the glow of a streetlight. Which is a ridiculous thought to have. And I would know. I'm an expert in ridiculous thoughts.

It would be so easy to kiss her. I think she would kiss me back. I've failed miserably at keeping my promise not to flirt with her. The more time I spend with her, the more time I *want* to spend with her.

I want to kiss her. I really fucking want to.

I almost do.

And then the thoughts come.

*What if she's been drinking?*

I've been with her all evening and she hasn't had a single drink.

*She could've had one earlier. She could've had one when she went to talk to the musicians.*

She's not drunk.

*What if you kiss her and get carried away? What if she wants you to stop? Do you really think you have that much self-control?*

I do. Of course, I do. I'm not an animal.

*Are you sure?*

I'm sure.

*If you're so sure, why would you even question it? Why would you be thinking what you're thinking right now?*

"Jack?" Raine says.

"Hmm?"

She searches my face. "Are you all right?"

I swallow. "I'm grand."

"Are you sure?"

*I'm not sure of anything, ever.* "I'm sure," I say.

She looks like she doesn't quite believe me, but instead of pushing the issue like I'm afraid she will, she simply takes my hand and starts walking, pulling me along after her. Once I catch up to her side, she laces her fingers through mine and says, "Have I already told you about the time I fell into the fountain at Trafalgar Square?"

"You did what, now?"

"Oh God." She laughs, and I tug her closer to my side so she won't accidentally step off the pavement and into the street. "It was so embarrassing, Jack. Absolutely mortifying."

I hold her hand tighter in mine. "Start from the beginning."

Raine launches into the story as we walk back to the pub. We don't acknowledge the hand-holding. Everything about her story-telling is big and loud. Her voice. How she talks with her free hand.

She's so animated, and the story is so winding, that it takes all of my attention to follow it.

It's only when we arrive back at the pub that she drops my hand. She turns to me, bouncing on her heels as she finishes her story. Afterward, there's a moment of quiet. Someone opens the door, and the music within the pub floats out to us.

"You don't have to stay," she says.

I look from her to the pub. I hate feeling like I want to come inside with her but can't. I hate that my own head is driving me away from everything I want. "I'd love to stay for a while, it's just . . ."

"A bad brain day."

I laugh. "A bad brain day. I like that. And . . . yeah, that's exactly the sort of day I'm having."

"It's probably for the best. If we spend *too* much time together, you'll get bored of me."

"I really doubt that, ciaróg."

We say goodnight, and after Raine disappears inside the pub, I linger out on the pavement. I want to say *fuck it* and go inside. I want to tell her I've changed my mind. About tonight. About being her *most professional coworker.*

The door swings open, and someone steps outside. Music floods out to me again. Everything I want is inside this pub right now. I catch a glimpse of red hair within the pub and know it's her. The door begins to swing shut, hiding her from view. The moment before it closes, I grab the edge of the door, pulling it open again so I can slip inside.

I make my way through the crowd, and the thoughts come. I let them, trying to do what I know works. I can do this. I've done this before. When I reach Raine, I lean close so she can hear me. "You did great."

Raine spins to face me, whipping me in the face with her hair. "You stayed!" She's practically dancing in place, wearing a smile I know I'll spend the rest of the night thinking about. She stretches up on her toes so her mouth reaches my ear. "You'll be okay?"

I'm not sure, but I want to try. Already, the anxiety has my every sense painfully alert. "I think so."

She gives me a gentle smile. She turns to face the musicians again and, stepping closer to me, slips her fingers through mine.

I look over at her, but her eyes are on the music. Her hand in mine doesn't take the thoughts away or make me feel better. But it gives me something to hold on to when I have no idea if I'll sink or swim. It's a reminder of why I'm putting myself through this torture.

I'm not well. I haven't been able to admit that, not even to myself.

I'm not well.

But I'm going to get better.

# Thirteen

## RAINE

Jack makes it through most of the band's set before he disappears. Once the pub closes and everyone else has gone home, I sit at the bar and stare at my phone, contemplating whether or not I should text him.

"I should, right?" I say to the empty bar. But by the time I've finished my sentence, I've typed out my text and sent it.

> **RAINE**
> You okay?

"I'm okay."

I nearly drop my phone at the sound of Jack's voice. When I look up, I find him at the door to the kitchen.

"I thought you went home," I say.

"Nah." He stands behind the bar, directly opposite of where I'm sitting. When he rests his elbows on the bar, I drop my gaze to his hands and think about how it felt to hold his hand in mine. He must be thinking the same thing, because he leans a little closer and his hand brushes against mine and lingers there.

"Are you really okay?" I ask.

"I'm really okay," he says. "How'd the rest of the set go? Sounded like a success from where I was hiding out in my office."

I run through everything he missed, but I'm not sure either of us is actually paying attention to the conversation. I'm not, at least. Because when he slips his fingers through mine, something neither of us acknowledges, the only thing I can think about is how I don't want him to leave.

"Sebastian misses you, you know," I say when Jack glances at the door, even though Sebastian spent most of the evening at Jack's side and is presently curled up on the barstool beside me.

Jack eyes the cat. "Does he?"

I shouldn't be doing this. It's late. "You should come visit him in the flat. If you want, that is," I say.

Jack looks at the door, then back at me, then at Sebastian. "He's probably wondering why I never come up there anymore."

I have no idea if he really believes that, but I'll run with it. "Oh, definitely."

"Well, then, I have no choice, do I?"

We grab our coats and Sebastian follows us when we step outside. Nervous energy courses through me as I watch Jack lock up the pub, and then when I unlock the door beside the pub that leads up to the flat.

"I love your place," Jack says when he follows me inside the flat. "Very tasteful."

"The previous tenant had a great eye," I say, shooting him a grin as I push off my boots. I scan the flat and cringe. It's a mess in here. My new MIDI controller and laptop are on the coffee table. A pair of socks is beside the couch. My hair brush and a package of hair elastics are on one of the bookcases for some reason. My foot tambourine and a half-empty glass of water are on the side table next to the couch. Actually, now that I scan the flat, I realize I've got half-empty glasses of water everywhere. Jack has been up here a few times, and it's never perfectly tidy, but it's not usually this bad. Jeez, I must be desperate. There's no way I'd bring him up here when the place is like this otherwise.

"Sorry about . . . all of this," I say, gesturing to the room at large. At the look of confusion on Jack's face, I add, "The mess." Great, now I've brought attention to it when I didn't need to.

Jack shrugs. "It looks lived in," he says.

I grab the stack of books I have on the couch and return them to the bookcases, then pick up Sebastian, giving him a look that I hope he understands means *play it cool*, and carry him over to Jack.

Jack takes the cat in his arms and scratches him between the ears. "Hey, Princess Ugly," he says. "Have you been taking good care of Raine?"

"I thought *I* was the one taking care of *him*."

Jack glances at me before returning his attention to Sebastian. "Should we keep letting her think that?"

I roll my eyes and settle onto the couch, tucking my legs beneath me. Jack walks over, Sebastian still in his arms, and sits at the opposite end. "I think Raine's lying about you missing me, Bash, but that's all right."

"He really does miss you!" I say. "Look at him! He's beside himself that you've come home."

But Sebastian is the worst sidekick I've ever had, and leaps from Jack's arms to curl up beside me.

Jack looks at me with raised eyebrows.

"You'd make an awful actor," I tell Sebastian.

Jack drapes an arm over the side of the couch. "You don't have to make up reasons to hang out with me. You could always just ask."

I busy myself petting Sebastian. "Fine. Would you like to hang out, Jack Dunne?"

He pulls his phone from his pocket. "Let me see if I can fit you in."

"Oh, shut up." I grab a couch pillow from beside me and throw it at Jack, but he catches it. Sebastian lifts his head to see what all the commotion is, then closes his eyes as if we're the most underwhelming humans he's ever met.

Jack spins the pillow between his hands and grins at me. "Sure, I'll hang out with you. What are we doing?"

I grab the other couch pillow and hug it to my chest. "What do *you* want to do?"

He hums to himself for a moment. "We could build a cat tent out of a T-shirt."

I snort. "Been there, done that, ruined the T-shirt."

"Or look for all your missing socks."

"Impossible. They're scattered all over Europe."

Jack sighs. "That's all I've got."

Jeez, what do I have to do to make Jack get the hint, flat out say it? *Don't say it. Don't say it. You shouldn't say it.*

"We could always make out on the couch," I say. As soon as the words leave my mouth my heart starts racing. "For fun, of course. If you're into that kind of fun, I mean." *Stop talking stop talking stop talking.*

Jack stops spinning the couch pillow and stares at me.

"Or we could . . . not do that," I say. Why did I say it? Why? I knew I shouldn't have, and I did it anyway. *Thanks for nothing, frontal lobe.*

Sebastian gets to his feet and stretches, then flops down next to Jack. "You're really testing the limits of my moral fiber, you know," Jack says.

I hug the couch pillow tighter. "Me or the cat?"

Jack looks up at me. "You, of course. Sebastian is too lazy for that. The worst he does is make me overspend on cat toys."

I sigh. "Can we stop pretending we're not into each other?"

"I'm not pretending to not be into you," he says.

"So you're just actually not into me?"

He ruffles his hair with a hand. "That's not it. I've just been trying to . . . ignore . . . being into you. And doing a shite job of it, apparently."

"So, just to clarify, you *are* into me."

Jack laughs. "Very much. And you're . . . interested in me too."

"Correct. So we've established that we're both into each other."

He nods. "I suppose we have."

"Great."

"Grand."

"So . . ."

"It's just . . . I know we said I'm not your boss, but I kind of am, right?"

*Ah yes*, how could I forget that Jack is my *most professional coworker?* "Okay, so you own the pub."

"Exactly, which is why—"

I hold up a hand. "However, I think you can relax a little."

Jack doesn't look convinced.

"This is not my career," I continue. "It's not like anyone is vying for my job. *Everyone* has been pushing us at each other. Aoife, Nina, Róisín. No one cares if we have a little . . . fun."

"Fun," Jack says. He looks away to pet Sebastian but doesn't say anything. The silence stretches on until I can't take it anymore.

"Jack?"

He lifts his head and smiles. I wish I could read the emotion there, but I can't. He looks all mixed up, like he doesn't know what he thinks or feels.

"I'd really like to have fun with you, Raine," he says, "Whatever kind of fun that is. Laser tag. Ice skating."

I roll my eyes. "You know what type of fun I'm talking about."

Jack clears his throat. "Just checking." He gives Sebastian a pat, then gets to his feet. I find myself holding my breath when he comes nearer and sits beside me on the couch. "I'd like that type of fun too. Obviously. But . . ." He tugs gently on a strand of my hair, his hand so close that I feel the heat of it on my cheek. I search his face, but he doesn't meet my gaze. His eyes are on my hair between his fingers. He looks as if it pains him to touch it. I don't understand. The touch. The look. Why we can't give in to this attraction between us, when we both clearly want to.

"I haven't told you everything about my OCD," he says.

"Jack . . . Whatever it is, it'll be okay."

He shakes his head. "You don't know what I'm going to say."

"So tell me, and I'll show you."

"I want you to think the best of me." He lifts his gaze to mine. "Please, always think the best of me."

I search his face, trying to figure out what it is that has him so terrified. With OCD the possibilities are endless. Anything can be an obsession. But irrational thoughts are just thoughts. I know that. But I also know how hard it is to truly believe that when you're the one having the thoughts. Especially if not everyone in your life has been understanding.

"I do," I say. "Of course I do."

Jack is completely still for a moment, and then he drops his fingers from my hair. When he speaks again, his voice is quiet, like he's not sure he wants to say it at all. "My OCD . . . It's not just thoughts of bad things happening to people. That's a big part of it, but there's also . . . I have thoughts about hurting people. I see myself doing the worst things. Awful, violent things. I can't see a knife, or a pair of scissors, or walk into a crowded room without my first thought being . . ." He shakes his head, as if unable to finish his sentence. "I know I'd never hurt anyone, I'd never hurt you . . . but . . . what if I'm wrong? What if that violent person is the real me, and I'm just pretending to be someone else?" He glances up at me, his expression pleading. "You don't think I'm capable of hurting anyone, right?" As soon as he says it, he squeezes his eyes shut. "No, don't answer that. I'm not supposed to ask for reassurance like that."

*Oh, Jack.* I knew he worried about bad things happening to people, but this . . . I want to tell him that everything will be okay. I want to tell him that, no, I don't think he's capable of hurting someone. "I had no idea."

"I'm sorry I didn't tell you before. It wasn't always this bad. I was in recovery for a long time but . . ." He turns away from me and rubs a hand over his face. "I haven't told anyone this. I haven't even wanted to admit it to myself. It was just small stuff at first but . . . I think I may be having a bit of a . . . relapse."

*A bit of a relapse.* How very like Jack to minimize his own problems.

"The thoughts are harder to manage right now," he says. "And if I'm with someone, even casually, things will come up. I should've told you sooner, but I didn't want to scare you. I didn't want you to look at me and wonder if I was thinking about horrible things. I liked you too much, and it happened so fast, and I was . . . scared, about what was happening to me and what you would think. I didn't want things to change, and I'm sorry if I misled you, and . . . Well, the point is, I can't promise having fun with me would be very fun. So it's probably a bad idea. Not that you'd still be interested in me anyway." He laughs, but there's no humor to it. "Who wants to be with someone who thinks like I do, right? Even if it's just casual?"

"What your thoughts are about . . . that's no one's business." I say. "You don't *owe* that to anyone. You and your thoughts are not the same thing. If you don't want to be with someone right now because it's too much on top of everything else, that's one thing. But if it's because you think you don't deserve to be with someone . . . Jack, you don't have to be perfect. You don't have to be in recovery or have everything under control. You deserve to be happy. Not later, but right now. You deserve as much happiness as you can get. And for what it's worth, I think plenty of people would want to be with you exactly the way you are. Including me."

When Jack's eyes meet mine, I feel as if we're playing a game of chess, only I have no idea whose move it is. There are a thousand possibilities. I could lean forward and kiss him. Or I could pull him to me and kiss him. Or I could shove him down onto this couch and kiss him. Or I could—

The door buzzes, and Jack looks away. "Are you expecting someone?"

"No." I have no idea who could be buzzing at my door, but whoever it is, I am very annoyed with them. "Maybe they'll just go away if we ignore them."

Jack looks as if he's considering it when the buzzer sounds again. "It's late," he says. "I should at least check who it is. Stay here, okay?"

I follow Jack to the door, then watch as he descends the steps. "Just a second!" he hollers when the buzzer sounds again. He reaches the door, and after looking out the window, turns back to me and says, "There's some woman standing out there with a suitcase."

"What?"

He shrugs. "I don't know her. Maybe she's at the wrong place."

I'm nearly down the steps when Jack opens the door, but his body blocks whoever it is from view.

"Hello?" he says.

"Hello, yourself," a woman's voice replies.

I know who it is the instant I hear her voice. When I peer around Jack, I wonder if this entire night has been a dream. Because that neat brown hair and that scarf . . . they don't belong here.

"What are you doing here?" I say.

"Visiting you, of course! I hope I wasn't interrupting anything."

"I'm sorry," Jack says, "but who are you, exactly?"

She gives Jack a look that makes me want to tie a luggage tag around his wrist with my name on it. "Well, aren't you going to introduce me to your friend, Raine?"

"This is my . . ." I suddenly have no idea *what* he is. "Jack."

She laughs, and I hope I can zip through this moment and into a less embarrassing one.

"Jack, meet Clara. My sister."

# Fourteen

"Let me grab that for you," Jack says. He starts hauling Clara's concerningly large suitcase up the stairs before she can object.

Clara's eyes follow Jack, and she gives me a sly grin. "That's Jack? The Jack you were telling me about? The guy whose place you're living in, aka your boss? The cat dad?"

"Mm-hmm."

"Wow, that is *not* what I was picturing when you said the words *cat dad*. No wonder you didn't want to leave."

I elbow her in the side. "Quit ogling my boss!" I grab her by the arm and tug her up the steps alongside me.

Clara sighs. "If you insist."

When we reach the top step, Clara launches herself at me, wrapping me in a tight hug.

"I missed you, Rainey." She sounds as if she's about to cry. Clara never cries. I haven't seen her cry in years.

I hug her back, but don't squeeze too tight. I'm worried I'll break her because she is obviously fragile right now. "I missed you too."

I have no idea what's going on. Spontaneous visits are not Clara. Skipping school is not Clara. Displays of vulnerability are not Clara. At least, that hasn't been Clara for a long time. I have no idea who this person is, but whoever she is, I'm worried about her.

I stand there until Clara pulls away. She wipes at her eyes with the backs of her hands, and I glance at Jack, who gives me a hesitant look from the doorway.

"Come on." I put my arm around Clara's shoulders and steer her into the flat.

"Did you just get in?" I ask. "You've got to be hungry or tired or something."

She waves a hand. "All of it. I'm all of it." She looks at Jack. "Thanks for the help, Cat Dad," she says, and plops onto the yellow couch.

*Plopping* is another thing my sister doesn't do. But here she is, curled up on her side and tucking a couch pillow beneath her head. I've never seen her so uninhibited around someone she doesn't know.

I stare at her, unsure what to do. I'm used to being the hot mess. Clara is the one with the pep talks and motivational mantras. I've never read a Brené Brown book, and I'll never need to because all I have to do is be around Clara for a week to pick up on the highlights of whatever the latest self-help fad is.

I don't know what to say, because I have no idea what's wrong. And there is very obviously something wrong, because Clara shouldn't be here. She should be in school.

Food. That is the obvious first step here. "I'll be right back."

I gesture for Jack to follow me into the kitchen.

"I don't know what's going on," I say, voice hardly above a whisper as I haphazardly open and close cabinets, hoping to find snacks. You'd think I've never stayed here a day in my life. Plates. Bowls. I even open the microwave door and find a bowl of soup I heated up yesterday and forgot about. I pretend I don't see it and shut the door again.

"Are you all right?" Jack asks.

"No idea." I open the fridge and stare inside it, but I keep forgetting to actually look at what's there.

Jack strides across the kitchen to another cabinet and throws a tube of Pringles my way.

"She's not acting like herself. I invited her to come, but she never said she was coming. She's supposed to be in school. She doesn't have a break until the end of March."

"Is there anything I can do?"

I shake my head. "I don't think so."

Jack nods. "I'll let you get your sister settled, then. Don't come into work tomorrow, okay? Spend some time with her."

"Are you sure?"

He nods.

"Thanks."

"Of course, ciaróg."

When we return to the living room, Clara is in the same spot on the couch with Sebastian curled up beside her. Jack and I look at each other with raised eyebrows, and I feel a spark of jealousy that Sebastian seems to like my sister as much as he likes me.

"I'm gonna head on," Jack says. "It was nice to meet you, Clara. I hope I'll get to see more of you while you're here."

"You most definitely will."

Jack laughs, and I feel that jealousy zip through me again as he heads for the door.

Once Jack leaves, the flat is quiet. Clara doesn't look at me as she pets Sebastian. We share the Pringles between us.

"Clara, I'm glad to see you but . . . why are you here?"

"I'm on sabbatical," she says.

"That's . . . not a thing for medical students."

She sighs. "Fine. I quit school."

"You . . ." I stare at her, but the words don't make sense. Clara doesn't quit anything she starts. "No you didn't."

Clara rolls onto her back and stares up at the ceiling. She crosses her legs at the ankles and, in this moment, my sister is a contradiction. All guarded sarcasm and yet there's something vulnerable about the way she lies there, face up, her feet in my lap. "I'm *going* to drop out of medical school. I just have to make it official."

"Do Mom and Dad know you're here?"

She laughs. "No! Of course not!"

"Why are you dropping out of medical school?"

She shrugs. "I don't want to be a doctor."

She's lying. Clara isn't like me. She didn't just go to medical school because our parents wanted her to. She's always loved medicine. Clara loves blood and guts as much as she does Audrey Hepburn movies and cleaning products. While most aspiring surgeons want to specialize in plastic surgery or neurosurgery, Clara has always known she wanted to have her hands in a little bit of everything and become a general surgeon.

But if Clara doesn't want to tell me the real reason, then I'm not going to prod. Not tonight anyway. I file it away as *Conversations to have when Clara is not jet-lagged.*

"How long are you here for?" I ask.

"How long are you going to stay here?"

I almost say, *As soon as I replace all my gear,* and then I remember I haven't told her about everything that happened.

"Four weeks, give or take."

"Then that's how long I'll be here," Clara says.

"And then what will you do?"

"Where are you going next?"

"I . . . don't know. I was thinking I might do Galway, but it's all up in the air still."

"Galway it is. Wherever you go, I go."

Okay . . . now I'm even more confused. "And what will you be doing? I don't make enough money busking to feed both of us."

Clara squints at the ceiling as if she really hasn't thought of this. Another point for my theory that this is not Clara, but an imposter. Clara overplans to a fault. She checks everything a billion times. Tries to nail down every detail.

"I'll sing with you," she says.

I burst out laughing, then clap a hand over my mouth when she glares at me. "Sorry, it's just . . . Clara, you're an awful singer."

She sighs. "Oh yeah. Forgot."

Clara has a voice you could never forget, and not in a good way.

"What does that Krista woman you met in Dublin do? Juggling?"

"Hula-hooping."

Clara snaps. "That. I'll learn to hula-hoop while we're here. I'll hula-hoop eight hours every day. I'll hula-hoop like it's my job and be ready in time for us to hit the road. Do you think I could be ready in time?"

"No."

"I know! I'll be one of those human statues. I'll paint myself gold and just stand around. You can't tell me I won't be able to do that."

I can, but I won't. Clara is too busy to be a human statue. She's always got some goal to work toward or some event to go to or someone to meet up with. My sister is a machine of productivity. She even relaxes productively: collage-making, yoga, crochet.

And yet . . . here she is, eating Pringles straight from the tube on Jack's couch.

"We can call ourselves the Wandering Harts," she says. "Get it?

You'll play the music and I'll stand around and look interesting. People love sister duos. Tia and Tamera. Mary-Kate and Ashley. Beyoncé and Solange. Raine and Clara. Sounds great, doesn't it?"

Does it? I'm not so sure. All I know is it sounds like my sister is *going through it*, and I have no idea why or what to do.

"It sounds wonderful," I say, hopeful that she'll come to her senses by the time she wakes up tomorrow and I'll find out what's really going on.

It isn't long before Clara dozes off on the couch. I gently wake her and she smiles that imperfect smile I love when she sees me. We change into our pajamas and go to bed. I turn to face her and tell her I love her and that, whatever is going on, things will be okay, but her eyes are already shut.

I sigh and turn away. My phone lights up on the nightstand. I grab for it and find a message from Jack.

**JACK**
Everything okay over there?

I look at my sleeping sister. She has her hands tucked beneath her pillow and her mouth slightly open. A strand of dark hair falls over her face, fluttering gently with every breath.

**RAINE**
Clara says she dropped out of medical school
and wants to become a human statue, so . . .
probably not. She's asleep now. I'm hoping
I can get more out of her tomorrow.

**JACK**
Can I call you?

I glance at Clara, then quietly slip from the room. Sebastian, who was dozing between us, follows me into the kitchen, where the only light comes from above the stove. When I call Jack, he answers on the first ring.

"I was going to call you," he says.

"What does it matter?"

"I've never called you just to talk before."

*Just to talk.* Did he really call just because he wanted to talk to me? Smiling to myself, I end the call and sit on the kitchen floor, dangling one of Sebastian's toys in front of him as I wait for Jack to call.

Thirty seconds pass. And then a minute. Just as I'm about to call him again, my phone rings.

"Hello?" I say.

"Did you hang up on me?"

"You said you wanted to call me. I didn't want to steal your thunder."

"I didn't know you'd hung up. Took me a while to figure out I was talking to no one."

It's nearly one in the morning. I should be exhausted after getting hardly any sleep last night, but so much has happened in the last few hours that my brain is buzzing. Whenever something big or exciting or surprising happens, it's as if my brain says, *Sleep? Never heard of it.* As a kid, when I was too worked up to sleep, my mom used to tell me stories. She'd lie in bed beside me and tell me to close my eyes. The stories always began the same way: a giant bubble appears in my room and scoops me up, softly carrying me to beautiful places all around the world.

Jack's voice in my ear feels just like that. It's as if I'm in a bubble, where nothing and no one can bother me. I can stretch out on this kitchen floor and no one will think I'm weird for lying on the floor instead of sitting in a chair. It's so late that I don't have to think about anything but whatever Jack wants to talk about.

I roll onto my back and stare up at the ceiling, then press the phone closer to my ear. "What were you saying to no one?"

"That's between me and no one."

"You're ridiculous."

"Aithníonn ciaróg, ciaróg eile."

I pull my phone from my ear and find the Post-it he drew me earlier where I tucked it away beneath my phone case. I unfold it, staring at it in the dim light. "When you give me my first tattoo—"

*"When?"*

"Yes, *when*. I want flowers with my beetles."

"This is becoming very elaborate."

"Elaborate is my middle name."

"Your middle name is Susan."

"The point is I want an elaborate tattoo." I stick the Post-it to my chest and lift one leg in the air. My pajama pants slide down, revealing my depressingly pale skin. Might as well make it beautiful if I'm going to be so ghostly. "On my leg."

"A leg is a big limb, Raine. You might want to be more specific."

"Eh, I'll decide where on the day of."

Jack sighs, but he doesn't say *No*, or *I don't think so*, or *I don't tattoo anymore*. I look at the beetle drawing once more before sticking it in my phone case again.

"Can I ask you something?" Jack says.

"Sure."

"If I'd have kissed you tonight, would you have kissed me back?"

I laugh a little too loud and cover my mouth with a hand. "You're not serious."

Jack doesn't say anything.

"Jack . . . I literally asked you to make out with me on the couch."

"But that was before I told you . . . what I told you."

I think of the way Jack looked right before Clara arrived and wish

I could reach through the phone and hug him. We didn't really get to finish our conversation. "Yes, I would've kissed you back."

"And you don't feel like I've been pressuring you? Me owning the pub doesn't make you feel uncomfortable?"

"If you pressured me any less, I'd float away. Stop thinking about it and come kiss me or something."

It's a joke, but Jack doesn't laugh. He's quiet for so long, I pull the phone from my ear just to check he hasn't hung up on me.

"Jack?"

"Okay."

I pause with the cat toy in my hand. "Okay . . ."

"I'm coming to kiss you."

I sit up so fast I see stars. "You are?"

"If that's okay."

"Yes. That's . . . fine. Great!" I catch sight of my reflection in the oven door. Pajama pants. Mismatched fuzzy socks. A hoodie I found at the back of Jack's closet. Hair pineappled on top of my head. If Jack leaves Nina and Ollie's place now, he'll be here in five minutes. Well, this is what he gets for finally deciding to kiss me at one in the morning.

On the other end of the call, I hear the jingle of Jack's keys and the soft thud of a door closing. "I'll see you in a few, yeah?"

"Um . . . yeah," I say.

"Grand."

When Jack hangs up, I stare at the phone for a few moments. *Jack is coming over here to kiss me.*

I look at Sebastian. "Floofs, he's coming over here to kiss me."

Sebastian yawns.

I get to my feet and race downstairs, where I keep my gaze out the window.

When Jack appears a few minutes later, I don't think I've ever opened a door quicker in my life.

As soon as I see him, I can't keep from smiling. He looks like he rolled out of bed too. Hair messy. Gray pajama pants under his black coat. "Hi."

"Hi."

I'm not sure what to do next. Am I supposed to do something? How is this supposed to work? I didn't think this through. Really, it was just a silly comment.

"Is that my jumper?" he says.

I tug the sleeves of his hoodie over my hands. "I found it in your closet. It smells like you."

Jack laughs. "What do I smell like?"

"Like an Urban Outfitters." *Oh my God, why do I even have a mouth?*

Jack leans against the wall. "What?"

"I mean, you smell like an Urban Outfitters *looks*."

"And *how* would you describe what an Urban Outfitters looks like?"

"I don't know . . . interesting." I can't think when he's here to kiss me.

"I'm not sure if *interesting* is a good thing when it comes to smells."

"Fine! Fine. It looks like you could walk in there intending to buy a shirt, and walk out with a cat mug, a new shower curtain, and a Britney Spears adult coloring book."

"That is . . . oddly specific."

"Well, it's a good thing, okay? You smell nice and it makes my brain happy. And I hope it makes you happy that you've gotten me to admit that."

"As a matter of fact, it *does* make me happy."

"You know, *most* people try to *keep* me from going on tangents," I say. "*You* practically shove me into them."

"I like to see where that brain of yours will go. It's a surprise every time. And I like seeing you in my jumper."

"Well . . ." I say, but that's all I've got.

I look up at Jack, but he isn't giving me that teasing look anymore. He steps closer, and when the toes of his boots brush my socks, my brain is nothing but radio static.

He tugs on a strand of my hair. "I can't stop thinking about you."

"That's because I work at your pub and live in your flat."

He's so close that his laugh warms my cheek. "I don't think that's why."

When Jack leans in, I lean in too, but the wrong way, and we end up knocking noses. I yelp, and then I'm laughing and rubbing at my nose. When I look at Jack, he's rubbing his nose and laughing too.

"That's not exactly how I thought that would go," he says.

"Me either."

"If I try to kiss you again, do you promise not to attack me?"

"I didn't attack you!"

He catches my chin in his hand. "Stay very still," he says.

I stare into his blue eyes, and nothing is funny anymore. If he keeps talking to me like that, I'll do whatever he wants me to. "Okay."

"Tá tú go hálainn, ciaróg."

"What does that mean?"

"It means you're beautiful."

"Oh," I say, feeling myself blush. "Do you know a lot of Irish?"

"Just whatever I learned in school. And a few phrases to help me flirt with girls."

"Does it work?"

"Sometimes." He releases my chin. "Níl mé ag iarraidh go dté- ann tú."

"And that?"

He smiles. "Don't worry about it."

I'm about to argue with him, but then he leans in again and kisses me. The first brush of his lips against mine is gentle. He pulls away, but not much. He searches my face, and I think *yes, yes, yes,* unable to speak but hopeful he can hear me anyway.

The next kiss is anything but gentle. I try as hard as I can to stay still but can't help myself. I pull him to me until we're pressed up against the wall. His mouth is demanding, taking whatever I give him. When his hands find my hair, it isn't one strand, but as much as he can hold. One of his legs presses between mine, and the *yes, yes, yes* in my head becomes *more, more, more.* My hands are in his hair, and then I'm unbuttoning his coat. He tugs at the sweater I'm wearing— *his sweater*—but it's tricky in such a cramped space, and this is one of those hoodies without a zipper, so I help him pull it off before flinging it onto the stairs. He has me against the wall again, kissing me as his hands slip beneath my shirt, and the sound he makes when he touches me, the *way* he touches me, has me actually considering having sex with him in this stairwell.

But between the two of us, Jack has the most control, of course. When he pulls away, the noise in my brain is nothing but a pleasant hum.

He rakes a hand through his hair. "I think . . . maybe we should . . ."

"I know, I know," I say, even though I don't *want* to know. I *want* to convince him that Clara is a deep sleeper and that I am capable of being very quiet so he can finish what he's started, but neither is true.

I glance up the stairs to the flat. "I love my sister. But I also kind of hate her right now."

Jack smiles. He tucks my hair behind my ears, then leans in to kiss me once more. It is tender, and soft, and I feel like I'm in that bubble again, floating in a world filled with only good things. "Good night, ciaróg."

"Good night, Keurig."

When I shut the door behind him, I sit on the bottom step, too stunned to move. I don't think I've ever been drawn to someone the way I'm drawn to Jack. I'm not sure how a little flirtation led to this.

I have no idea what this means or where it's going, but I want to find out. I don't want this to end, but the only thing I know for sure is that it will.

Four weeks has never felt shorter.

# Fifteen

## JACK

I slip into Nina and Ollie's quietly. I don't even bother to stop and take off my boots and coat. I head right to my room and toss them into a corner before falling into bed. I run that kiss over and over again in my mind. Her waiting for me at the door. Her in my jumper. The mess of hair on top of her head. How sweet she tasted. How soft she felt.

It isn't until I'm nearly asleep that the thought comes.

*You said you were coming over to kiss her. You did more than kiss her.*

I sit up, blinking in the dark. She was into it, right? I think of how she helped me take off the jumper, and the way she leaned into me when my hands slipped beneath her shirt. That's obvious, yeah?

*Maybe she was afraid to say no.*

I can imagine it, a parallel scenario, one I am pretty sure is fake. What if she was breathing faster because she was scared, not because she was enjoying herself? What if I read everything all wrong? There's so much evidence to the contrary, and yet . . . all I need is the tiniest pinprick of doubt to spiral into a full-on panic.

I rub my hands over my face. I tug at my hair because I want to tap my fingers against something and undo the very thought that I went too far. Why can't I be sure of anything good? It's always the bad things. I really only went over there to kiss her. I truly didn't expect anything beyond that. I wasn't exactly thinking, though, so what if I missed something?

"It's just an intrusive thought," I say into the dark.

My least favorite part of exposure response therapy is the scripts. Rather than fight against the thoughts, I'm supposed to agree with them. I'm supposed to run through a script of everything I'm afraid of and say it without undoing it. Sometimes, I have to write it down. Sometimes I have to record it and listen to it multiple times a day. I have to hear myself say the awful things I think. I should agree with this intrusive thought. I should say it aloud, but I'm scared to, because what if that makes it true? It's too horrible. Too unthinkable. I can't say it. I won't.

I grab my phone and turn it over in my hands. I could just text Raine and make sure. I *should* text her, right? I don't have to ask her outright if she feels taken advantage of. I could talk around it. Feel it out.

I check the time. It's nearly two in the morning. I shouldn't text her right now. She's probably asleep, unlike me. Unless she's not. Unless she's awake because she's upset.

My phone vibrates in my hand. Raine's name appears on the screen. My hands are trembling as I open the message, every worst-case scenario fighting for real estate in my mind. I read the message four times, each time convinced I've read it wrong, and when the words finally sink in, I feel like crying. I don't remember the last time I cried.

**RAINE**
I'm glad you came over.

I should feel relieved, but I don't. I'm exhausted. I'm so fucking tired of every good moment being darkened by doubt. I don't know if I'll ever have something good without doubting it, but when I was in recovery, I could keep it from ruining things.

I can relearn how to keep it from ruining things.

I exit out of my chat with Raine and type out an email to Martina before I can change my mind. After I hit send, I notice the unread email at the top of my inbox. It's a reply to one of the posts I made on a message board for local musicians. The subject line reads, Re: Stolen Gibson guitar, Ireland sticker on back.

I open the email, scanning the words so quickly, I have to read them twice.

I think I found your friend's guitar. There's a link attached. I click it, trying not to get my hopes up. The link takes me to a listing on an instrument resale site, and even though I've never seen Raine's guitar in person, I have seen it in videos, and I know it's hers right away. I don't believe it, though. After weeks of relentlessly searching, it can't be this easy. I click through the photo gallery, and when I get to the photo of the back of the guitar, there it is . . . the Irish flag sticker.

I click through the gallery a second time to be sure. I read through every word of the description. I look through the seller's other items, but they only sell guitars. No sign of her other gear, so this probably isn't the person who stole it. I look at the asking price for the guitar and laugh. I reread the title of the listing: **Rare Gibson. Buy as is**. Raine wasn't kidding when she said you can't just replace something like that.

But all I have to do is think about how happy she'll be to see her guitar again. *Jesus, this girl is going to cost me a lot of money.*

I want to tell her I've found it, but what if something goes wrong? I don't want to get her hopes up, only for her to be more disappointed than ever.

That, and I want to see the look on her face when she finds out she doesn't have to replace her guitar.

*She doesn't have to replace her guitar.*

The elation I felt a moment ago fades. The guitar is the last big thing Raine needs. I told her she didn't have to stay all twelve weeks if she had all her gear, but she said that with the guitars she was thinking of getting, she'd have to work the full twelve weeks to save up for it.

But now she won't have to replace her guitar. She won't have to work at the pub anymore.

Once Raine has her guitar, it will be easy for her to leave. I've been pretending her leaving isn't happening. I don't want her to go . . . but at the same time, I do, because when I picture Raine's future, it's filled with stages and bright lights and ticket stubs. When I picture mine, it looks like almost every other day of the last five years.

My phone buzzes. Another message from Raine.

**RAINE**

Floof Update—2:03am Sitting on my head as if I'm a pillow and not at all concerned about my ability to breathe.

*Jesus, I love this girl*, I think. And then I panic.

This is the worst thing that's happened to me all day, and I can't even tell myself it isn't true. Because of course the one thing I *should* doubt, I don't. Why else would the thought of her leaving make me absolutely miserable?

I don't want Raine to go, but I can't ask her to stay, can I? We like each other, sure. But we've known each other for less than two months. It would be ridiculous for her to turn her life upside down for that. I wouldn't want her to.

But what if she didn't have to turn her life upside down to stay? Didn't she tell me that if she had the courage, she'd stop traveling and find somewhere to stay for a while so she could work on an album? I'm not sure what making an album consists of, but why couldn't she do it here? I could convince her. She could stay in the flat awhile longer. I'd give her all the time and space she'd need to focus on her music. She could record it in Cork, or hell, I'd drive her up to Dublin if I had to. It would only buy me a bit more time with her, but time is exactly what I need. Time to figure out what these feelings mean. Time to figure out what I want. To figure out what *she* wants.

*You realize you're bending over backward to make this work, right? Please tell me you know this makes absolutely no sense.*

That's what Ollie said the night Raine and I met, and everything turned out great. Why wouldn't this be the same?

# Sixteen

## RAINE

When I wake up, I find a Post-it note from Clara stuck to my forehead.

*Got hungry waiting for you to wake up.*
*Went downstairs. Fed the cat. xx*

When I grab my phone, I discover it's just after ten in the morning. I remember Jack coming over to kiss me and can't stop grinning. I'm glad my sister isn't here, because it would only take her one look to know something happened. I rub my hands over my face and roll out of bed, then wander into the living room. Sebastian isn't on the cat perch, or on the couch, or in the windowsill. I wonder how Clara knew exactly what he needed, then catch sight of the Post-it notes I have stuck all over the kitchen with everything I need to remember about Sebastian and the flat.

I splash water on my face and brush my teeth, then hurriedly change before heading downstairs. Clara's laugh rings out as soon as I open the door to the pub. I find her at the bar with Sebastian on the stool beside her. One of her legs swings beneath her as she perches on her stool and chats with Ollie and Róisín as if she's been here for months.

I push away the unreasonable jealousy I feel. I can be extra sensitive to rejection, even when it isn't actually rejection. For the last few weeks I've been thinking of the Local as *my* place, and these people as *my* people. But they aren't, really. This is just twelve weeks of my life.

*Just because Clara is fitting in great already doesn't mean you don't*, the voice of reason says.

I mentally roll my eyes. I hate when the voice of reason is so . . . reasonable.

"Look who finally decided to wake up," Clara says when I take the seat beside her. In front of her is a plate of half-eaten French toast with berries and some sort of custard and something else I don't recognize. She shoves the plate over to me. Half of me wants to say I don't need her leftovers. The other half is hungry and doesn't care. I go with the hungry half because, really, this French toast looks amazing.

"Is this new?" I ask Ollie and Róisín.

"It's incredible, Rainey," Clara says. "I'm going to think about this breakfast for the rest of my life." She turns to Róisín and looks them over. "I like your eyeliner. I can never get my wings even like that."

Róisín blushes furiously. "Oh . . . Thanks. I could show you sometime. If you wanted."

Clara smiles. "That would be nice."

Ollie claps a hand on Róisín's shoulder. "Don't want you leaving, Ro, but you need to stop fucking around and go to school. Dunno why you're wasting your time in this fecking place."

Róisín turns even redder. "I dunno. I like it here."

Ollie shakes his head. "Well, if you insist on staying, get back in the kitchen and quit wasting time out here flirting with girls."

"I wasn't . . ." Róisín shakes their head. "It was nice to meet you," they say to Clara. "Hope you'll be around for a while."

"If you keep cooking for me, I don't think I'll ever leave," Clara says.

Róisín tucks their hair behind one ear. "Oh . . . I . . . Happy to cook whenever. And the eyeliner thing. Teach you the eyeliner thing, not cook the . . . eyeliner."

"Oh, for fuck's sake," Ollie mumbles. He steers Róisín in the direction of the kitchen. When they push through the kitchen doors, I can just hear Ollie saying, "I thought I was teaching you to cook. Don't tell me I have to teach you how to pick up girls too."

When Ollie returns a few minutes later, he gives Clara a stern look. "If you're gonna be a distraction, I'm gonna have to kick you out, you know."

"Who says I'm a distraction? Maybe I'll be Róisín's muse. I've always wanted to be someone's muse."

"Speaking of muses . . ." I turn to find Jack settling onto the stool beside me. "I'm here. Let the inspiration flow."

I look him over. Everything from last night—the phone call, the kiss, him pinning me against the wall—flashes through me again in an instant.

Jack smiles, but his eyes are hesitant. I have no idea what I'm supposed to do. Is what happened last night a secret? We probably need to talk about it, but when?

"The only thing *you* inspire me to do is pull out my hair," Ollie says to Jack.

Jack hangs his coat beneath the bar with a sigh. "Uh-uh, don't go blaming me for your thinning hair, big brother."

Ollie runs a hand through his hair. "My hair's not . . . Oh, feck off, Jackie."

Clara props her cheek in her hand. "How old is Róisín, anyway? They're cute."

Ollie laughs and leaves for the kitchen again.

"Twenty-three," Jack says.

Clara eyes the kitchen door, but all she says is, "Mm." I'm not sure what that means, and I don't really want to know the details of my sister's actual or potential sex life. She sighs, then leans around me to look at Jack. "Cat Dad, are you going to the *Titanic* Experience with us?"

Jack laughs.

"I wasn't aware we were going to the *Titanic* Experience today," I say.

"You promised! Today is the first day of my new life, and I want to spend it at the *Titanic* Experience."

*New life?* I really need to figure out what Clara's deal is. And I get the feeling that she's avoiding being alone with me for some reason. "You want to spend the first day of your new life at a museum dedicated to a horrific tragedy?"

"Mm . . . yes." She turns to Jack. "So? Are you coming?"

He looks from Clara to me. "Sure, yeah. So long as you don't mind. I don't need to be here until this afternoon anyway."

"We don't mind," Clara says. She hooks her arm around my shoulders and squeezes me tight against her side. "We're going to have so much fun!"

Clara fills the entire walk to the *Titanic* Experience with chatter. She looks so much like the Clara I know, those Audrey Hepburn sunglasses over her eyes, the scarf I gave her around her neck, hair neat and tidy. But she's more upbeat and energetic than she's been in a long time. It's as if middle school Clara, the Clara I remember from when we were kids, has been resurrected.

We take Clara to the Deck of Cards, then backtrack around the park across the street so Clara can get the perfect photo of the houses and cathedral. When she stands on tiptoe to hold her phone over the wall, Jack's fingers lightly brush against mine.

"Hi, ciaróg."

"How'd you sleep last night?" I ask.

Jack laughs. "I hardly slept at all. Something kept me up late." He bumps his shoulder against mine. There's that hesitation in his eyes.

I take his hand in mine.

"You don't care if she sees?" he asks.

"I don't care if anyone sees. Do you?"

"I don't."

"Great."

"Grand."

"Got it!" Clara turns to face us. Her eyes immediately dart to my hand in Jack's. A look I don't understand passes over her face, but she turns away and starts walking before I can even begin to decipher it.

When we arrive at the museum, Jack tries to pay for our tickets, but Clara whips out her phone so the cashier can scan the digital tickets she's already bought. Pre-purchasing tickets is very Clara. The cashier hands each of us a postcard. On it is the image of an actual boarding pass that belonged to one of the passengers who boarded the *Titanic* from Cobh.

Clara looks at her boarding pass and grins. "First-class passenger. My destiny."

"Your destiny is to be a first-class passenger on a sinking ship?" I say.

She fans herself with the boarding pass. "If I survive, yes. If I don't, no."

I read my own boarding pass. "I'm in third class. My name is Margaret Rice, and I am traveling with . . . my five sons." I shake my head. "This better not be my destiny." I elbow Jack. "What about you?"

Jack looks up from his boarding pass. "First class. William Edward Minahan."

Clara gasps, and it startles both of us. She claps a hand over her mouth. "You're my husband, Jack! Sorry, sis. Didn't mean to steal your man."

Clara slips her arm through Jack's. "I'll give him back later," she says, as we walk over to a fake luggage display to wait for the tour guide.

Clara's just messing around, but it has me on edge anyway. Of course Clara is a first-class passenger while I'm stuck in third class with my brood of children. Of course Jack is her fake husband. None of it matters, because none of it is real, but suddenly I feel as if I'm reliving high school and college all over again. Everything is fine, and then Clara shows up, and it's all *Raine, your sister is so funny! Raine, is Clara single? Will Clara be there? Raine, make sure you invite Clara!*

It isn't Clara's fault, I know. But I'm petty. So petty that Clara being accepted at the same medical school as me was the last straw, the thing that made me realize I didn't really care for medicine after all.

A few other visitors wait nearby. When the tour guide comes, our little group shuffles into the exhibit, which is way more interesting than I expected. We see replicas of the sleeping quarters and dining areas on board the *Titanic*. I'm so absorbed in the stories the tour guide tells us about the various passengers on the ship that I forget to be annoyed whenever Clara *oohs* and *aahs* over the first-class passenger amenities. When the tour guide asks if the Minahans are present, Clara loops her arm through Jack's again and raises her hand, and we all have the pleasure of learning that they are the only first-class passengers today. Apparently there were only three first-class passengers who boarded the *Titanic* from here. How lucky that my sister gets to be one of them.

Clara is delighted by this information, and it's too bad we're not on a real boat, because then I could jump off it and into the water. No iceberg necessary.

Jack is quiet as we move through the museum. When we step

outside to look at Heartbreak Pier, where the passengers who boarded here embarked, I catch his eye and ask if he's okay, but he says he's just tired.

By the time we take our seats in the "lifeboat" at the end of the guided tour, I am very invested in Margaret Rice and my—*her*—five young sons. The room goes dark, and a video about the night the *Titanic* sank begins to play. Eyewitness accounts from survivors narrate as we watch the *Titanic* sinking from the perspective of one of the lifeboats. The ship slowly rises. There's the music of the band on board. The panicked screams of passengers. The creaking of the ship. The flickering lights. It's overwhelming. I know the video I'm watching is just a simulation, but these events really happened. And they happened to real people. People who had plans and hopes and dreams, just like me. When one of the eyewitness accounts talks about seeing a mother and her five children huddled in a corridor and I learn Margaret Rice and her five sons perished, I start ugly crying right in the middle of this fake lifeboat.

The tour guide clears her throat. I feel everyone's eyes on me as the film continues. I'm so embarrassed that I get to my feet just as the ship snaps in half, pushing through the door at the side of the room before anyone can stop me. I find myself in an exhibit hall filled with displays. Fortunately, I'm the only one here. And fortunately, the room is so filled with exhibits that it's easy to hide myself from view while I wait for Jack and Clara to leave that hellish fake lifeboat/theater.

I wander to the far end of the room but don't really take in what I'm seeing. I'm still crying when I make it to the final display, a large board on the wall that lists the names of all the passengers who boarded the *Titanic* here in Cobh and their fates. Standing here looking at these names is not going to help me calm down, especially now that I recognize so many of them, and I really need to calm down before Jack and Clara find me. I turn away, hoping to find a less depressing display, and end up running right into Jack.

Fabulous. Wonderful. Less than twelve hours ago we were making out in a stairwell, and now he's seen me have a meltdown in a fake lifeboat. I'm really busting out all the moves now.

I cover my face in my hands. "I'm so embarrassed."

Jack puts his arms around me. I bury my face in his shoulder, concentrating on the circles he rubs over my back as I try to slow my breathing.

"What happened?"

"Nothing happened. It's just . . . like, it's so easy to forget these were real people, and . . ." I laugh. "I feel too much, and sometimes this happens, and it's embarrassing, and . . ." My throat tightens, and I can't go on, or I'll start ugly crying again.

"Nothing wrong with that," Jack says. "Most people are desensitized to trauma. Maybe the world would be a better place if they felt a bit more."

"I don't know," I say. "I don't like feeling this way. I don't want anyone else to feel this way."

"What happened?" Clara says.

I don't look up from where my face is still pressed against Jack's shoulder. "She's just a little overwhelmed," he says when I don't answer.

I'm not sure who I'm more embarrassed to fall apart around, Jack or Clara. Really, I can't think of two people I'd hate to see me burst into tears during a museum simulation more.

"Oh, Rainey," Clara says. "She's always been like that," she adds to Jack. "She has a big heart."

This makes me laugh. *Big-hearted* is not how I would describe my attitude toward my sister this morning.

I groan and lift my head, nearly blinded when I drop my hands from my face. "I'm good now," I say, and avoid making eye contact with either of them.

Jack steps back and Clara swoops her arm around my shoulders as we exit the room and step inside the gift shop. I'm sure Clara would like to stay and buy a few things, but she doesn't stop. "It was the fucking video, wasn't it? Honestly, I was close to crying too."

"No you weren't."

Clara sighs. "Teensy lie for sisterly solidarity. You don't have to call me out on it. But really, you can't be blamed. They pulled out all the stops. Just like in—"

"*Tarzan*," we both say.

Clara laughs. "Phil Collins broke her," she explains to Jack. "He didn't have to go that hard."

"I'll never forgive him, even if he is a genius," I say.

As soon as we step outside, Clara and I look at each other and start singing "You'll Be in My Heart" at top volume. Jack raises his eyebrows in surprise at Clara's awful singing (and rightfully so).

"You two are something else," he says.

That evening, Clara and I occupy one of the snugs at the Local for dinner and drinks. Sebastian is curled up beside me. He's been going between me and Jack, who is working behind the bar tonight, all evening.

I've gotten no closer to figuring out why Clara's really here, but after my hot mess of a morning, I've had enough emotions for the day and don't want to risk asking directly. Instead I watch Jack as he pours pints for a group that's just walked in. It's busier in the Local than it used to be. I close my eyes and can barely hear the music playing overhead. I strain to hear it, and as soon as I make out the song, my eyes fly open.

"What?" Clara says.

"Listen!"

"To what?"

"The music!"

"What about it?"

"It's me! That's one of my covers!" My eyes find Jack, who is busy making drinks. He mouths along to the words as he pulls a pint, and I catch myself audibly sighing.

Clara follows my gaze. "Okay, I've been very respectful, but I need to know what the deal is with you and Cat Dad."

I roll my eyes. "Stop calling him that."

"*You* called him that first. It isn't my fault it's catchy," Clara says. She takes a sip of her drink. When she sets it down again, she says, "So . . . is this serious?"

I look away from Jack. "Of course not. I can't just . . . stay in Cobh. I love traveling. And Jack's got responsibilities here. Our lives don't match up."

Clara stirs her gin and tonic with her straw. "Mm . . . but do you *feel* serious about him?"

"I . . . don't know." I adjust in my seat, pulling both feet up under myself. "I don't think it matters."

"Of course it matters."

I don't say anything.

"Is he why you won't come home?" Clara asks.

I look at her. "I haven't even been here two months. I'll be back on the road soon. Why would he be the reason?"

There's an awkward silence between us as Clara takes another slow sip of her drink, and I get the sense that Jack isn't really what Clara wants to talk about.

"Why are you here, Clara? What happened?"

She sets her drink on the table. "I told you. I'm quitting med school to become a human statue."

"But *why* are you quitting med school?"

"Because I don't want to be a doctor."

"That's not true. You've always wanted to be a doctor. You want to be a doctor more than Mom and Dad like talking about being doctors. And that's . . . a lot."

Clara's gaze is sharp when it meets mine. "Why'd *you* quit med school, Raine?"

The question takes me off guard. I don't see what me quitting med school has to do with anything. "This isn't about me."

"Of course it's about you!" Clara says. "I'm here to see *you*! I thought I'd be going to med school with *you*, and then out of nowhere, you're off on some magical travel adventure! I thought I was supposed to go to Ireland with *you*, and you come here without me."

Now I'm upset. "I was tired of waiting for you! I tried to plan a trip for the summer after you graduated high school, but you decided to take summer classes. When we were in college together, I tried to plan it for our spring break, but you always chose to do alternative spring break instead. I tried to plan a trip the summer before I started med school, and you were too busy with your internship. Don't act like this is all on me."

Clara continues as if she hasn't heard me. "The last time I saw you, you were going on and on about how excited you were to start rotations, and the next thing I know, you've dropped out and become a street performer."

Sebastian yowls from beside me, and I scratch him between the ears, willing my heart to slow. "I know you don't take me seriously, but—"

"It's not that I don't take you seriously, Raine. I just don't get it. I don't understand. How can I? You don't tell me anything. You finished two *years* of medical school. You were just about to get to the fun part. *Something* had to have happened."

"I had a mental breakdown, Clara!"

A hush falls over the pub. Clara blinks at me. I feel myself turning red, but don't dare look around.

"A breakdown?" Clara says. "What do you mean, you had a breakdown? I thought you just . . . didn't want to do it anymore."

I lean toward Clara over the table, lowering my voice to a reasonable volume. "I was anxious all the time. I had a thousand things to do, a thousand thoughts swirling in my head. And yeah, I know med school is hard for everyone, but it wasn't just med school that was hard. It was everything. Laundry, and bills, and, yes, school. I was going, going, going until I hit a wall. I couldn't do it anymore. I'd take out my books but couldn't make myself study. I'd wake up for class but couldn't make myself get dressed. And then I found out *you* were starting in the fall, and I couldn't do that again. I had to get away from my life and find a new one."

"You couldn't do *what* again?"

"Be the disappointment!"

Clara shakes her head. "I don't understand."

"Come *on*, Clara. As soon as you show up, I get compared to you. And how am I supposed to measure up to Miss Most Likely to Succeed? Miss Popular? Miss Best All Around? And don't even argue that, because you've literally won all of those superlatives at some point. So no, I didn't want to live in your shadow again, especially when I was already failing. Really, you did me a favor. I would've left anyway, but you getting accepted really sped things up."

"You left because of me?"

As soon as I see the hurt in Clara's eyes, I wish I could take back every word. "No, Clara. That's not what I mean. I'm sorry, I'm just—"

"All I ever wanted is to be your friend." Clara's voice sounds close to breaking. "You stopped being my friend, and I didn't know why . . ."

"We're sisters, isn't that better than friends?"

She glares at me. "You know what I mean."

"I didn't stop being your friend. You were always so busy. You fit in so easily. Everyone just loved you. And yeah, I had friends, but even *they* seemed to like you more. And don't get me started on Mom and Dad . . ." I look up at her, but she's turned her face to the wall. "It's all so *easy* for you—school, making friends, meeting expectations. It felt like whenever you came around, I was suddenly not good enough. It happened in high school, and then the same thing happened in college. And I just wanted something to be *mine*. God, it sounds so stupid, but I just wanted to be someone's favorite for once."

Clara laughs. Tears slip down her cheeks, and when she turns to me, there's anger in her face. "You wanted to be someone's favorite? You were *my* favorite."

Clara scoots out of the booth, and when she stands beside the table, I feel impossibly small. "Do you *seriously* think everything is easy for me? I did summer school and internships and alternative spring breaks because I had to if I wanted to keep up. Just because Mom and Dad were always comparing us doesn't mean everyone else was. *You* were the only person I could let my guard down around, and then you just . . . *left* me. And I needed you. I need you right now. But you know what? I don't want to step on your toes. I don't want to take anything away from you."

When Clara turns and heads for the door, I shoo Sebastian out of the way and follow after her. "Where are you going?"

"I'm grabbing my suitcase and going to find some gold body paint so I can be a human statue all by myself!" She reaches the door on the last word and pushes through it. It swings shut behind her like some kind of mic drop.

I stand there for a moment, stunned. I feel everyone's eyes on me. It's so quiet that the only sounds are Jack asking me what happened and my own stupid song playing overhead.

———

When I catch up to Clara, she's sitting beside the door to the flat.

"Forgot I don't have a key," she says.

I don't say anything as I pull the key from my pocket. Clara gets to her feet and rushes past me when I open the door. I step in behind her, trying to figure out what to say as I watch her make a beeline for the bedroom. While I watch at the door, she tosses the few things she unpacked back into her suitcase.

She zips her suitcase with finality and sets it upright, pulling up the handle with a snap.

"Can we talk? Please?"

Clara looks away from me. "You haven't seemed very interested in talking to me lately, so I don't know, you tell me."

"I want to talk." I cross the room, and she doesn't resist when I take the suitcase from her and set it back down. I sit on the end of the bed and rest my feet on top of the suitcase so she'll be less inclined to pick it up and flee. "Let's talk," I say, and pat the bed.

Clara looks at the spot on the bed beside me but doesn't sit down. Instead she leans against the wall opposite me and stares at a strand of hair that's come loose from her bun. "You go first."

"I'm sorry," I say.

"For what?"

Clara winds that loose strand of hair between her fingers. If she won't look at me, maybe this conversation will be easier if I don't look at her either. Eye contact can be so . . . distracting, especially when I'm going to have to say things I'm not sure I want to say. I lie back on the bed and stare up at the ceiling. "For hurting you. For pulling away. I had no idea you felt that way. I didn't think you really cared."

"Of course I cared. And you would've known that if you ever bothered to have a real conversation with me."

"You're right." My heart feels tender and raw, like my fingers often do after I've played guitar for too long. It's probably just as callused too. "I'm sorry. It's just . . . it was already hard feeling like I couldn't live up to expectations without being compared to you, and you just always seemed to fit in better than me. And I know that's not your fault, but telling myself that you were the problem was less painful than having to look at myself."

I try to blink back tears, but it's no use. "If you're the problem, then I don't have to ask myself what I'm doing wrong. Why I'm such a mess. Why I can't just get my life together. I mean, look at me!" I spread my arms out on the bed. "I'm twenty-eight! I don't feel twenty-eight. I'm voluntarily homeless. I've never had a real job. I've never been in a real relationship. Not a good one, anyway. And I'm just . . . deluding myself thinking I can make a career out of this music thing. I'm too scared to put out my own music. I can't even stick to a regular posting schedule! Not that I've even *had* anything good to post since my guitar got stolen."

"Wait . . . what?"

*Crap.* I forgot I hadn't told her. Though what does it really matter now? She's been here less than twenty-four hours and I've already had two public meltdowns. "The real reason I'm in Cobh is because all my stuff got stolen. I met Jack. He offered me a job. And that's the only reason I didn't have to go home."

"Raine, why didn't you tell me? I would've helped you. I would've sent you money."

I sit up on my elbows. "I didn't want you to know. You were so upset when I dropped out of med school. I didn't want anyone knowing what a fuckup I am."

Clara drops the strand of hair between her fingers and sits beside me. "You're not a fuckup, Raine."

I laugh. "Really? Come on, Miss Perfect."

She shakes her head. "I'm really not. I . . ." She pauses to let out a puff of breath. "I'm a fraud."

"What do you mean?"

"I missed a quiz for anatomy because I was finishing my term paper for histology. And then I flaked out on a group project for biochem because I got my weeks mixed up and . . ." She closes her eyes. "You said you hit a wall. Well, I hit a wall. You at least made it through two years. Congrats, you're better than me, because I can't even make it through one. I'm not cut out for medicine."

I look at my sister. "But . . . Mom and Dad said you were doing amazing. *You* said things were going great! What changed?"

Clara picks at a loose thread on the comforter and doesn't look at me. "I lied."

"Why?"

"For the same reasons you did. I didn't want anyone to know what a fuckup I am."

"If you didn't want me to know, why did you come here?"

Clara sighs. "I wanted to know how you did it."

"Did what?"

"How you moved on. How you let go of everyone else's expectations and just . . . did what you wanted to do."

I laugh. "Clara, I didn't let go of everyone else's expectations. I just ran away from them. If I *really* didn't care what other people thought, I'd be putting out my own music." I wait for Clara to say something, but she doesn't. "Do you *really* want to drop out of med school?"

"No," she says. "I want to be a doctor. I've wanted to be a doctor my whole life, but it's scary. What if I keep trying and all that happens is I keep failing?"

"Then you'll fail knowing you gave it your all. You won't wonder what could've been if you'd just been a little braver. Don't give up something you love just because it's difficult. You can get through med school. I know you can. Don't give up yet."

Clara wipes at her eyes and groans. "God, look at us. Jack was right, we're something else."

She sighs and stares at the wall in front of her. It hurts to think of the space that's grown between us, space I let grow because of my own fear. If there's one thing I know about Clara, it's that she wants to be a doctor more than anything. I can't picture her doing anything else. I can't imagine a person better-suited to the job.

I nudge her shoulder. "Will you please go back and try again? It's just a bump in the road. If anyone can manage it, it's you."

"Fine." She gives me a sharp look. "But only if *you* don't give up."

I shake my head. "Clara . . . I dropped out of med school over a year ago, somehow I don't think I can just pick up where I left off."

"Not med school, *music*."

"That's different."

"It's not," she says. "Just . . . try to put your own stuff out there."

"I don't know . . ."

"You have to set a good example for your little sister," she says, and gives me a pinch on the arm.

"Ouch! Okay, fine! I promise I'll *try*. I can't promise I'll succeed. Deal?"

"Deal." Clara goes quiet for a moment. "I'm sorry I made such a scene downstairs. I wasn't thinking . . ."

"It's okay."

"It won't ruin anything with Cat Dad for you, will it?"

I shrug. "What's there to ruin?"

She rolls her eyes. "Come on, Raine, don't kid yourself."

"I'm not kidding! He's just a fling. A travel romance." I grin at her. "I'm very worldly now, you see."

"If you say so." Clara gives my leg a pat, then sits up with a sigh. "Want to have a movie night? We can continue this cry fest and watch *Tarzan*."

"I'm not sure I have any tears left."

Clara gives me a skeptical look. "Raine, you always have more tears. And it's *Tarzan*. Don't kid yourself."

When she gets to her feet and crosses the room, I call out after her. "Hey, Clara."

She pauses at the door to the bedroom. "Yeah?"

"I'm glad you're here."

Clara smiles that imperfect smile I've always loved. "Me too."

# Seventeen

## JACK

It's just past midnight when Raine calls me.

"I didn't wake you, did I?" she says.

"I was reading." Until I dozed off, anyway. The book is still open on my chest. I grab the Post-it I've been using as a bookmark. I found it stuck to my coat a few days ago when I was about to head home from work. Right away I recognized Raine's handwriting. She must have left it before going upstairs for the night. *I think you'd like this,* it read. Beneath the message, she'd written a song title and artist. I listened to it on repeat for two days. It's been stuck in my head ever since.

I stick the note in the book to mark my page, then set the book on my nightstand.

"Everything okay over there?" I ask, thinking of how she and Clara left the pub earlier. I texted Raine as soon as she left, but she didn't answer. An hour or so afterward, she came downstairs to get Sebastian, but only stuck around long enough to tell me she'd call me later when I asked if she was okay. I kept checking my phone all night, waiting to hear from her. I lingered at the pub for a while after it closed, just in case she called, but ran out of excuses to hang around.

"I'm really sorry for what happened," she says. "I didn't mean for things to get so heated."

"I own a pub. Believe me, I've seen worse."

Raine laughs.

"But everything's okay?" I ask.

"Everything's okay."

"Good."

There's a brief pause. "Are you busy right now?" she asks.

I eye the book on my nightstand. "Very."

"Too busy for a walking meeting?"

It takes me a moment to work out what she's said, but as soon as I put it together, I roll from the bed, searching the floor for the black trousers I tossed there earlier. "I think I can reschedule some things."

"Great. See you soon. I'll meet you downstairs."

When I near the door that leads upstairs to the flat a few minutes later, Raine flies out of it and skips over.

"So, where are we walking to?" I ask.

"The waterfront?"

I nod, and we set off down the street.

"And Clara?" I ask.

"Fast asleep with Princess Ugly. That cat is a traitor." She turns to me, all excitement. "Oh! Do you want to listen to some music?"

"Sure," I say.

She digs in the pocket of her coat, pulling out her phone and a tangled-up pair of headphones. "Sorry they're the wired kind. I had a nice pair of wireless ones, but, you know."

"I don't mind." Especially if it means she'll have to stick closer to my side.

She pauses beside me, muttering to herself as she untangles the headphones. Once she's gotten them in order, she passes an earbud to me and places the other in her ear. She frowns at her phone as she scrolls, then finally chooses a playlist. The music is calm and electronic. I don't think it's in English, because I don't understand it.

She tucks her phone back into her coat pocket. "Do you know this one?"

"I don't." We walk in silence as the music plays, but I can't focus on it. All I can think about is her guitar, and how tomorrow morning I'll be driving all the way to Dublin to pick it up. When the song ends, Raine pulls out her phone again, and I realize her hands are bare. "Where are your gloves?" I ask.

"Oh, I don't know. I lost them," she says. "It's fine, though, my coat pockets are warm."

I halt in the middle of the pavement, and she stops too. I take her bare hands and warm them between my gloved ones. "What am I supposed to do with you, ciaróg?"

"Whatever you want."

I let go of her with a laugh, then pull off my gloves and slip them over her hands.

"But you'll be cold," she says. "And I've already stolen your hoodie."

"You said I could do whatever I want with you. And what I want is to give you my gloves without you complaining about it."

She smiles up at me. "Is that all you want to do with me?"

"That's a ridiculous question," I say.

"Why?"

"I think you know why." I put my arm around her shoulders and pull her to my side as we walk.

We let the music fill the silence on our way to the waterfront. When we get there, we lean against the railing and look out at the dark water ahead.

Raine turns to me when the song we're listening to ends. She takes my hands and presses one against her cheek. "You're freezing." She looks at my hands and blows hot air on them.

"Why'd you get 'Last Call' tattooed on your knuckles?" she asks. She pulls me closer and tucks my hands into her coat pockets, even though I have my own coat pockets. But I'm not about to remind her of that.

I sigh. We're so close that I can't tell where her cloud of breath ends and mine begins. "I got it right after Da died and I decided to move home and run the pub. As a joke. To lighten the mood. Didn't really work, though."

Raine is quiet for a moment. "You didn't have a good relationship with him."

"That's an understatement."

"You don't have to talk about it," she says. "I shouldn't have brought it up."

Normally, I wouldn't talk about it. Normally, I'd say, *We didn't see eye to eye*, and leave it at that. But I *want* to tell Raine. I want her to know, even though a part of me is terrified that when I tell her what my da was like, she'll start to wonder if I'm capable of the horrible things I think, if I've got some genetic predisposition for evil. I couldn't blame her if she did. I wonder the same thing.

"He was violent," I say. "At home."

Raine stills. "Oh."

"He was charming and funny too, especially at the pub. For a long time, I wondered what we were doing wrong to make him act so different at home. He and Ollie always got into it the most, but things didn't get any better once Ollie left."

"Was that why Ollie left?"

I nod. "He tried to convince Mum to leave and come with him when he went to culinary school, but she couldn't go through with it. I didn't know that until after Da died. I really looked up to Ollie when I was a kid. And then when he left, I never heard from him again. I had no idea . . . I spent years thinking he just forgot about me, or that I'd done something wrong."

Raine steps closer and rests her head on my shoulder, and it makes it easier to keep talking, because I don't have to watch her expression. I don't have to worry about mine.

"After Da died, me and Mum were going through his stuff when I came across some of Ollie's things. I must've said something about him, I don't remember what, and that's when Mum told me about it. I'd spent fifteen years upset with Ollie, only to find out I had everything wrong. I remember Mum asking me if I was okay, but I just got up and left. I walked for hours, not even thinking. Just walking."

"You two seem pretty close now," Raine says.

"I understand why he left. I know it isn't his fault. But I do wonder sometimes . . . I wonder if I'd have developed the OCD if he'd stayed. Or if it wouldn't have been so bad. Or if I would've gotten diagnosed sooner. Mum didn't like taking us to the doctor. She didn't want anyone guessing . . ." I don't say any more. Raine can fill in the blanks.

Raine doesn't say anything, and I'm glad. I don't need to hear how sorry she is, or how sad it makes her.

"Do the windmills ever stop spinning?" she asks.

"I don't know," I say. "I've never thought about it."

She doesn't say anything. I watch the windmills turn and think about how much I want her to stay. I want her to ask me random questions like this every day. I want to think about things I'd never think about unless she asked.

"Can I hear one of your songs?" I ask. When she doesn't answer, I look down and find that she's looking up at me, hesitation written on her face. "Please?"

"I don't have an entire song. Just bits and pieces."

"That's fine."

She stares at her phone in her hands. "They're not good."

"Let me be the judge of that."

"Will you be honest?"

When she looks up at me, I'm not sure what to make of her expression. The hesitation is still there but . . . there's something like anticipation too. That creative, wide-open part of her that is always talking, always sharing, always giving. It takes everything in me not to kiss her.

"I very rarely say things I don't mean," I tell her.

She's still for a moment. I think we're both holding our breath. And then she pulls the earbud from her ear and puts it in mine. "I can't listen to it while you're listening to it," she says, looking away from me to scroll through her phone.

I don't want to say something wrong, so I don't say anything. A moment later, Raine's voice sounds in my ears. I look down at her, but she's got her eyes on the screen of her phone.

I expected Raine's music to be good. I knew she could sing. I knew she could play well. But I didn't expect *this*. I didn't know she could take everything she is and turn it into music. Because that's exactly what her music sounds like. There's no other way to describe it. It's everything I think of when I think of her. Full and energetic and warm and a little unexpected.

When the music stops, she looks up at me, and the anxiety in her eyes makes me laugh.

"Told you it's bad," she says, and looks away.

"That's not why I'm laughing," I say. "I'm laughing because I can't believe you don't know."

Her eyes search mine. "Don't know what?"

"How talented you are."

"You're just being nice," she says.

"I'm not."

A slight smile forms on her lips. "You're biased."

"I am, but that doesn't change the fact that I'm right, and if you'd just share your music with more people, you'd see."

"I don't know . . ."

"Play for the pub," I say.

"I *have* played for the pub."

I lean in closer. "Play *this* for the pub." She opens her mouth to respond, but I cut her off. "Don't answer me now," I say. "Just promise me you'll think about it."

"I'll think about it. But that's *all* I'll promise."

"That's all I'm asking for."

Raine sighs and rests her head on my shoulder again. I try not to feel too hopeful that my plan to convince her to stay will work, but I can't help it. Until now, she's never let me hear her music. Until now, she's never suggested she'd even *think* about playing her own music for an audience.

"Are you tired?" I ask when Raine yawns.

"Mm-hmm."

"Let's get you home, then."

She lifts her head from my shoulder. I keep my arm around her waist as we walk back toward the pub.

"What's your family like?" I ask.

"Well, you've obviously met Clara."

"She seems nice."

"She is. She's also . . . complicated. We were really close as kids, and then we weren't. But I think we're coming back around to each other again."

"And your parents?"

She sighs. "They're wonderful. Really. I know I make it sound like they aren't sometimes, but they are. They love us. They mean well. They want the best for us. But they also put a lot of pressure on us too. They have a very specific idea of what *best* looks like."

"And it doesn't look like quitting medical school to become a traveling musician?"

She laughs. "Definitely not."

"I bet *best* doesn't look like some Irish publican covered in tattoos either." I don't know why I say it. I shouldn't be thinking about Raine's parents, people I will never meet, and what they might think of me. I can't help but wonder, though. There's a part of me that wants to be good enough.

"Actually, I think they'd love you."

"You don't have to lie to me, Raine. I know what people think when they see me."

"I'm not lying," she says. "They're very narrow-minded in what they think *we* should do—school, job-wise, stuff like that. They want us to have every opportunity. But they wouldn't judge you for how you look or your job."

"What would they judge me on, then?"

"Well, they love to laugh, and I think you'd make them laugh. That would earn you some points for sure. But even if you didn't make them laugh, they've always said they want us to have people in our lives who are kind and make us happy."

We arrive in front of the door that leads to the flat. Raine starts to take off my gloves, but I tell her to hold on to them until she finds hers.

"Can I ask you something?" I say.

"Sure."

"Are you happy right now?"

She smiles up at me, and I'm overwhelmed by the way I feel when I look at her. "Yeah, I am."

"Good."

There's a moment of silence as we look at each other. Raine fights back a yawn. She rolls her eyes when I laugh at her and says, "Are you going to kiss me good night, or what? I need my beauty sleep."

"I'll think about it," I say. I take her by the waist, walking her backward until she's against the wall. "And you certainly don't need any beauty sleep."

"Well, you ought to make up your mind soon," she says. "I'm tired."

When I kiss her, she brings her hands to my face and pulls me closer. I let my hands roam over as much of her as I can. All of her is soft and lovely. I try to stay present. I want to remember the way she feels after she's gone. It kills me to pull away, but it's late, and I know she's tired, and I am too, for that matter.

"I'll see you tomorrow?" she asks.

I think of the message on my phone, confirming the time and place I'm meeting with the seller to buy Raine's guitar. "In the evening," I say. "I've got some errands out of town. Now go upstairs and get in bed."

She scrunches her nose at me. "You're so bossy."

I shake my head. "*Good night*, Raine."

She sighs. "All right, all right. Good night."

But when she turns to go, I catch her hand and pull her to me, kissing her again. Because once she has her guitar, she can leave whenever she wants. Because tomorrow, all of this might be over.

# Eighteen

As soon as I return to Cobh from picking up Raine's guitar, I scan the pub for any sign of her. It's just after two. The lunch crowd has already returned to work, and things won't pick up again until about five. Other than Aoife and Róisín, the pub is empty.

Róisín looks up from a cookbook when I step behind the bar.

"Have you seen Raine?" I ask.

"She and Clara went to Fota Wildlife Park a few hours ago."

"And they seemed . . ."

"They're good now," Róisín says. "That's what Clara said anyway." They tap their phone and check the time. "She said they'd be back around four so she can get ready for dinner." Róisín's cheeks turn pink.

Aoife doesn't even look up from the newspaper she has in front of her when she says, "Róisín and Clara are going on a date tonight."

"I mean . . . I'm not sure I'd call it a *date* exactly," Róisín says.

"For the last time, Ro, it's definitely a date." Aoife closes her newspaper with a sigh and looks at me. "I was here when Clara told Róisín she was taking them out for dinner and drinks tonight."

"She didn't *say* it would just be us . . ."

"She didn't have to, dear! It was implied!" Aoife grins at me. "You should've seen it, Jackie. Those two were looking very cozy."

"I wouldn't say cozy . . ."

"You were sitting on the same side of the table, Róisín!"

Róisín shrugs.

"Anyway, Raine comes in so they can leave for Fota, and Clara just stands up and tells Róisín she's taking them out for dinner. Doesn't ask, *tells*! I thought Róisín was going to faint. Anyway, Ro's been like this all day. Tell them it's a date."

I look at Róisín. "Sounds like a date to me, Ro."

"I don't know if that makes me feel better or worse," they mumble.

Róisín's gaze drops to the guitar case in my hands. "Is that . . . ?"

I pat the guitar case. "It is."

Aoife's eyes widen when she sees the guitar case. "Oh, Jackie," she says. "You've got it bad." She opens her newspaper again. "Maybe you and Raine can have a double date with Clara and Róisín."

"This pub isn't a fecking dating show," Ollie, who has just come in from the kitchen, says. He eyes the guitar case in my hand, then looks at me. "You found it?"

I set the guitar case on the bar. The entire drive to meet up with the seller, I found myself half wishing I'd get there and realize I'd made a mistake, as awful as it sounds. But as soon as I flipped the guitar around, I spotted the Irish flag on the back, the letters R.H. written in permanent marker on one corner of the sticker.

The door to the pub swings open, and I whirl around, thinking it's Raine, and I can finally get this over with, but Nina walks through the door with Josie and Jacqueline.

As soon as Jacqueline sees Ollie, she shouts, "Daddy!" and races over to him.

Nina pushes her sunglasses on top of her head. "I gestated these

children for nine months, and they both come out looking like him."
She sighs. "Mother nature is cruel."

Ollie picks up Jacqueline and ruffles her hair. "Maybe we just
need to try again."

"Hilarious, Oliver," Nina deadpans. "I'm dying of laughter."

Josie, who stays by Nina's side, points at the guitar case on the
counter. "What's that?"

"It's a guitar," I say.

Nina stares at the guitar case. "Is it . . ."

"For the love of God, yes, it's Raine's guitar. Jesus, how many
times am I going to have to say it? If I'd have known I was going to
have such a large audience, I would've snuck in through the back."

"How are you going to give it to her?" Nina asks.

"When she comes back from Fota, I'm going to hand her the guitar case."

Nina looks at me as if she's never heard of a worse idea in her
entire life. "Don't be ridiculous. This is your chance to make a big
romantic gesture!"

"Why would he do that?" Ollie says.

Nina gestures at me. "Because he's in love, obviously!"

Everyone looks at me. I flip one of the latches on the case up and
down but don't say anything.

"You can't just *hand it to her*, Jack," Nina says.

"Actually, annoying sister-in-law, I can." I flip the latch down,
then pick up the guitar case and step around Ollie to push through
the kitchen door and head straight for my office.

Once inside, I set the guitar case on the floor and just stand there
staring down at it. The door eases open, but I don't turn around.

"Jackie," Ollie says.

"What?" Why won't everyone just leave me alone?

Ollie sighs, and I turn to find him standing in the doorway with

Jacqueline still in his arms. She has her head on his shoulder, her thumb stuck in her mouth as she watches me, looking as if she's fighting off sleep.

"If you really do love her, maybe you ought to talk to her," Ollie says.

"Thank you for that unasked-for advice," I say.

"I'm serious, Jackie." He steps inside and shuts the door behind him.

"What is there to talk about? Her whole life is traveling. My whole life is here, whether I want it to be or not."

"All I'm saying is that if you want to be with her, you should tell her. It can't be as black-and-white as that. Let her decide what she wants." Ollie smooths Jacqueline's hair, and her eyes slowly drift shut. "And don't act like I'm the one keeping you here. I told you I'd buy your half of the pub if you wanted."

I sink into the office chair and stare at the mess of Post-its on the desk. For the last week, Raine and I have been having a conversation through sticky notes that has somehow become a competition to see who can leave the most ridiculous note. It started simply enough. I found a note Raine left that said, *Shaggy Angel HitClip? Where?* I had no idea what it was about, but I left a another nearby that said, *Did you check inside the cat tent?* It escalated rather quickly from there, and now the desk is covered in ridiculous brightly colored notes. I notice a new one beside the keyboard. *Glowsticks? Yes no maybe?* I flick it with a finger and laugh.

There's silence, except for the sound of Jacqueline sucking her thumb. *Just tell her.* Easy enough for Ollie to say. Ollie with his happy marriage and his two kids and his comfortable house he doesn't hate on principle and his normal fucking brain.

As soon as I think it, I worry I've wished him ill and all those good things will get taken away from him.

I want to undo it in my mind, but I know I shouldn't.

"Well," Ollie says. "Do you want me to buy you out, Jackie?"

I shake my head. "I don't know what I want anymore." I pick up a pen and circle *maybe* on the Post-it Raine left about the glowsticks.

That's not entirely true. I want to undo any potential harm I've wished out into the universe. I want to *know* that I am good. That I'm truly not capable of the things I think. I want my first appointment with Martina to hurry up and get here already. I want to trust myself again.

"Well, I suggest you start thinking about it," Ollie says. "Hopefully you'll figure it out before she leaves."

# Nineteen

## RAINE

**JACK**

Are you home? There was a delivery for you.

I frown at the message. I can't remember ordering anything other than a HitClip of Shaggy's "Angel" I impulsively purchased after finding it on eBay, but I thought it had gotten lost in the mail. I reply, telling Jack that I'll come down and get whatever it is once Clara leaves for her date with Róisín, but he replies seconds later to tell me it's heavy and he'll bring it up for me.

Two minutes later, there's a knock at the door. "It's open!" I call, unable to pull myself away from the kitchen table, where I'm tweaking the design for our St. Patrick's Day pub quiz flier. "You can leave whatever it is by the door," I say when I hear Jack come inside. "Thanks for bringing it up, by the way. It's gotta be something I forgot I ordered, because I can't think of what it would be."

"I think you'll want to see it," Jack says.

"In a minute. I just need to finish this."

"Raine," he says, his voice uncharacteristically serious. "I really need you to come out here."

"Oh, fine." I save the file and shut the lid to my laptop. "What's all the fuss?" I ask when I step into the living room, but as soon as the words leave my mouth, my eyes land on the guitar case in Jack's hand.

"No," I say, because I can't be seeing what I think I'm seeing.

"Yes," Jack says. He sets the guitar case on the coffee table and steps aside, grinning as he watches me.

"No!" I shout.

Clara, who has been applying her makeup in the bathroom, races into the living room and looks between us. "What happened?"

Neither me nor Jack answers her. "It's not," I say. "It can't be."

"It is," Jack says.

"Will someone please let me know what's going on?" Clara follows my gaze to the coffee table and gasps. "Oh my God." She looks at Jack. "You found it?"

"It can't be," I say again.

Jack flips up the latches of the guitar case and lifts the lid, and the moment I see it, my breath catches in my chest.

"Oh!" I say, sure if I look away from the guitar, it will disappear. With all my other gear replaced, the guitar was the last thing on my list. I'd been delaying making a decision for as long as possible, because no matter how many guitars I looked at online, nice, new, beautiful guitars, I couldn't narrow my choices down.

I look up, and as soon as my eyes meet Jack's, I jolt into motion, crossing over to the coffee table and running my hand along the fretboard. I pluck at a string, and it's horribly out of tune, but it's the most beautiful sound I've ever heard.

Jack stands nearby, and though I'm not looking at him, I can hear the smile in his voice. "The night we met, I set a bunch of Google alerts and made a few posts online about your guitar," he says. "I never had any luck, but the other day, I got an email from someone who said they thought they'd found it."

"Oh!" I don't know what else to say. I'm overwhelmed. This is . . . unbelievable. I want to pick up the guitar and tune it. I want to feel the strings vibrating beneath my fingers. But before I do, I spin to face Jack, who lets out an *oof* when I barrel into him and wrap my arms as tight as I can around his middle.

"Well, I'm off," Clara says. "Don't wait up. Not sure when or if I'll be back." She pulls me in for a hug and whispers, "I'm really happy for you, Rainey." When she pulls away, the look she gives me has me unsure if she's talking about the guitar or Jack.

As soon as the door shuts behind Clara, I lift the guitar from its case. I have no idea what to focus on first. The guitar? Jack? What is he thinking? I talk nonstop the entire time I tune the guitar, telling him every little thing about it. I'm not sure I'm even making sense.

Once the guitar is in tune, my fingers are in motion. The music comes automatically, a chord progression I've played a million times. The vibration of the strings beneath my fingers makes me feel more grounded than I've been in weeks. I know this guitar as if it's an extension of my own body. My fingers know exactly where to go and what to do without my having to think about it. Sometimes, I feel as if I think in music. It starts inside me and comes out of my fingers and into the world. When I talk, I say things I don't mean. I trip over my words. I get distracted. I'll think I've said something when I haven't. I'll forget what I've said as soon as I say it. But music . . . music is the language of my heart.

"Play it for the pub, please," Jack says.

It takes me a moment to understand what he's said. As soon as I do, I realize the song I've been playing is the one I let Jack listen to last night.

"Please?" he says again.

I'm so overwhelmed—by the way he asks, by having my guitar again—that I don't hesitate. "Okay."

Jack's eyebrows raise in surprise. "Really? You mean it? You're sure."

"I'm sure." And in this moment, I am.

Jack doesn't say anything else, so I keep on strumming. It feels so good, so so good to have this guitar in my hands, to finally feel like *myself* again, that after a few minutes I have to set the guitar down because I start crying so hard I can't play.

"Is something wrong with it?" Jack, who has been quietly watching, asks.

He sits beside me on the couch, and I turn my face away to wipe at my eyes with the sleeve of his hoodie. "No, it's . . . perfect. I'm happy. These are happy tears." I try to hold them back, because I must seem like an absolute disaster human after all the crying I've done in the last twenty-four hours. "Thank you, Jack. You have no idea . . ." But then the tears threaten to overwhelm me again, and I can't finish my sentence. I get to my feet, needing to put some space between us before I say or do anything else embarrassing.

I set the guitar in its case and run my fingers over the strings, hesitant to close the lid. I never want this guitar out of my sight again. "I'm sorry," I say. "God, I've cried, like, what? Three times in the last forty-eight hours?"

"There's nothing wrong with that."

I feel his hand on my arm but don't turn to face him. "Don't look at me. I'm a mess," I say.

"You're not a mess."

I laugh. "How can you say that? Look at me!"

"I thought you didn't want me to look at you."

I cover my face with my hands. "Oh, you know what I mean," I mumble.

Jack takes me by the shoulders, and I don't fight it when he turns me around. "You're not a mess," he says, and gently pulls my hands from my face.

I can't meet his gaze, so I look away, eyes landing on the gallery wall. All those beautiful drawings. I've spent a lot of time looking at them over the last few weeks. Not all of the subjects are beautiful—but the drawings . . . they always are. I'm not sure how he does it. How does he turn everything into something beautiful?

I want to believe what Jack says about me, but it doesn't fit with what I know. I think of all the times I've been told to be quiet, to calm down, to stop being so sensitive, to act my age. I think of all the times I've tried to be like everyone else and failed. I look down at my hands and notice I've picked a loose thread on the cuff of his sweater into an unsightly snag. I let go of the thread with a sigh and tug the sleeves over my hands so I can't do any more damage.

"It's okay," I say. "It's not personal or anything. I know who I am. I'm a mess. I overreact, even to good things. I'm too sensitive."

"You feel a lot. Why is that a bad thing?"

"I don't know," I say. "I just know that it is. I just know I'm too much."

"Raine, look at me."

I shake my head, eyes on my hands hidden in the sleeves of his sweater.

"Ciaróg." He takes my face in his hands. The quiet between us is something tangible, as deliberate and meaningful as a rest in music.

His eyes roam my face before meeting mine again, and the way he looks at me makes my chest ache. He wipes the tears from beneath my eyes, then cradles my face in his hands. "How can you think you're too much, when I can't get enough of you?"

*That's the look*, I think. The one I've always wanted. He looks at me as if I'm his favorite person. *Me*, this crying mess of a human being. "Jack . . ."

"Hmm?"

"What is happening between us?"

He pauses for a moment before answering. When he lets go of my face and leans away, all of me is waiting for what he'll say next.

"Whatever you want." He looks me over. Everywhere his gaze lingers feels electric, glowing beneath his attention but desperate for more. When his eyes meet mine again, there's that look, the one that makes me feel like everything. "What do you want, Raine?"

# Twenty

## JACK

Raine doesn't answer me. Instead, she wraps her arms around my neck and kisses me, and I forget whatever it was I asked her in the first place.

"I need more than this," she says when she pulls away.

I don't have enough blood flowing to my brain to know what she's talking about. "Than . . . ?"

"Kissing. I need more than kissing."

"Are you sure?" I ask.

"Very sure," she says.

"Okay." We move to the couch, and I tug her into my lap and kiss her again. Raine refuses to wear real clothes whenever she's in the flat, and thank God for that, because she's wearing these little sleep shorts that leave hardly anything to the imagination. I slip a hand beneath the jumper and cup one of her breasts. She grinds into me, and I feel as if I'm half out of my mind already, and we're both still fully dressed.

*What do you think you're doing?*

Not now.

*She's your employee.*

We've talked about it. It's fine.

*Are you sure? What if you only heard what you wanted to hear?*

She told me she wants more.

*But what if you get carried away? What if she changes her mind and you can't stop? How can you be sure this is consensual?*

I pause.

"Jack," Raine says.

I lift my gaze to hers. "Are you sure you want to—"

"Yes."

"You don't feel pressured or—"

"I don't feel pressured."

"But what if you do, and you just don't realize it? What if you only realize after—"

"I won't."

"But what if I hurt you?"

"You won't."

"What if—"

"No more *what if*s," Raine says. I search her face, trying to figure out if I've annoyed her, while at the same time looking for any signs that my OCD is right. "I want you. I trust you. And anything that makes you doubt either is a lie."

"You're sure—"

"I am explicitly giving you my enthusiastic consent to do unspeakable things to me, provided they are sexual in nature, of course."

I can't help but laugh at that, and when she smiles, I feel myself relax. But only a little, because the thought that I might hurt her comes boomeranging back around again.

"You don't think I'll hurt you?" I say.

"I know you won't."

"Will you tell me if you don't like something?" I ask.

"Yes."

"You promise?"

"I promise. I also promise to tell you when I *do* like something. Like what you were doing with my boobs. That was great," she says, and leans into my touch. "Though I have to tell you, at a certain point I might not be able to communicate what I like in words. Shocking for someone who talks nonstop, I know."

"Only you would be making jokes when I'm having intrusive thoughts while we're making out on my fecking couch."

She gives me a teasing smile. "What's the joke? I'm not kidding."

Something in her expression changes, and she leans away. My hand falls to her waist. For a moment, I worry that my OCD was right, and she's realized she does feel pressured into this. But then she says, "Do *you* want to do this? I don't mean to assume. We don't have to. I won't take it personally."

My jumper is so big on her that it swallows up those little sleep shorts. "I really, really want to," I say. "You look really fucking sexy in that jumper," I say. "I've spent all day imagining you in nothing but that jumper."

"You don't have to imagine it," she says.

"So, just to confirm—"

"Jack."

"Sorry, sorry."

She crosses her arms over her chest, and I'm sure I've done it now. I've annoyed her with the constant reassurance-seeking and have killed the mood and the moment is over and I'll never get another one.

But then she surprises me by saying, "*You* haven't given *me* your enthusiastic consent to let me do unspeakable things to you yet."

"Oh, you definitely have my enthusiastic consent to do unspeakable things to me."

She squints at me. "I don't know . . . that didn't sound very enthu-siastic."

"You want enthusiasm?" I say. "I'll show you enthusiasm, ciaróg." She opens her mouth to respond, but before she can say anything, I change positions and pin her beneath me.

I'm done letting the thoughts ruin a moment I've been dreaming of for weeks. Done asking her to reassure me through every little fucking thing. I'm done feeling out of control, when all I want is to take it. I want to make her feel like she's mine, even if I have to let her go sooner than I'd like. I want her to belong to me, at least right here and now. When she's in Timbuktu or some other place I'll never go, I want her to think of me, and when she does, I want this to be what she thinks of first. When she's with someone else, I want her to be chasing the way *I* made her feel.

I tug at the jumper. "Take this fecking thing off," I say.

She arches a brow at me. "I thought you wanted me in nothing but your jumper?"

"I changed my mind."

She laughs when we both struggle to get the jumper over her head.

"Fuck this thing," I say, hurling it across the room once I've freed her of it.

"I approve of the enthusiasm," Raine says.

When I look down at her again, whatever reply I had falls out of my head, because her nipples are visible beneath the thin white camisole she's wearing. Another *what if* floats through my head, but I tell it to fuck off. I pull off her camisole and throw that across the room too.

"Fuck, you're beautiful." For a moment I just look at her beneath me, her stomach, and breasts, and all that red hair splayed out on my yellow couch.

It isn't enough to touch her with my hands. I want my mouth on her. It isn't enough to get these small sighs. I want her to call out my name. I kiss my way down her neck to her chest and take one of her breasts in my mouth, paying close attention to how each flick of my tongue makes her react. She has her fingers in my hair. Whenever she really likes something, she pulls it harder, and I decide that if I don't have a headache after this, I haven't done a good enough job.

"We should've done this sooner," she says when I kiss my way across her chest to her other breast. "I wanted you to invite me over the night we met so we could do just this," she says. "I've been thinking about it every night since we met."

"I wanted to invite you over," I murmur.

*I've been thinking about it every night* . . . I don't know if it's what she meant, but an image of her alone in my bed comes to mind. "Do you make yourself come in my bed?"

She seems surprised by the question. I'm about to apologize for asking when she looks me in the eye and says, "Yes."

I'm half convinced I'm dreaming. "And what do you think about when you're touching yourself?"

The color rises in her cheeks. "You."

I brush a hand lightly along one of her knees, and she spreads her legs wider. I tug at her sleep shorts and she lifts her hips so I can slide them off and throw them across the room.

"And what am I doing when you think about me?" I ask.

I touch her over her underwear, and she presses up into my hand. "Fucking me," she says.

I don't know how much more of this I can take, but I am willing to find out. "Will you show me?"

"Show you . . ."

"How you touch yourself. It's okay if you don't want to. I just . . . fuck, I really want to see what you look like when you're thinking about me."

"I thought you were my most professional coworker," she says.

I laugh. "I don't think I've ever uttered such nonsense."

"I have the text messages to prove it."

"I don't think so," I say. "Because the things I want to do to you are very unprofessional."

She searches my face for a moment. "Okay."

"Okay?"

She laughs. "I don't think I've ever seen you look more excited, and that's saying something."

"I don't think I've ever been more excited," I say.

I move to give her space, but she pulls me back to her and tells me to stay. I can't be dreaming. I couldn't come up with a dream this good. I must be dead. If I am, I can't say I mind.

Raine makes room for me beside her. She drapes one of her legs over my hip and slips her hand into her underwear.

*What if . . .*

Fuck off.

*But . . .*

She said she trusts me. She promised she'd tell me if she didn't want to do something.

*But what if . . .*

Fuck off. Fuck off. Fuck off. Fuck off. And then, because I really, really just need to be able to enjoy this, I think, *undo, undo, undo, undo.*

I watch as she strokes herself in small circles, and I have no idea what I've done to deserve this, but I hope that whatever it is, I do it again. I'm unsure where to keep my focus. All of her is beautiful. Her face, the movement of her hand, the way her chest rises and falls with each breath she takes.

"Are you thinking about me?" I ask.

"Yes."

"Where?"

The color rises in her cheeks, and she bites her lip.

"Please." I loosen my grip on her thigh when I realize how tightly I've been holding on to her. "Please tell me."

"Your office," she says.

There goes any chance of me getting work done in there ever again. "Where in my office?"

Her blush deepens. "The desk."

I kiss her shoulder, then her neck. When my mouth finds her ear, I whisper into it, "Is that what you want? Do you want me to fuck you on my desk?"

The only answer she gives me is a whimper.

"Because I will, if you want me to," I say. She replies with another whimper.

"Are you close?" I ask when her rhythm picks up and her breathing quickens.

"Mm-hmm."

"Stop. Please."

She pulls her hand away and presses her thighs together.

"Look at me," I say.

When she opens her eyes, I brush the hair from her face, wanting to take in as much of her as I can. "I've thought about fucking you right here a thousand times."

"I don't have any condoms. Do you?"

"I do, but we don't need one now."

"Why not?"

She looks so desperate and, God, I want to fuck her so bad, but not as much as I want to please her. "Because I want to feel you come on my mouth first," I say.

Her eyes goes wide.

"If that's okay," I add.

"That's . . . more than okay."

I sit back to take one of her legs in my hand, then press a kiss to her ankle before working my way up her leg. I pause with my mouth on the soft skin of her inner thigh. "Do you want me to stop?"

"If you stop, I'll never speak to you again," she says.

When I arrive at her underwear, I want to laugh. "Raine. It's Friday. Why are you wearing Tuesday underwear?"

She laughs, and the sound drives me wild. I remind myself to slow down, but I'm quickly losing anything resembling rational thought, not that I ever had much of it in the first place.

"If I had the answer to that, I wouldn't be me," she says.

"And thank God you're you," I say. "Wear Monday underwear on Thursday, and Thursday on Sunday. Hell, wear them all at once. Better yet, never wear them again."

"What are you talking about?"

"I don't know." I can see how wet she is through her underwear, and I can't focus on anything other than what is right in front of me. "I don't know what I'm talking about. I'm talking about nothing."

"Then stop talking," she says.

"Only if you tell me exactly what you want." I brush my mouth over her. The touch is light, a whisper of contact. When she arches up to meet my mouth, I pull away, and she groans.

"Tell me what you want," I say.

"I want you to take these off," she says, and wriggles her hips beneath me.

I slip off her underwear, and the sight of her completely naked beneath me has me absolutely desperate to go right where I most want to be. But I also want to make her feel as good as I can for as long as possible, until she's begging me to push her over the edge. It's as if I've never wanted anything else in my entire life. As if the only thing I've ever wanted is to make this woman dizzy with pleasure.

"Fuck, Raine. You're . . ." I can't think of the right word for what she is. I'm not sure there is one.

She sighs as I kiss my way along her thighs, and after I've kissed and licked her everywhere but where she really wants me for as long as she can stand, her fingers are in my hair again.

"Please," she breathes. "Jack, please."

I don't make her wait any longer. I don't think I could make *myself* wait any longer. Raine seems to lose all sense of herself once my mouth is between her legs, and I lose all sense of anything but her. How she tastes. Every sound that escapes her. The way she moves her hips to pull as much pleasure from me as she can.

When Raine comes, I have no idea if she says my name. She squeezes me between her thighs so hard that I can't hear a thing.

# Twenty-One

## RAINE

When I finally come down from the best orgasm of my life, I realize I've practically crushed poor Jack.

"I'm so sorry," I say once my knees fall apart, freeing him from my death grip.

Jack sits up and looks down at me. "You take that back right now."

The look on his face makes me laugh.

"I'm serious!" he says. He ruffles his hair with a hand, making it look even wilder than it did a moment ago. "Take back your apology, I don't want it."

"All right, all right, I take it back."

"Thank you," he says.

"Now come here," I say, making room for him to lie down beside me on the couch.

He trails a finger down my side. "You are absolutely incredible."

"How can you say that? I didn't even do anything."

"Oh, you did a lot of things, ciaróg, and I liked every single one of them."

I run a hand along the collar of his shirt. "Will you take this off already?"

"You don't need a break?"

"This is the break, and the break is over."

He laughs. Then presses a kiss to my nose before sitting up to tug off his shirt.

I take in the many tattoos I haven't seen before. I trace the outline of a rose on the lower left side of his stomach. When my eyes are drawn to the tattoo above that, I have to laugh. "Is this an astronaut cat?"

"Too weird?"

I shake my head, unable to take my eyes off him. This man is the very definition of eye candy—colorful and sweet. "It's the perfect amount of weird."

Above the astronaut cat is a serpent. And then I let my hand drift up to where, on either side of his chest, he has finger guns pointing toward each other.

My hands make their way down his chest to his side. "Jack."

"Hmm?"

"Is this a bagel with airplane wings?"

"It's a plane bagel."

I look up at him, and as soon as I do, I burst out laughing.

"Don't you dare make fun of me, ciaróg," he says.

"Why not? What are you going to do to me?"

"Oh, I have a list of things I'd like to do to you."

"Is it a very long list?"

"Impossibly so."

I tug at the belt loops on his jeans. "Just a heads-up that I will be making a thorough examination of your tattoos later."

"That sounds like exactly my sort of fun."

"My sort of fun is you naked on this couch," I say.

Jack laughs, but instead of pulling me to him like I think he will, he picks me up and tosses me over his shoulder. "No way, ciaróg. I'm not fucking you tonight."

He carries me into the bedroom and when he sets me on the bed, I feel a bit deflated. "You're . . . not?"

Jack stands between my legs and runs his fingers through my hair. When he catches my eye, he leans down and kisses me. "I would love to sleep with you," he says. "So long as you aren't opposed—"

"I'm not opposed. I am very much in favor."

He laughs, then takes my chin in his hand and leans closer. "And I am *more* than happy to fuck you another night. Maybe even on my desk. But right now, I want to take my time. I want to make sure you're comfortable. I want to enjoy every inch of you."

I bite back a laugh, and Jack narrows his eyes. "Don't you dare—"

"That's what she said," I whisper.

*"Ciaróg."*

"Sorry, sorry," I say. "Go on."

"Anyway," he says, "I don't think I'd call that fucking."

"What would you call it?"

"I think it's easier to show you," he says.

"So show me."

When Jack kisses me, the urgency from the living room settles into something languid. I finish undressing him, and having his skin against mine, having nothing between us, is a new and different kind of pleasure.

Even though this is the first time we've been together, I don't feel awkward or worry about what will happen next. When I look at Jack, I don't worry about a thing. It's as if nothing else exists.

He rests his weight against mine and kisses me slowly, as if we have all the time in the world. At his touch, the universe in my head is distilled to a single star. Every movement is unhurried and attentive. I delight in every detail of him. The feel of his hair between my fingers. The way he looks at me when he rolls on a condom and pushes into me slowly. The sound of his breath in my ear.

He lingers everywhere, and I think I understand what he was trying to say about not wanting to fuck me, because this doesn't feel at all like what happened on his couch. I've never had sex like this. Like there's no destination, like every sensation is the whole point. I have been touched in these places but not in this way. I have been a means to an end, but I have never been *everything*. This is what it must feel like for someone to make love to you. It occurs to me that no one ever has.

He stills and tucks a strand of hair behind my ear. "Are you okay, ciaróg? You're crying."

"I'm just feeling," I say. "Good feelings. It's nice to just feel and not think." I trace the tattoo of a swallow on his shoulder. "That probably doesn't make sense."

"I understand you perfectly. I'm a champion overthinker, after all."

When I laugh, the tears slip down my cheeks in earnest. "Oh God. This is embarrassing," I say.

I search his face for any sign of annoyance or disappointment and find none.

"Feel whatever you want to feel," he says. His voice in my ear is the best kind of secret. One that belongs only to me. "But if something doesn't feel good you'll tell me, yeah?"

I nod.

"Good." He brushes away my tears even as more come. "I love how much you feel. It's my favorite thing about you."

"What else do you love about me?" I say, then pull him closer. "Don't stop. Please."

He rocks back into me and lowers his head so that his nose touches mine. "I love your freckles," he says. "I love your voice." He presses a kiss to my mouth and throat, and then he's whispering into my ear. "I love the sounds you make. I love the way you look when you come. I love being inside you."

*And me?* I think. *Do you love me?*

I don't ask, because I think I know. I feel it in the way he kisses me, in how his fingers brush my hair, in the rhythm of his breath and the deliberate, unhurried way he moves with me. I wonder if he can tell I love him, because I do.

Except I'm not sure it matters. Because as much as I love it here, I can't stay. I already feel the heartache in my chest. It's tender to the touch, like a bruise you know is coming but can't yet see.

When I come again, I don't know if I'm falling apart or being put back together. All the parts of myself that seemed out of tune before find their place. Or maybe they were never out of tune at all. Maybe I've been listening for the wrong key—A minor instead of C major. Maybe I'm not playing the wrong notes, but starting in the wrong place. All that dissonance because I've been trying to play someone else's song.

When Jack finds his own release, he buries his face in my neck, and I hold him as close as I can. I hold him and don't let go when he stills. I hold him and don't let go as our breathing slows. I hold him and don't let go as this moment passes into the next.

I don't want to let go.

Afterward, we lie beside each other in silence. Jack's gaze follows his finger as it trails along my bare shoulder, and I wonder what he's thinking about. He mutters something under his breath, as if he's trying to count the freckles that pass beneath it.

Finally, he lifts his gaze to mine. "Where will you go?"

"Hmm?"

"When you leave Cobh."

"Oh." I was wondering when we'd talk about this. "Vienna, I think."

"Not Galway?"

"I don't think it could live up to Cobh," I say.

"Why Vienna?"

*Because it's far from here, and I need to distance myself from you and this place as much as possible, or I won't be able to at all.* "It's a very musical city," I say.

"And . . . *when* are you thinking of going?"

"When my twelve weeks are up in April. That's what we agreed to."

Jack is quiet for a moment. "That's really generous of you," he says. "But you have everything you need, and you've done everything I hoped you'd do here. I don't want to hold you back. It would be selfish of me to have you stay when there's nothing keeping you here anymore." His hand drifts up and down my arm as he speaks. "You've got to make up for all the adventures you missed while you were stuck here in this silly pub with me."

"I don't know. I think I can count being stuck here with you as one of my adventures."

"I hope it's been a good one," he says.

"One of the best."

I think about my new travel case and MIDI keyboard and microphone. I think about my new street amp and backpack and phone charger. I think about my old guitar and foot tambourine. I have my life back. I should be happy about it, and . . . I am happy. I'm excited to see new places and meet new people. I'm excited to get back to music. I've missed never knowing what the next week will bring.

I want him to ask me to stay, because I want him to *want* me to stay. But I also *don't* want him to ask, because I know I can't. I love the pub, but I don't want to work at it forever. I love Cobh, and the Local, and Jack, but I can't give up traveling. I can't imagine settling into a normal life. What if I stay and come to resent this place I love? To resent him?

I don't think I could bear it.

"Clara's flight back to Boston leaves Monday afternoon," I say. "So I guess I'll head out the week after that."

"Okay," he says.

We fall quiet again. I trace each of his tattoos, first the outline, then the details.

"How many tattoos do you have?" I ask.

He hums to himself in thought for a moment. "I have no idea. I lost count."

A tattoo of a light switch on his thigh catches my attention. It's a lot more faded than the others. The lines aren't as clean.

I trace the banner at the bottom of the light switch. "Fuck off," I mutter, reading the words that stretch across it.

When I raise my gaze to Jack's, he's watching me thoughtfully.

"That's my first tattoo," he says. "I did it myself with one of my mum's sewing needles when I was fourteen. Fecking stupid. It's a miracle it didn't get infected. If Shauna ever knew about that, I doubt she'd have given me an apprenticeship. Hell, she'd be pissed off if she knew about it now." He narrows his eyes at me. "So you better not tell Róisín."

"Your secret is safe with me," I say.

He laughs, then turns to face me. "I can't believe I was ever capable of something like that. Now I can't even tattoo with all the proper sanitation. I can't tattoo even with over-the-top sanitation."

"Did you do it because of the light switch compulsion?"

"Thought it would feel good to tell the thoughts to fuck off." He sighs. "It did feel good, you know."

My eyes drift to the tattoo of a pair of scissors on his forearm, then to the dagger on his neck. "Is that why you have the scissors and the dagger?"

He runs a hand through his hair. "It is. It felt like taking control, but . . ." He pauses to run a hand through his hair. "Martina, my therapist, she'd say that what I actually need to do is accept I don't have any control, and that's okay."

"She sounds like a smart therapist," I say.

"She is." He looks away, eyes on his finger as he traces my collar-bone. "I've decided to start seeing her again, actually."

"Jack, that's great."

"You make it easier."

I laugh. "Me? How do *I* make seeing your therapist easier?"

He takes my hand and kisses it, then laces his fingers through mine and holds my hand to his chest. "You make it feel okay."

"Because it is okay."

"It is, but . . ." He sighs. "Not everyone makes it feel that way. Nina and Ollie . . . if they knew how bad things were, they'd badger me about therapy until I give in, whether I'm actually ready for it or not. They'd make my relapse this big thing. And yeah, it's a big thing, I guess, but it's *my* big thing. It's also just . . . part of my life. It's not normal, but it's normal for *me*. And you make it feel completely normal."

"It is normal."

There's a beat of silence before he speaks again. "Can I ask you something?"

"Sure."

"Did you really mean it when you said you'd play your song for the pub?"

I don't fully understand the look he gives me. It's hopeful and pleading, and I don't want to disappoint him. "Yes."

"Wednesday? Could you do it then?"

"I don't see why not." Even though the thought of it already has me nauseous.

Jack grins at me, but then his smile falters. "I know you were hoping I'd tattoo you before you go."

"Jack, it's okay."

"I'm going to work on it in therapy. I didn't even try last time, but . . . I do miss it. I just won't be ready before you go. But I do want to be able to give you your beetle tattoo one day," he says. "Maybe right . . . here," he says, and kisses me on my neck where I'm ticklish.

I roll over and try to wriggle away, but he pulls me closer. I bury my face in his neck, and for a while just listen to the rhythm of his breathing, thinking about how soon, it'll just be me and my guitar again. Which is exactly what I wanted when I left Boston. It's exactly what I wanted when I stepped inside the Local for the first time. So why do I feel like I want more for my life? I want *everything*. I want travel and music. But I want home and a family too. I want to always see something new, but at the same time, I want to find a place that is so familiar, it feels like a part of me.

I don't want to feel heartache right now. I already spend so much of my time feeling bruised. I don't want to ruin *now* by thinking about what's to come. Because when I'm with Jack, I feel like something wonderful. He makes me feel perfectly at home in this body. In my mismatched socks and dingy brown boots with faded red laces. In his hoodie and his gloves. In nothing at all. With Jack, I feel perfectly at home in who I am. In my music and unfiltered words and careless mistakes. I don't know if I can take the feeling with me when I leave, so just in case it stays behind with him, I decide to immerse myself in it now.

I don't want to let go.

But I know that sooner than I'd like, I won't have a choice.

On Monday morning, Jack and I take Clara to the airport. I stand beside her as she checks in for her flight, and we stop outside the entrance to security to say goodbye.

"I'm really going to miss you, Rainey," Clara says.

"I'm going to miss you too. But you're going to kick med school's ass, so at least I'm giving you up for a good cause."

She laughs. "Yeah, we'll see. At least I've got being a human statue as a backup career."

"I wouldn't count on it," I say. "But you don't need a backup career."

"Thanks," she says.

"Go before I start crying," I say. But it's no use, because when I notice Clara wiping the tears from her eyes, I start laughing *and* crying.

"Ugh!" she says, tipping her face to the ceiling to hold more tears at bay. "You've infected me with your feelings."

After one last forceful hug, I watch as Clara disappears through security, then go outside to find Jack.

"You okay?" Jack asks when I slide into the passenger seat with a sigh.

"I think so."

He reaches over and squeezes my hand before letting go to pull out of the airport. When I leave, I wonder if he will come inside with me, like I did with Clara. Will we linger beside the check-in counter? Or will he drop me off at the curb for an unceremonious goodbye? I try to imagine that but can't. At the very least he would step out of the car to help me unload my gear, even though I don't need the help. I've carried everything on my own before and will carry it all on my own again.

It would be nice to have a little help, though. Some company in all those new places.

Jack must sense me watching him. He looks over and smiles.

"I've heard Vienna has some cool street art," I say. "A lot of surrealist stuff."

"Does it?"

"Oh yeah," I say. "Some of it is really weird. Gutsy. And I mean that literally."

He glances at me, then returns his gaze to the road. "Now that I'd love to see."

I don't say anything. Instead, I lean forward and turn up the music, imagining what it would be like for him to come with me. We could explore the whole city if we wanted. I'd drag him around every street corner and we'd look for the weirdest art we could find. He'd probably make me impatient. He'd see something no one else would notice, an abandoned sock or some other ugly discarded thing, and we'd have to stop so he could find some beauty in it. I'd pace up and down the block while he perched on a bench or a curb and made a quick sketch. The same thing has happened on so many of our walks around Cobh that I can see it, really see it. Like it's a vision. Something destined to come true.

We're quiet the whole drive back to Cobh. Jack keeps his eyes ahead and doesn't so much as glance at me. I catch sight of the tattoo on his neck—a dagger pierced through a heart. *That's how it feels to leave*, I think, then scold myself for the melodramatic thought.

But leaving doesn't have to feel that way. Not if Jack comes with me. He's capable of more than he thinks. He can travel. He can see and do all the things he wants. He just has to believe he can. But I can't just ask him to come with me to Vienna. I have to start small and *show* him he can.

When I return to the flat, the first thing I do (after greeting

Sebastian, of course) is buy two round-trip tickets to London. I'll play for the pub on Wednesday. We'll leave Thursday, stay one night, and be home in time to work the night shift on Friday.

It's just a quick little getaway. A small step to feel things out. At least it's *something*.

I just hope it'll be enough.

# Twenty-Two

## JACK

An hour before Raine is supposed to perform at the pub, I get stuck in the guest room at Nina and Ollie's house with my hand on the light switch. For the last ten minutes I've been telling myself that I need to leave so I can make it to the pub on time and yet . . . here I am.

I could step through this open door and into the hall. It would take less than a second. But I can't pull my hand away. No matter how many times I flick the light switch, it doesn't feel right. And I can't leave until it feels right, otherwise . . . Otherwise what? *Nothing*, the rational part of my brain says. *Nothing bad will happen*. But my OCD doesn't agree.

Earlier, when I picked up my phone after taking a shower, I found a missed call from my mum. No text. No voice mail. Which isn't unusual. I called her back, but she didn't pick up. Also not unusual. Since she and Ed started dating, she's been busier than she used to be. We miss each other's calls all the time. I didn't think much of it as I got dressed. But then, just as I opened the door to the guest room, I thought, *What if Mum's been hurt? What if she's bleeding out some-where and was calling for help?*

Instead of leaving the room, I called her a few more times. Still, no answer. I called Ed—something I try to avoid as much as possible—but he didn't pick up either.

I started playing games in my head when I was ten years old. The first of these games was the mug game. The rules were simple: If Mum handed Da the red mug, it meant he'd have a bad day. If she handed him the blue one, it meant he'd have a good day. Da having a bad day usually meant Mum and I would have a bad day too, and eventually, I offered to make Da's coffee myself, just so I could make sure he got the blue mug—even if that meant ignoring the four clean mugs in the cabinet and washing it.

I knew it wouldn't actually keep Da from getting angry, but I did it anyway. I didn't mind. It made it easier to move on with my day. But then I'd get to school and wonder if I'd actually given him the blue mug. I'd run through the events of the morning in my mind over and over, but could never be sure. What if I was thinking of yester-day, not today? Nearly failed because of it.

Today's game is called *If you don't flick this light switch the right way, your mum is dead.* This game is a cousin to the ever-popular *Step on a crack and break your mother's back.* The rules of my game are a bit more complicated. All I have to do is flick this fucking light switch in multiples of four until I get the sense that my mother is out of danger.

There are many problems with this game. One, it isn't real. Two, it's time consuming. Three, it makes me feel like I've lost my mind. Four—there are always four rules—I never know what multiple of four will be the magic number to keep whatever horrible thing I've thought from happening. Today, we're upwards of forty and still go-ing. *On-off-on-off. On-off-on-off. On-off-on-off. On-off-on-off.* Again and again and again and again. It's the world's worst fucking rave. It's giving me a fucking headache.

I could stop right now. I *should* stop right now. I should let go on an odd number and put on my boots the wrong way—left before right. I should say to myself, *Yes, my mother is bleeding out somewhere in the Canary Islands because I didn't answer her phone call. Perhaps I could prevent it from happening by flicking this light switch, but I refuse. If she dies, it will haunt me for the rest of my life. But alas, I will just have to suffer the consequences.*

I should do all of those things, but I don't. Because I'm very close to getting it right. I'm sure of it. And then I can go to the pub and not worry about whether or not Mum is dead. If I resist the compulsions like I'm supposed to, my anxiety will be worse in the short-term, and I'm simply too busy for that.

My phone buzzes in my hand. I answer the call and press the phone to my ear. "Ed?"

"Jack, is everything all right?"

"Where's Mum?"

"She went for a swim. Why? Is there something wrong?"

"And Mum's okay?"

"She's . . . fine, Jack."

"Are you with her right now?"

"I'm not. But I can see her from here."

"Can I talk to her?"

"Is everything okay there?"

"Everything's fine."

Ed sighs. "You called twelve times, Jack."

I could've sworn it was eight, but I wasn't exactly thinking straight. I don't say anything.

"And Ollie and the girls are okay?" Ed asks.

"Everyone's grand. Can I talk to Mum?"

Ed sighs. "Jack . . . I'll have her call you later."

"But—"

"You worry her, you know."

"I'm fine."

"I know you're the worrying sort—"

"Ed, can we not—"

"But it seems worse lately. You call a lot more. You seem agitated. Your Mum is totally safe here. I'm looking out for her, okay?"

It's not okay. Because it isn't just her being away that's the problem. I worry about her being away with *him*. I've never seen him so much as angry, but you can't really know what a person is like. Da was the most charming fella you'd ever meet, until he started beating the shite out of you. And me . . . the horrible things I think. How am I supposed to believe Ed is safe and trustworthy, when I can't even trust myself?

"You can't be responsible for everyone, Jack. You'll kill yourself trying. You've got to live with a little uncertainty."

"Where'd you get that one from?"

Ed laughs. "I'm not sure, but I'm going to say I came up with it myself. Just take care of yourself, okay? You don't have to take care of your mum anymore."

*You don't have to take care of your mum anymore.* Ed might think he knows what we went through with Da, but he doesn't. He only knows what Mum tells him, and Mum only sees what she wants to see. She only acknowledges as much as she can stand to.

I step from the room and shut the door behind me. My thoughts are spiraling as I make my way downstairs, where I put on my boots, starting with the right one.

When I finally make it to the pub, I'm surprised to find it's busier than I expect. Every stool at the bar is taken. Every table is occupied. It's not the first time this has happened, especially over the last few weeks. But there is something different about tonight. I'm not sure what.

I'm also not sure I can stay out here long enough to figure it out. The incident with the light switch and the phone call with Ed feel stuck to my nerves, as if the fear and circling thoughts are still right there waiting, and anyone—anything—can bring them back. Just the thought of the thoughts has my heart picking up the pace.

I should've come in through the back. I glance at the front door, tempted to slip out and walk around so I can close myself in my office before anyone can notice me. Better yet, I can escape the pub completely and walk back to Nina and Ollie's place. The thoughts will follow me no matter where I go, but at least there won't be anyone to see it. And by anyone, I mostly mean Raine. Somehow I don't think another mental breakdown will add to the allure of staying in Cobh.

I eye the door to the pub. The temptation to take the easy way out and walk away is strong. But I'm the one who put Raine up to this, and if I can just get her to see that she can play her own music, then maybe she'll work up the courage to record it, and maybe she'll decide to stick around here to do it. But now, I see how truly awful this scheme is. How can I ask her to stay in Cobh for a few more weeks when I can't even stay in this pub for a few minutes?

Just as I take my first step toward the door, I hear my brother call my name. I pretend I don't hear him and take another step.

I shouldn't be here. I'm not in the right headspace.

Before I can reach the door, Ollie's hand is on my shoulder, and I can't pretend I don't hear him now.

"Where the fuck do you think you're going?" he says.

"Home." I try to take another step, but Ollie's grip on my shoulder keeps me in place.

"Oh, no you don't, Jackie. You're not leaving me to close up after this mob all on my own. You know Aoife's leaving early tonight."

If I thought I could escape this without having a conversation with Ollie, I would. Ollie's right. But he can manage on his own.

He'll understand. I'll explain to him what is going on, just a quick conversation, and he'll let me leave like he always does on days like today. Then I can go home without the guilt.

I turn to face him, and his already furrowed brow deepens. "What's with you?"

"Oh, you know, the usual."

Ollie looks me over, then nods. "C'mon."

"Where are you—"

"Hush up, now. We need to talk."

I'm too tired to fight it when Ollie steps around me and places his hands on my shoulders. He steers me behind the bar and toward the door to the kitchen, deftly avoiding running into Aoife, who is in her element as she whizzes around taking orders and pouring drinks.

I hold my breath as soon as Ollie pushes me through the door. The kitchen is quieter than out front. Róisín doesn't look up as we pass by them. I try not to catch sight of the knife in their hands, and avert my gaze to my boots. *Bad-boy aesthetic my arse*, I think. All the black clothes and tattoos can't hide the fact that I'm a coward.

Ollie lets go of me to open the office door. He gestures for me to step inside, and I do so, but not without a sigh. Neither of us says anything when he steps in behind me and closes the door. I busy myself by loitering around the desk and pretending to read over the jumbled mess of Post-its stuck to it.

I don't look at Ollie when he sinks into the chair behind the desk, though I can feel him watching me. I'm not sure how long the silence between us stretches on. Thirty seconds? Three minutes? I'm too stuck in my own head to know.

"Why don't you take a seat, Jackie?" Ollie finally says.

I shake my head but do as he says anyway.

"Now tell me what's going on."

"The usual. Like I said."

"What's the usual?"

When I look at Ollie, I feel outside of myself. It's been five years since he came home, but every now and then it hits me out of nowhere that he's here. He came home. For me. Because I asked.

"I need to go home."

Ollie doesn't say okay like he usually does. He looks me over, and does that brow-furrowing thing again. "Are you sure that's what you really *need*, Jackie?"

"What do you mean?"

Ollie tips his face up to the ceiling and sighs. "I know I'm not good at this stuff."

"What . . . stuff?"

"Your OCD. I know I'm not good at . . . doing whatever it is I'm supposed to do. I wanna do right by you, Jackie, but it's hard. I don't wanna make things worse. Reassuring you . . . helping you avoid triggers . . . it *feels* like the right thing to do, even if it isn't."

I'm too stunned to speak. For the last few years, Ollie and I have talked *around* my OCD. We never touch on it directly unless it is absolutely necessary. I know it's not because he's ashamed of me. I know it's his own shame that he wasn't here, and that if he had been, maybe things wouldn't have been so bad.

"You're seeing your therapist again, yeah?" he asks.

"First appointment was yesterday."

"Right. So . . . what would your therapist say you need? Do you really *need* to go home?"

I stare at my brother for a moment. "I don't understand."

"Jesus, I'm not making sense, am I? You said you need to go home. Is that really what you need or—"

"Not that," I say. "I don't understand . . . this."

He gives me a blank stare.

"*You.* I don't understand you." I slump into the chair and cross my arms over my chest. "It's a bit inconsiderate of you to start doing exactly what you're supposed to when I really was hoping you'd continue enabling me."

Ollie rolls his eyes. "Is that really what you want?"

*It is,* I want to say, but when I open my mouth, the truth spills out. "It's not."

"Then what do you want, Jackie?"

"I told you, I don't know anymore."

"I think you do."

Ollie holds my gaze. I want to look away, but I can't. Ollie is gruff and abrasive, but he's as loyal as they come. "I want to be well," I say.

"And will going home right now get you closer to that?"

I shake my head.

"Then don't go home, Jackie. Stay. Just for a while."

"I don't know if I can."

"You can."

I can't look at Ollie anymore. I'm not used to this. I'm not used to him pushing me in this way.

"You wanna know why you should stay?" Ollie says.

"Because exposure response prevention therapy is incredibly effective."

"Yeah, sure. But that's not the only reason."

"Go on."

Ollie plants his elbows on the desk and leans forward. "If you leave, you're walking away from everything you wanted. Did you see it out there?"

"It's busy, sure, but—"

"It's not busy, Jackie. It's alive. There's a difference. I know I wasn't here for a long time, but I grew up in this pub too. I remember what it was like when Da was running the place, and yeah, it was busy at times, but it was never *alive*. It was a place to go, but not a place to belong. You've turned this into a place to *belong*, Jackie. You and Raine both."

*Raine.* "Shite, she should be playing now, shouldn't she?"

Ollie smiles. "And you'll miss seeing your girl perform. That was gonna be reason number two you ought to stay."

"Oh, shut your fecking gob, Ollie Wollie."

"I don't think I will."

We look at each other for a moment.

"Oh, fine, I'll stay. But I'm not sure how long I can manage."

"You can manage plenty, if you want to."

"You're right annoying, you are," I tell him.

"I do know, yeah. It's clearly genetic. Now, get your arse out there. We've got a pub to run."

# Twenty-Three

## RAINE

Over the last year I've performed in places I could never have imagined—on Tower Bridge in London, the Pont Neuf bridge in Paris, the Charles Bridge in Prague. (A lot of bridges, really.) But now, as I look out at the familiar faces before me, I can't help but think that the Local is my favorite.

When my set ends, I find myself in a seemingly endless swirl of conversation. It's only once the pub closes that I'm finally able go looking for Jack, who disappeared as soon as I finished my final song of the night. At first, I think he's gone home without saying goodbye. The kitchen is quiet, save for the steady sound of the sink as Róisín cleans up. His office is empty. I'm about to give up and trudge upstairs for the night when I notice the back door to the pub is slightly ajar.

Jack lifts his head when I ease the door open and sit beside him on the top step. He's hunched forward with his hands laced between his knees. He flexes his fingers slowly, and I can tell he's resisting the urge to tap out one of his rhythms. I can't help but feel that whatever is bothering him is my fault. He wanted me to play *my* song, and I just . . . couldn't. As soon as I said I had one more song and strummed the opening chords, I noticed the faces at the tables before me, faces of people I have come to know and love, people I really, *really* want to like me, and my fingers shifted to something different. Someone else's song.

"I'm sorry," I say, and press my shoulder gently against his.

Jack searches my face as if he has no idea what I'm apologizing for.

"My song . . . I didn't play it."

"That's all right. I shouldn't have pushed. I was just hoping . . ." He lets the words trail off. He looks away from me and swipes a hand through his hair. I notice the hilt of the dagger on his neck and want to trace it with my fingers.

"You were just hoping . . . what?"

He laces his fingers together again. "Nothing . . . I was just hoping you had a good time, is all."

"I did."

"Good."

I'm skeptical that's all he was hoping for, because he seems so . . . sad. He smiles at me, but I'm not sure what to make of it. I think of the tickets to London I purchased and already know he's in no place to travel. But there's a small part of me that hopes I'm wrong, and unfortunately that little glimmer of hope is enough for me to open my mouth.

I drop my gaze to my boots and notice I'm fidgeting with the frayed end of one of my laces. "Do you ever wish you could just . . . get away from it all?"

He's quiet for a moment. I feel his attention shift to my boots too, and I let go of my torn-up laces to stuff my hands into the kangaroo pocket of his hoodie.

"All the time," he says. He nudges my shoulder with his. "It must be nice to live by your own rules."

"It's okay." I wiggle my toes in my boots. The voice of reason tells me not to bring up London or traveling, but the words are out of my mouth before I can stop myself. "You could, if you wanted. Get away from it all. Maybe we could do a little overnight to London? I could show you all of my favorite busking spots."

My heart is racing when I glance at Jack. At the pained look on his face, I feel as beat-up and worn down as my dingy hiking boots. "Never mind. That was a silly idea."

"Raine—"

"Who cares about busking spots, right? Totally not worth the plane ticket."

Jack places his hand on my cheek, and the absolute certainty of his touch stills me. "It's not silly. I want to see your favorite markets, and parks, and bridges, and whatever else you want to show me."

"You do?"

His thumb strokes my cheek. "Of course I do."

"Then come with me," I say. As soon as the words leave my mouth, that sadness returns to Jack's face, and I want to take them back.

"I wish I could," he murmurs. "But—"

"No need to explain," I say. My face is warm with embarrassment. I turn away and his hand falls from my cheek. "I wasn't thinking."

"I would love to travel but—"

"You've got a real life here," I say. "You have the pub and your family. You can't just . . . spend your life fucking around, like I do."

"Raine."

"I wasn't really asking you to come with me," I say. "I was just talking. It didn't mean anything."

"Raine, slow down and look at me."

I don't want to, but I do it anyway. He tucks my hair behind my ear. "Even if I didn't have the pub, I don't see how I could go with you. I'm not very good at uncertainty. I wish I was. And as much as I want to tell you I can be that person one day, I don't know if I can." He gives me a gentle smile, but it's a sad one. "I'm sorry I can't be the one to have adventures with you."

"But maybe you can be. Not now, of course, but maybe one day."

"Maybe," he says. "But one day could be years from now."

"Or in a few months."

"Or never."

"I know it's not as simple as a few therapy sessions, but you said it yourself, therapy changed your life."

"It did. And I know it will help. But I don't know how much, and I don't know how long it'll take. I don't want you to wait around for something that might never happen."

"We could do long distance. I could come back here once a month or something."

Jack shakes his head. "I can't ask you to do that. It wouldn't be fair."

"I wouldn't mind—"

"It's never going to go away completely, Raine. There will always be ups and downs."

"I know that."

"And you deserve better," he says.

*"Bullshit."*

A flash of anger courses through me, and I look away. I don't know why he does this. Why he denies everything he deserves, why he thinks he can't be happy.

Jack sighs. He catches my chin in his hand, and I don't fight it when he makes me look at him. "You'll meet someone as brave and adventurous as you are, and you'll have an amazing life."

"Jack—"

He leans in closer and whispers, "Just so you know, I already hate the guy."

Jack kisses me. The moment his mouth leaves mine, I'm hit with the weight of a loss that has yet to arrive, and the tears I've tried to hold back slip down my cheeks.

"Ah, crap," I whisper.

Jack swipes the tears away. "I'm no good for you anyway. I keep making you cry."

"Oh, everything makes me cry," I say. "A really good cup of coffee makes me cry. That doesn't mean it's bad for me."

I bury my face in his shoulder. Jack puts his arm around me and pulls me close to his side. "You're the silliest person I've ever met," he says.

"A role I take very seriously."

"Quit stealing my jokes."

"Jack?"

"Hmm?"

I tip my face up to his. "You promise you won't go to Tokyo without me?"

"Promise."

When I hold out my hand for a pinkie promise, he takes my arm instead, making me squeal when he pulls me into his lap. He kisses my chin, then grabs my arm and kisses my elbow.

"What are you doing?"

"Just making sure I haven't missed anywhere," he says, and kisses my other elbow. When he pulls back, he pins me with a stern glare. "No more being sad."

"Or what?"

"Or else you're fired," he says.

"Oh, please."

I want to make the most of the time we have together, even if it isn't much. Being with Jack reminds me of my very favorite days. Perfect ones with perfect weather. When I look up at him, his arms loosely wrapped around my waist, it feels like tilting my face up to the sun, like standing in the middle of a new city that somehow feels like home.

# Twenty-Four

I spend my last night in Cobh at the Local, perched on the very same stool I took my first night here. I've hardly left it since my shift ended, and that was nearly four hours ago now. Aoife, who took over behind the bar when Ollie went home at five, has been talking my ear off since she arrived. I try to pay attention, but then my phone buzzes on the bar top with a message from Jack.

**JACK**
Running late. Be there soon.

"You good, girl?" Aoife asks.

I stare at the text for a moment, then click the screen dark without replying and look up at Aoife, who sets yet another pint in front of me. I'm starting to suspect she's trying to get me drunk so I'll miss my flight. When I suggest as much, all she says is, "Someone certainly thinks they know everything about everyone," and winks.

All evening I've tuned in and out of the conversations around me. The toppling of the Jenga tower sounds from the game room, followed by a wave of laughter. I think of that first night in Cobh and how the first thing I noticed when I walked in here was the music playing overhead and can't help but get a little emotional at how much this place has changed. I haven't been here long, but I know this place. I know the origin of every item on these cluttered walls. I know which games are missing pieces. Which customers will drift in when. I know exactly what song Dave will play first when he pulls out his guitar and the look on Aoife's face that says she's just remembered a particularly good piece of town gossip.

I know how it feels to sit on the floor in front of the fireplace, my boots in a heap beside me, and not get any strange looks. I know that when I tear a napkin into little bits that form a pile on the bar top, I can just set them on the nearest empty plate, whether it be mine or someone else's. I know to expect someone will join in when I'm singing to myself and that I'll hear my named hollered from across the room as soon as I walk in the door.

I know what it feels like to be here, not as a tourist or passerby, but as someone who belongs.

The later it gets, the more I feel like crying. When Róisín calls for Aoife from the kitchen, I slip from my stool and step outside, hoping a quick loop around the block will keep me from making a fool of myself in public again. With every step, I try to remind myself that this was all part of the plan. I was only supposed to stay here for a little while. I was never supposed to stay here at all.

I turn a corner, and when the cathedral comes into view, I slow to a stop and watch it glow above the town. I don't stay for long. It's just a moment. One small, brief pause in a bigger journey to somewhere else.

Jack is waiting for me when I reach the door to the pub again. "There you are. It's almost last call and everyone is waiting for you."

"Why is everyone waiting for me?"

"Don't worry about it."

I squint at him. "You're making me nervous."

"Don't be nervous."

He presses a kiss to my forehead, then takes my hand in his and leads me inside. I'm surprised to find that Jack wasn't kidding. *Everyone* is here. And not just Aoife and Róisín and the regulars who were already here when I went for my walk. Dave and Nina and even Ollie (who already spent his entire day here) sit beside each other at the bar.

"There's our Raine," Aoife calls when she spots us. "I was wondering where you ran off to, girl."

"What's everyone doing here? Aren't we closing in five minutes?"

Jack doesn't get the chance to answer my questions because Nina jumps up from her stool and races over.

"I'm stealing your girl," she tells Jack, then loops her arm through mine and drags me to the bar, despite the fact that Jack and I were already headed in that direction.

I'm not sure what all the fuss is about, but when Nina makes me take the empty barstool beside her, she waggles her eyebrows at me and whispers, "Are you ready for your first lock-in?"

"Really?" I spin around to look for Jack, who is busy locking the door and shuttering the windows. I've heard about lock-ins of course, but I've never experienced one. Last call at the Local is at eleven thirty during the week, as it is in most pubs here in Ireland. But sometimes, when folks aren't quite ready to go home for the night, the owner or bartender will keep the party going. Once closing time comes and anyone not in the know leaves, the door is locked, the windows are shuttered, and everyone inside enjoys a few more rounds. My grandfather used to tell me about them, and I've always wanted to be a part of one. But they happen rarely and are mostly reserved for locals.

The evening is filled with stories and laughter and music. When Dave asks me to play my guitar, I'm just tipsy enough that I find the courage to play my own song. Between the praise from Dave and the look on Jack's face, I'm too embarrassed and emotional to strum another chord once I finish it.

It's late when I say my tearful goodbyes, and then it's just me, Jack, and Sebastian in the pub. Jack disappears into his office and returns with three small gifts that he sets on the bar.

"What's this?" I ask.

"Something small," he says. "A going-away present." He sinks onto the stool beside me and slides one of the gifts toward me. "Here. Open this one first."

I'm not sure what to say, so I don't say anything. I tear open the paper to the first gift and laugh at the sight of brand-new bright red boot laces.

"You need them," he says. "Can't go gallivanting about with those dingy laces."

I stare down at my boots. "I thought you liked my dingy boots with their dingy laces," I say.

Jack grabs one of my feet and, setting it in his lap, begins undoing the laces. "I do, but your safety is my top priority, and *these* are just not up to code."

"You're ridiculous," I say. "Thank you."

Sebastian leaps into my lap, purring gently as Jack replaces the laces of one boot, then the other. He sets the old laces out of sight on the empty stool beside him, then passes the second gift my way. I try not to disturb Sebastian when I reach for it, but it's no use, and after one giant stretch, the cat makes the short jump from my lap to Jack's.

The second gift is a tiny red spiral-bound notebook the size of my palm. I pass my hand over the cover, then glance at Jack, confused.

"It's for the ugly stuff," he says.

I don't say anything because I still don't understand.

"Open the other," he says, and nods to the last gift.

When I unwrap it, I'm surprised to find another notebook. It's nicer than the first. The cover is a soft leather in a rich brown. I run my finger over the words etched right in the center—*Songs*, and beneath it, *Raine Hart*. My name.

"When did you get this?"

If Jack answers, I don't hear. I open the notebook and read the note in Jack's handwriting on the first page. For your future top-40 hits, ciaróg. I flip to the next page and realize that this is no ordinary notebook. The paper inside isn't regular paper at all.

"I thought it would save you time," he says. "If you didn't have to write out all the lines for the . . . music paper? I don't know what it's called."

"Staff paper," I mutter. I eye the plain red notebook. "Why two?"

"You said you used to have a notebook where you wrote out your song ideas, but you didn't like it to be messy. That's why you write on the receipts and scrap paper first right?"

"Right."

"But you're always losing your scrap paper with your ideas, so I thought having one notebook for the ugly stuff would help keep it all in one place. And then you could transfer it over to the other one when you're ready."

I look up at him. "Jack, this is . . ."

"Too much?"

"No." I run my hand along the smooth leather of the notebook. "It's perfect."

"Don't you have to get up early?" Jack says when I drag him upstairs and into bed.

"I can sleep on the plane," I say. "Now that I don't have a boss, I have all the time in the world for sleeping."

Eventually, Jack does fall asleep, but I lie awake in bed beside him and think about my sister crying at the airport. If *she* cries saying goodbye to me, her sister, someone she will most definitely see again, then how am I, champion crybaby, supposed to say goodbye to Jack in a few hours without it being a mess? I'll probably cry the whole way through security. Everyone will be so alarmed, they'll send me for a secondary screening. It'll be embarrassing. For me, and probably for Jack too.

I'd rather that not be the memory I leave him with.

It's five in the morning when I slip out of bed. Sebastian yowls when I reach the door, and I shush him, not wanting to wake Jack. He follows me out into the living room, where my travel case and guitar and backpack are waiting for me by the door. I unzip the pocket of the backpack and pull out the ugly notebook Jack gave me last night. Sebastian is at my heels when I walk to the kitchen and take a seat at the table.

I know I can't say goodbye without falling apart. So I write it instead.

# Twenty-Five

## JACK

I wake up to Sebastian in my face. "Are you trying to suffocate me?" I say, and shove him off of me. When he chirps at me, I shush him, not wanting him to wake Raine. She has a long enough day ahead of her.

*Raine.* I reach out, but don't feel her beside me. I blink awake, and it's brighter than it should be. I grab my phone from the nightstand, bolting upright when I see it's nearly ten. I leave the bedroom to look for her, even though I know she isn't here. Sebastian follows, nearly tripping me when he darts between my legs.

"Will ya quit it, Bash?" I scan the living room. Her boots are no longer in a heap beside the door, but I do spot one of her socks balled up beside the TV.

Sebastian chirps again. I turn toward the sound and find him staring at me from the kitchen table. "I'm coming, I'm coming. Jesus, you act like I haven't fed you in years."

But when I step into the kitchen and fill his food bowl, Sebastian doesn't hover behind me like he usually does. He just keeps sitting there on the kitchen table, staring at me like he's never encountered such a frustrating human before. He chirps again, and when I cross the kitchen to try and figure out what the hell is wrong with my cat, I spot the letter on the table. Raine's handwriting.

Keurig,

I know you wanted to drive me to the airport, but I don't think I can handle goodbye with you, so I took the train. Sorry.

I've been thinking about what you said about accommodations when we first met. I know I never took you up on the offer, but only because you were already making accommodations for me without even meaning to. Every time you reminded me to eat, or talked through my ideas with me, or fact-checked pub quiz questions. You knew what I needed without me having to ask.

You might not be the most professional coworker I've ever had, but you are an incredible boss, and I think that, given enough time, the Local would've been fine without me because you are the heart of that place. AND DON'T YOU DARE BRUSH OFF THE COMPLIMENT! I'm being one hundred percent serious here. Everyone who steps through that door adores you. How could they not want to come back? It's like knowing what people need is your superpower. DON'T LAUGH. IT'S NOT A JOKE. You created an opportunity for Róisín when they weren't sure they wanted to go to culinary school. You gave Aoife a job with a schedule that meant she could support her kids after her husband died. You left your life in Dublin to take care of your mom, to take care of this place, even when you had every reason not to.

But, Jack, please don't forget to take care of yourself. I can already feel you rolling your eyes, and I haven't even finished writing this yet. And I'm not talking about your

OCD. I'm talking about you. Go be selfish. Buy a dozen poppy-seed bagels and share them with absolutely no one. Waste a few hours making a cat tent out of a T-shirt. Take a day off work to read a trashy book you'll forget as soon as you finish the last page. Make art that is useless and silly and important. You deserve every good thing, even when you're having dark thoughts. You deserve to be happy, even when you aren't well.

And love—you deserve that too.

See you in Tokyo.
Ciaróg

I take a seat at the table once I finish reading, then give Sebastian a scratch between the ears. "Sorry for being cross with you. You're a very good cat, you know." He leans into my hand with a yowl.

"I know," I say. "I already miss her too."

I have a feeling I'm going to miss her for a long, long time.

**RAINE**

Good morning from Vienna! I think living
in your flat has ruined me for hostels.
(Tell floofs he is the best roommate
I've ever had, even with all the
cup-knocking-over he does.)

**JACK**

Guess how many of your socks I've
found since you left yesterday.

**RAINE**

Zero. I am very thorough at
packing.

**JACK**

Then why did I find a neon
pink sock beside my TV?

**RAINE**

It was a parting gift for Sebastian.

                                          **JACK**

                              He says thank you.

                    And thank you for your letter.

               Also, did you steal my jumper?

**RAINE**

Maybe.

                                          **JACK**

                    I expect you to return it.

                                  In person.

**RAINE**

I'll bring it back when I come
to get my tattoo.

# APRIL

**JACK**

Floof update—2:23pm Irish Standard
Time/3:23pm in Berlin. Sitting at your
favorite stool and missing you.

**RAINE**

Raine update—Standing next to a very
talkative man on the bus and missing
floofs too. And you.

**JACK**

If he bothers you, call me, and I'll pretend
to be your boyfriend. You can tell him I
keep a giant knife on me at all times.

**RAINE**

I take it therapy is
going well.

Is that a knife in your pocket or are
you just happy to see me?

                                    JACK
                    You are so inappropriate.

RAINE

This is why I will never have a real job.

                                    JACK
                        Your job is real.

RAINE
Okay, a normal job, then.

                                    JACK
                            Better.
                Now back to this fella on the bus.

RAINE
His name is Elias.
He's tall, well-spoken, impeccably dressed.
And he's also eighty years old and
won't stop talking about his late wife,
though he may just be reciting the plot of
The Notebook. Too soon to tell.

MAY

**RAINE**

I'm just gonna drop this file here and
run away forever. K thanks, byeeeee.

**JACK**

Is this . . . a complete recording of
a Raine Hart original song???

**RAINE**

No.

**JACK**

I think it is.

**RAINE**

It's not.

**JACK**

I'm pretty sure it is.

**RAINE**

If you like it, it's mine. If you don't,
it's not.

**JACK**

Thanks for the new ringtone.

**RAINE**

Don't you dare!

**JACK**

Too late. You know, might be the
perfect alarm too.

**RAINE**

Wanting to wake up to the sound
of my voice, huh?

**JACK**

Maybe.

**RAINE**

Hopefully not because it's so grating
it'll motivate you to get out of bed.

**JACK**

Raine. It's wonderful.

**RAINE**

It's not.

**JACK**

It really, really is.

# JUNE

**RAINE**

JACK OMG YOU WILL NEVER BELIEVE
WHAT JUST HAPPENED.

**JACK**

A really famous music producer happened
to be in Copenhagen, heard you playing one
of your original songs, and you now have
an amazing record deal.

**RAINE**

NO.
Though I maybe have started playing
some original stuff . . .

**JACK**

Have you now?

**RAINE**

Anyway . . . will you please GUESS
WHAT JUST HAPPENED TO ME?

                                                    **JACK**

                                        I'm stumped.

**RAINE**

A SEAGULL.
JUST.
ATE.
MY.
LUNCH.

                                                    **JACK**

                                        You're kidding.

**RAINE**

I'll send you a photo. It's the smug-looking
one eating a hotdog.

                                                    **JACK**

                                        Wow. That's just . . . rude.

**RAINE**

You predicted that the night
we met! Remember?

                                                    **JACK**

                                        Of course I remember.

**RAINE**

You're psychic.

JACK

I suppose I am.

RAINE

Do you have any other
predictions for me?

JACK

Hmm.

I do have one, actually.

RAINE

Go on.

JACK

I predict a handsome, charming, amazing
man is going to buy you dinner tonight.

RAINE

Ha ha.

JACK

Don't doubt me, ciaróg. I know things.

RAINE

Did you just send me fifty
euro over PayPal?

JACK

Told you I know things. And here's the link to a
restaurant that has five stars on Tripadvisor.

# JULY

**RAINE**

Happy birthday, Keurig! You are
finally as old and wise as me.

                                   **JACK**

                   For four whole months.

**RAINE**

Did you get my present?

                                   **JACK**

                                 ???

**RAINE**

Hold on.

Okay, it's on its way.

JACK

What's on its way?

?

Hello???

Raine.

Lorraine.

I'm going to keep texting you if you
don't respond.

Lorraine Susan Hart.

**RAINE**

Be patient!

JACK

I don't want to be patient.

Why is someone knocking on
my door?

**RAINE**

JACK

Lorraine.

**RAINE**

JACK

How am I supposed to eat this
many bagels????

**RAINE**

Sounds like a YOU problem.

So, did all your birthday wishes come true?

                                        **JACK**

                        Where are you right now?

**RAINE**

Amsterdam.

                                        **JACK**

                        Then no. Not even close.

# AUGUST

**JACK**

Are you a ghost?

**RAINE**

????

**JACK**

It's the only explanation I can think of
for why I am STILL finding your
socks five months after you left.
That or you have secret
teleportation skills.

**RAINE**

How do you know they're MY socks?
They could be the socks of
some other woman you've
had in your flat.

**JACK**

The one I just found behind a box

in my closet has avocados on it.

And you're the last woman

who was up here.

**RAINE**

Has it really been five months?

OMG. I mean five months since I left!

Not five months since you've had sex!

It's not like your flat is the only location you

could have sex with someone.

And you can have as much sex as you want,

obviously. And wherever you want.

Lawfully, of course.

Wow I am only making this so much worse.

Anyway . . . why are you digging around

in your closet?

**JACK**

I was taking out my tattoo machines.

And there hasn't been anyone else.

In case you were wondering.

**RAINE**

Oh.

Same.

In case you were wondering.

# SEPTEMBER

  JACK

                                   Guess what?


RAINE

You've developed an intense
love of flamenco dancing.


                                        JACK

                                        . . .


RAINE

I'm in Madrid.


                                        JACK

                                       Right.

                 Sadly, I have not developed an intense
                          love of flamenco dancing.

**RAINE**

Damn.

What then?

                                                            **JACK**

                                              My books are open.

**RAINE**

Well, that is how you read them.

By opening them.

                                                            **JACK**

                                              Not those books.

**RAINE**

 . . .

Oh!

You're tattooing again?????

JACK!!!!!!!

KEURRRRIIIIGGGGGG!!!!!!

                                                            **JACK**

                                              I should've called you.

**RAINE**

JACK KEURIG DUNNE!!!!!!!

So when is my appointment?

                                                            **JACK**

                                              Whenever you want.

**RAINE**

JAAAAACCCCKKKKKKKKKKK

> **JACK**
>
> I'm calling you.

**RAINE**

Can't talk. I'm busy packing.

> **JACK**
>
> Where are you going?

**RAINE**

COBH!

> **JACK**
>
> You're not serious.

**RAINE**

Wanna bet?

> **JACK**
>
> You're seriously planning to
> come to Ireland . . . now?

**RAINE**

Well, not now. I have to wait until
there's a flight, Jack.

> **JACK**
>
> You don't have to drop everything
> and fly to Ireland for a tattoo.

**RAINE**

But I do! Once the masses hear that Jack Dunne
is tattooing again, they'll be knocking down
your door for appointments. If I don't hurry,
you won't be able to fit me in.

                                                          **JACK**

                                          You're ridiculous.
                            And I'll always be able to fit you in.
                                                          Wait.
                                                          Don't.

**RAINE**

That's what she said.

                                                          **JACK**

                                          Damn it, Lorraine.

**RAINE**

Real talk—There's a flight this afternoon.
I'd land in Cork at 10:20pm.
I can always come some other time.
You're probably busy. I don't mean
to intrude upon your life.

                                                          **JACK**

                                          Book it.

**RAINE**

Really?

JACK

Yes.

RAINE

Ahhhhhhhhh! Okay.

AHHHHH!

And . . . booked! AHHHHH!!

AHHHHHH!

JACK

See you tonight, ciaróg.

# Twenty-Six

## RAINE

When I arrive in Cork, Jack is waiting for me inside the terminal. As soon as I see him, I'm grinning, and when he sees me, he's grinning too, and we must look absolutely ridiculous grinning at each other. If I weren't so concerned about my gear, I'd drop it and run over, but I'm basically speed walking as it is, and I think I may have a literal bounce in my step.

As soon as he's within arm's reach, I drop my things on the floor and launch myself at him, hugging him as hard as I can. He squeezes the breath out of me when he hugs me back and lifts me off my feet.

When he sets me down, I tip my face up to his to tell him I missed him, but he's kissing me before I can get a word out.

"Hi, Jack," I say when we pull away from each other.

"Hello, Raine," he says.

Jack insists on carrying all of my gear to the car. The backpack and travel case and guitar. I tell him to at least let me carry *something*, but he refuses.

"You always get to carry this stuff," he says. "Let me carry it for a while. I can pretend I've just come back from my world tour."

I laugh. "You'd make a very handsome touring musician."

"I would, wouldn't I?" He hefts the backpack higher onto his shoulders. "Jesus, this is heavy. What do you have in here?"

"Before I left Madrid, I stuffed as much Jamón Ibérico into it as I could."

Jack only sighs and shakes his head as we exit the airport.

When we reach his car, I stand and watch as he packs my things into the trunk. In the six months since I left Cobh, I've mostly traveled to new places, but I've also visited familiar places to see friends, some from my old life, and some I've made since leaving the US. It's been nice staying in someone's home every now and then. Nice to see familiar places and revisit cities I loved the first time around.

But returning to Ireland feels entirely different. Seeing Jack feels entirely different. It isn't the familiarity of a place I vaguely know or the excitement of catching up with a friend. Even when I travel to a place I've been to before, I always feel in flux. Everywhere is a pit stop to the next place. But Ireland feels like a destination. If my life is a song, then the places I've been are the verses, new and varied. But Ireland—Ireland is a chorus, something to return to again and again, a place to land.

Or maybe it isn't Ireland. Maybe it's Jack.

We talk the entire drive back to Cobh, though I'm not sure what there is to catch up on, seeing as we've been in touch almost constantly since I left. Even so, this is different. No wandering around for better signal. No time differences to keep in mind. No delay in the back and forth. He's here, in the driver's seat beside me. I can reach out and touch him, so I do. I take his hand in mine and don't let go.

God, I've missed him.

St. Colman's Cathedral is the first thing I see when we pass into Cobh. It glows above the town, as beautiful as I remember. Jack must see the excitement on my face, or maybe I make a sound (I'm too caught up in the moment to know), because he laughs and squeezes my hand tighter.

"What are you laughing at?"

He glances at me, then eyes the cathedral. "I've lost count of all the places you've been in the last six months, and you're all excited over our wee little cathedral."

I gesture to it out the window. "It's not little. And how dare you! That's a great cathedral. Definitely in my top three favorite cathedrals. And that's saying something, because I have seen a lot of cathedrals."

"What's it competing with?"

"Notre-Dame and Sagrada Família, of course."

Jack laughs so hard, I'm worried he won't be able to drive. "You're telling me that cathedral is right up there with Notre-Dame and Sagrada Família?"

"Yes!" I try to look upset, but it's no use. I still have that ridiculous grin on my face. I don't think it's disappeared since I saw him at the airport. "Actually, now that I've thought about it, I think St. Colman's is number one. Sorry, Notre-Dame."

Jack sighs. "Jesus, Lorraine. I don't know what to do about you."

"I thought you had an impossibly long list of things you wanted to do about me," I say. "Maybe you should start there."

Jack eyes me as he pulls into a parking space behind the pub. "Aoife and Róisín are working, if you want to see them." When I glare at him, he laughs. "What's that look for?"

"As much as I love Aoife and Ro, I did not impulsively buy a last-minute flight from Madrid to see them. If you don't take me upstairs right now, I'll die."

"I can't let that happen," Jack says, unbuckling his seat belt and stepping from the car so quickly it startles me.

As soon as the door to the flat swings shut behind us, Jack sets my things on the floor, and then he's kissing me again. I kick off my boots, and one goes sailing across the living room, where it smacks against one of Jack's bookcases, and a stack of books goes tumbling to the floor.

"I haven't even been here for sixty seconds, and I'm already making messes."

"I don't care," Jack says. "Go ahead and trash the place, but can we maybe save it for later?"

"Wait. Where's Sebastian?"

"Are you seriously thinking about my cat right now?" Jack says.

"I don't want to psychologically damage him."

"I have no idea where he is. It's fine. He's a very respectful roommate." Jack backs me up against the wall in the entryway of the flat. "I need you," he says. "Please let me fuck you. Or do you need to say hello to my cat first?"

I sigh. "I suppose the cat can wait."

He looks me over, and I don't think I've ever seen him with so much pent-up energy. I could melt beneath the intensity of that gaze. He takes a strand of my hair between his fingers, looking at it for a moment before his eyes meet mine again. "I am really, really sorry, but I don't think I'm going to last very long."

"I take that as a compliment."

I shimmy my leggings down my hips as he unbuttons his jeans. We don't even manage to get our clothes off before he puts on a condom, turns me around, and pins my wrists to the wall. As soon as he's inside me, he buries his face into my neck with a groan.

"Fuck, you feel . . . just . . . fuck," he says.

He says something else, but it makes absolutely no sense. He hardly lasts two minutes, and I love that I can do this to him just by existing. I love that I can unravel this man who is always so busy trying to keep himself in control. I love that he can't help but give himself over to the way I make him feel.

When he stills, he rests his chin on my shoulder. "I'm sorry," he says, the words warm against my skin. "I promise I'll make it up to you."

And he does. He makes it up to me on the couch. And on the kitchen table. He makes it up to me sweetly. And urgently. And possessively. He makes it up to me until I'm sure neither of us can take any more. And then he carries me to his bed and makes it up to me one more time before I fall asleep in his arms.

"I'm glad you're here," he whispers.

I burrow closer to his chest. "Me too."

When I fall asleep, I feel as if I spend hours dreaming. Missed flights. Lost key cards. Broken guitar strings. I dream about my gear being stolen, only this time I'm in some other town I know nothing about. I'm not even sure it exists.

I haven't had a good night's sleep since I left Cobh. Some nights, I wake up in the middle of seemingly endless dreams and can't fall back asleep no matter how hard I try. It's too disorienting when you're never in the same place for more than a few days. Too many unfamiliar beds in unfamiliar hostels filled with unfamiliar people.

Tonight, the dreams must make me restless, because I hear Jack's voice in my ear before I wake up on my own.

"It's all right. It's just a dream."

I want to ask him what I've said, but he sweeps his fingers through my hair, the lightest touch in the steadiest rhythm, and I'm too tired to find the right words.

"It's just a dream," he repeats. "I'm right here."

When I drift off again, I dream of home. At least, it *feels* like home. I don't dream of Boston. I don't even dream of Cobh. I dream of Jack's fingers in my hair gently undoing every snag and tangle until they pass through the strands with ease.

# Twenty-Seven

## JACK

Raine isn't the first person I've worked on since taking up tattooing again, but when I bring her to the private studio I've rented to set up shop, I'm nervous, hyperaware of her beside me as I unlock the door.

She passes her hand over the words I've stuck on the window. "Black Cat Tattoo," she reads. "Jack, this is incredible. Why didn't you tell me you opened a studio?"

I shrug. "Didn't want to get your hopes up in case things didn't work out. It's just me in here, so it really isn't that big a deal."

When I swing open the door, the bell above it chimes. The studio is small but nice. I only have one tattoo bed. It doesn't have the same feel as a shop with other artists. But right now, I need to lessen the triggers if I can, and Martina helped me realize that perhaps an open studio wasn't the best environment for me.

I move to let Raine inside, and though I've said the shop is no big deal, it feels like a big deal to show her this place. I already know she'll love it. The girl loves almost everything. But I feel as if I'm introducing her to a different side of myself. She knows Jack, owner of the Local. She even knows Jack the artist. But she doesn't really

know Jack the tattoo artist. There's a difference. Tattooing is inti-
mate. When a client sits for a tattoo, they are putting an immense
amount of trust into my hands. It always awes me a little when someone trusts me to make a permanent change to their body. Over the
last month, I've been amazed at how easily people have put their
trust in me. Ollie volunteered himself as my first client. *I don't really
care what it is,* he said when I asked what sort of tattoo he'd like. *I care!*
Nina hollered from the next room. Ollie only sighed and said, *I
dunno, Jackie, just put the girls' names on me or some shite like that.*

Tattooing myself was easy. Giving Ollie his first tattoo was a
little anxiety-inducing, but it wasn't so bad. I spell-checked the girls'
names about thirty times. My mentor, Shauna, came to help me get
things up and running at the studio and sat for a bigger piece. It
shouldn't have taken as long as it did, but Shauna didn't mind that I
needed more breaks than an artist normally would. With each tattoo, I've had to trust myself a little more. But tattooing Raine . . . it
feels a lot more intimidating than tattooing myself, or my brother, or
Shauna.

Raine takes a few steps into the shop, then comes to a halt. She's
still as she takes everything in, but when she turns to me, she does
an excited little dance and skips back over, nearly knocking me down
when she hugs me tight around my middle.

"I take it you like it," I wheeze.

She still has her arms around me when she tilts her face up to
mine. "You're right. This isn't a big deal. It's a huge deal!"

"Oh, I don't know."

She lets go of me with a contented sigh. "Well, I *do* know, and this
is a huge deal. You now own *two* businesses, Jack. Two!"

"But they're just—"

"Shh!" Raine points at me, eyes narrowed in warning. "You shut
your mouth. Rule number one of Black Cat Tattoo is no brushing off
compliments."

I laugh. "Rule number one of Black Cat Tattoo is always wear gloves. And I don't believe you have the authority to make the rules around here, ciaróg."

"We'll see about that." She spins away from me and slowly wanders the studio. Like the day I showed her the flat, I follow her around as she examines everything closely. She doesn't say much, but every now and then she gives a little hum of approval.

"Are you ready to see the design I came up with?" I say once she's finished her inspection of the studio.

She gives me a confused look. And then I'm confused when she pulls her phone from her pocket and pries off the case. She takes out a small neon green paper. No, not a paper, a Post-it. She hands it to me, and when I unfold it, I realize it's the drawing of a beetle I made for her that first music night at the pub.

"You still have this?"

"Of course! I was gonna hand it to you and say, *I'll have exactly this, please.*"

"I think you'll like what I came up with better," I say, though when I hand her back the Post-it and grab my iPad from my desk, I start to worry she won't like it. Which would be fine. She's the client. It's her body. But I was just so sure she'd love this. I started it the day she left Cobh. I can't count how many times I've drawn and redrawn it.

I walk over to her, tapping into the drawing program to find the design. "Right. Here." I pass the iPad into her hands. "We can adjust whatever you like. And I can tweak it depending on the placement. I know you said you wanted it on your leg, but like I said, that's a big limb, so I'm not sure *where* you want it on your leg. I'll print out a few stencils in different sizes."

Raine stares at the drawing. I'm not sure she's heard a word I've said. She just stares and stares.

"Raine?"

She snaps out of whatever thought she's gotten stuck in and grins at me. "This is *way* better than the Post-it."

I laugh. "I certainly hope so."

She drops her gaze to the iPad again. "When did you do this?"

"Oh . . . months ago. Probably right after you left."

"It's beautiful."

"I based the design on some old travel journals I found online. I thought you might like that." I move to stand beside her. "And the flowers are all native to Ireland. If you'd prefer other flowers—"

"Don't be ridiculous, Keurig, of course I want Irish flowers." She passes me the iPad. "It's perfect. So, when do we get started?"

"Now, I suppose. Let me just print out these stencils so we can choose a size and location, and I'll get my station set up."

"Perfect," she says.

Raine wanders the studio again while I get everything set up. She pauses in front of where I have my flash taped to the wall and sticks the Post-it beside one of the designs, but it flutters to the ground a few seconds later.

"Damn it," she says. I don't bother asking what she's doing. Who knows. She finds some tape I have on my desk and tapes it to the wall. "There, it's yours now. You better tell me as soon as someone picks it for a tattoo."

I laugh from where I'm cutting out the stencils. "I sincerely doubt anyone is gonna look at my flash and choose a hastily drawn beetle from a faded Post-it."

"You never know," she says. "People can surprise you."

"Maybe," I say. "But I don't think I could tattoo that on someone anyway. I drew it for you. It would feel weird to tattoo it on someone else."

Once we've settled on the size and location, I have Raine stand beside the tattoo bed. She starts giggling when I grab a disposable razor and squat down in front of her to shave the part of her thigh I'll be tattooing.

"Sorry," she says. "I don't know why it's funny. It's not. I was just thinking about how I should just get a tattoo whenever I'm too lazy to shave."

"Could be a good idea," I say. "So long as you only plan on having part of your leg shaved."

"Also, you look really great in this position."

I glare up at her. "Are you *trying* to distract me? You know tattoos are permanent, right?"

"Sorry! Sorry," she says.

I clean her skin, and even though I've done this a million times before, I hold my breath as I apply the stencil and step back to take a look.

"What do you think?" I say.

Raine turns toward the mirror and examines the stencil on her leg. "I love it," she sings.

I have Raine sit on the tattoo bed. A few minutes later, I'm in front of her, everything I need set up beside me, tattoo machine in hand.

I look up at her. "You ready?"

"I've been ready ever since I found out you were a *sort of* tattoo artist," she says. "I suppose you're just a tattoo artist now."

"All right, first line, here we go." I brace my hand against her thigh and get to work before I have the chance to doubt myself. I glance up at her after the first line, and she smiles at me, so I continue working. After a few minutes, the nerves lessen. Raine is quiet and still. Which is . . . very unlike her.

"Are you doing okay?" I ask.

"This hurts way less than I expected," she says. "I mean, I wouldn't exactly call it fun, but it's not so bad. I just don't want to throw you off your game."

"You can talk. Just try not to talk with your hands as much as you usually do. If you whack me in the head, the results won't be pretty. And I mean that quite literally."

My OCD must know how keyed up I've been about this, because half an hour in, just as I'm starting to think this will be a breeze, it comes out swinging. Raine must sense the change because she says, "You okay?"

I sigh but keep my eyes on my work and don't look up at her. "The usual."

"Anything good?"

"I wouldn't call it *good*. I'm worried I'll tattoo something awful."

"I don't care if it's ugly."

"Not that kind of awful."

"Well, now you have me intrigued. You don't have to tell me what it is. Though, maybe I want it. I could go for something a little scandalous."

I feel myself turning red. "I really don't think you want the word *slut* tattooed on your thigh."

"Slut? Wow."

"I obviously don't think you're a slut. Not that there's anything wrong with being one, of course. I . . . Jesus, I don't even know what I'm saying right now." I pause to look up at her. "You know I don't really think anything negative about you, right? You don't think I'd tattoo something awful like that, do you?"

I try to read her expression, but all she says is, "We agreed I wouldn't answer questions like that."

I both love and hate how good she is at sticking to the rules. "Right, right, sorry."

"Maybe you will tattoo the word *slut* on me. Unfortunately for your OCD, I don't care. We can just put one of those little banners around it. Oh, I know! We can turn it into a sassy candy heart."

"I don't think *sassy* is the right word."

"Meh. I can always get a coverup. Now chop-chop! Back to work! Can't wait to find out if I get that gorgeous beetle tattoo or the word *slut*. Maybe I'll get both. A beetle slut tattoo. Oh, that sounds like a fabulous band name."

Jesus, I have no idea how I've gone without seeing this girl for six months. How was I not bored out of my mind every day? "Does it?"

"Mm . . . maybe not. Good thing I'm a solo artist."

I resume tattooing her and don't undo the thoughts when they come. I let them hang out in my head like it's totally normal to worry you'll tattoo the word *slut* on the woman you're in love with.

"You sit better than Ollie, you know," I say.

"Really?"

"Oh, yeah. He was swearing at me the whole time. Feared for my life, to tell you the truth."

Raine laughs. "I would've paid good money to see that."

We settle into a comfortable quiet then. I check in with her every so often. An hour into it, she says, "I think I kind of like the feeling? Is that normal? It's sort of relaxing, even if it's uncomfortable."

"That's the endorphins," I say.

"Jack?"

"Hmm?"

She doesn't respond at first, and I wonder if the pain is getting to her. Her skin doesn't feel clammy, so I don't think she's in danger of fainting, but maybe I'm wrong. I just need to finish pulling this line, and then I'll—

"I love you."

I'm so startled that it takes all of my focus to finish pulling the line. As soon as it's finished, I lift my hands from her. "Jesus, Lorraine! You could've ended up with a line straight across your leg!"

"Sorry," she says. Once the shock wears off, I notice her cheeks have turned pink. I turn off the machine and set it aside. It's so quiet in here that I can hear my pulse in my ears.

When I look up at her, I don't know what to think. Not about *her.* I'm certain about that. I love the girl. I've lost count of how many times over the last six months I've nearly blurted it out over the phone. But hearing her say it . . . I don't feel elation like I should. Eight months ago, I walked into my pub, and there she was talking to my cat. It took less than two months to fall in love with her. Not even six months apart could put a dent in it. We've had more conversations over the phone than we've had in person. It feels like a cruel trick from the universe for her to love me back when we can't be together.

"I love you too, ciaróg," I say. "You know that, right?"

"I know," she says. There's a moment of silence, and then she sighs and says, "Jack, what are we doing?"

I search her face. She looks exhausted, and I don't think it's from the tattooing. "What do you mean?"

"Why aren't we together?"

I don't want to talk about this. I don't want to talk about how I can't be the man she deserves when I want to be that person more than anything. "I know it might seem like I've got everything together, and yes, I'm doing a lot better than the last time we saw each other, but . . . Raine, I don't think I'll ever be able to keep up with you. I'm *certain* I'll never be able to. And you can't give up your life for me. I won't let you. I just don't see how we can have a normal relationship."

"Is that all?"

I laugh. "Raine, that's a pretty big thing."

"When did I ever say I wanted normal? What about my life is normal? My job isn't normal. My living situation isn't normal. My inability to keep track of a single pair of matching socks *definitely* isn't normal."

I groan. "Be serious."

"I am being serious! Nothing about my life is normal. Why would I want a normal relationship?"

I shake my head. "You deserve to be with someone who can do all the things you do. You deserve someone who can travel the world with you. Someone who can be there for you every day, no matter what city you're in—"

"What about what I *want*? What about what *you* want? What about what *you* deserve? Stop thinking about what you can't do. Stop thinking about what we can't be. It's been six months, and nothing has changed. I've met so many people, but I can't even look at someone else. I can't even think about thinking about someone else. It's you, Jack. That's all there is to it. So our relationship wouldn't be normal. Who cares?"

"But I can't give you everything—"

"Who can give anyone *everything*? Why does that mean we should have nothing instead? I hopped on a flight to Ireland at the first excuse I had. I would've come sooner. I wanted to. I can come more often."

"But that's not fair—"

"Not everything has to be fair. We just need . . . accommodations."

"What?"

She sways from side to side in excitement. "Relationship accommodations! That's what we need!"

"That's not a thing."

"Says who?"

"Everyone?"

"Clearly not *everyone*, since I say it's a thing. You give what you can give, and I'll give what I can give. In some places, you'll be the one giving more, and in others it'll be me. And I'm not pretending it'll be easy, because it won't. But nothing ever is. Every relationship has these sorts of problems. Sure, ours might look a little strange to everyone else, but who cares? If we're happy together, even if we aren't always physically together, then what does it matter? And if you can travel sometimes, you will. And when you can't, I'll come home more often."

I'm unsure what to say. Everything in me wants to believe she's right, but the doubt . . . it's right there on top, holding me down. Holding me back from saying yes. *You can't be enough for her*, it says. *You'll only hold her back*, it tells me. And it's so loud. The doubt is so, so loud.

*And what do we do with doubt?* imaginary Martina says.

This isn't an intrusive thought, I tell her. This is different.

*It's not that different, Jack.*

Easy for you to say, Martina.

Raine's words echo in my head. *I'll come home more often.* I look up at her. "Home?"

The confidence in her expression slips, and she fumbles for words. "I didn't . . . sorry, I didn't mean to assume this would be home or anything. Don't get me wrong, I love traveling. I don't want to stop traveling altogether. But it would be nice to have somewhere to land now and then, for a few weeks or months or whatever."

*What do we do with doubt, Jack?* Martina says.

Jesus, Imaginary Martina, you are rather persistent today.

*Jack.*

Fine. *Fine.* Acknowledge it. Accept it. Keep going anyway.

I look at Raine, and for a moment my only thought is that word, *home. Home home home home.* I try to make it fit, but it turns out I don't have to try at all. The idea is already there. It's her socks in weird places around the flat. It's her cuddled up with Sebastian on my yellow couch. It's her sitting in the strangest ways at the kitchen table. It's happy tears, and sad tears, and tears for no reason at all.

And music. Everywhere, all the time. In her pockets—a tambourine that shakes every time she moves, the jingle of coins in that ridiculous Ziploc bag she uses as a wallet. It's in her mouth—humming, and laughing, and singing. So much singing. Quietly, absentmindedly.

Singing instead of thinking. Singing instead of talking. Singing instead of shouting. All that music everywhere she goes. All that music she leaves behind. I hear it even when she's gone.

"Move in with me," I say. "Make Cobh home. Travel all you want. Come back whenever you want, for as long as you want. But let's maybe not go six months without seeing each other next time."

She opens her mouth, then closes it, then opens it again, but no sound comes out.

"Raine?"

"Do you mean that?" she says.

"I told you the night we met that I very rarely say things I don't mean. I used to hate that fecking flat, you know. But when you're in it . . . I don't know. You make it feel like home."

"But I won't be here a lot of the time."

"Doesn't matter," I say. "It's knowing you'll be back. That, and I'm sure you'll have your things all over the place to keep me company while you're gone. Besides, it's been a few weeks since I've found one of your socks lying around, and I kinda miss it. So . . . what do you think?"

She frowns, brow furrowed in thought, and I discover that I am still a brow-furrowing man.

"Do you have a Christmas tree? Or is it too much trouble with Sebastian?" she says.

"A Christmas tree?"

"Yes, a Christmas tree!"

"Raine, why are you talking about Christmas trees right now?"

She gives me an exasperated look. "I'll obviously be home for Christmas! This may surprise you, but for someone who hardly ever stays put, I am *very* enthusiastic about decorating for holidays."

I sigh. "Just to clarify, that is a yes on the moving in with me?"

She looks at me as if it's preposterous I'd even ask. "Yes, it's a yes!"

"Well, that's a relief."

She grins at me, and I grin back, and then she says, "Can you kiss me? I'd kiss *you* but I have a half-finished tattoo on my thigh and would rather not move."

I stand up, careful not to touch anything with my hands when I kiss her. I've never been more grateful to have a private studio, because we must look ridiculous with my hands held up in the air at my sides.

When I sit back down I give her my sternest look. "No more surprises, ciaróg. I'd like to finish this tattoo and take you home so you can get started throwing your socks all over the place."

She rolls her eyes. "It isn't *that* bad."

"It is, ciaróg. It's that bad."

"And yet you *still* asked me to move in with you."

"That's how much I love you," I say.

She smiles at me. And that mouth . . . I have no idea what she'll say next.

But I can't wait to find out.

# DECEMBER

# Twenty-Eight

---

## RAINE

When I step inside the pub, the first thing I notice is the conversation. It's loud, with vibrant laughter and lively debate that makes me want to join in, even though I can't make out the words. The Local is busier than I expect, even for a Friday night in Ireland, but this has become our new normal.

I cross the pub, take a seat at the bar, and after ordering a Guinness from Ollie, pull my phone from the pocket of my coat to text Jack. When the screen doesn't illuminate, I instinctively reach for the phone charger he always keeps behind the bar, only to find it isn't there.

"Welcome home, Raine," Ollie says when he fills my pint glass halfway. He sets it aside and moves down the bar to the next customer. While I wait, I peer around the pub. It's clean and well-lit and filled with things to see. In addition to the chalkboard menu and the two Irish flags on the ceiling, the walls are decorated with art and photos and vintage items and knickknacks I've collected from all over. And speaking of things to see, there are people everywhere I look. I don't think I could have stumbled upon somewhere livelier if

I tried. I ought to get up and go looking for Jack, but I've been traveling for the last three weeks, and now that I'm seated, I simply don't have the will to get up.

Ollie returns a few minutes later, fills my pint the rest of the way, and sets it before me. I thank him, but he only grunts and disappears to the kitchen again.

I prod my dead phone with a finger. I've just finished my beer and am working up the motivation to hunt down Jack when I'm startled by a blur of movement to my right. When I turn, I find Sebastian perched on the barstool beside me.

"Hey, floofs," I say. He swishes his tail lazily behind him, staring at me with his large green eyes as if he's been waiting for me to come home since I left.

I sigh at him. I can't help it, I'm in love with this cat. I pull him into my lap and say, "I missed you, floofy boy. Did you miss me too? You better have."

Sebastian blinks at me, then makes one of his trilling sounds. When he rubs his face against my hand, I give him a scratch beneath his chin. "Speaking of missing people, you don't happen to know where your dad is, do you, floofy boy?"

I nearly fall off my stool when I hear Jack's voice in my ear. "I'm right here, ciaróg."

When I turn, I find him lowering himself onto the stool beside me. I hug Sebastian close to my chest as I tip from my stool and into his arms. I tug the beanie from his head and run my fingers through his dark hair. And when he grins at me with those clear blue eyes and that easy expression, I decide that I was right, this cat is lucky, because without him, who knows if Jack would've sat beside me the night I first walked in here.

Jack props an elbow on the bar, posture confident and casual because he owns the place. He's sex on a stool, and I know he knows it. I take in the swoop of hair that falls into his eyes, the black peacoat and black jeans and black wingtip boots, and, damn, this sophisticated-bad-boy look still does it for me.

"I like your everything," I say.

He pushes the hair from his eyes and looks me over. "I like your everything too," he says. Jack nods to Sebastian. "He missed you terribly. Isn't that right, Princess Ugly?"

"And you?"

He shoots me a playful smile. "Oh, I missed you horrendously. And tremendously. And dreadfully."

I fantasized plenty of times about meeting a cute local and falling into a whirlwind travel romance, but I never imagined it would actually happen. I never thought it would begin with a cute local catching me in conversation with a cat.

When Sebastian chirps at Jack, he gives the cat a scratch between its ears, then eyes my phone on the bar. "Let me guess, it's dead."

I grin at him, and he sighs. "Do you need the phone charger?"

I tap my fingers along the screen of my dead phone with a sigh. "Nah, my fiancé is here, and he's the only one I want to talk to anyway."

"Lucky him."

I raise an eyebrow. "Are you flirting with me?"

Jack laughs. "Definitely. Do you mind?"

"Not at all."

He holds out his hand, and when I place mine in his, he eyes the ring on my finger. "Wow, your fiancé has great taste. What an elegant and sturdy ring, well-suited for travel."

He flips my hand over so that it rests palm-up on top of his.

"This again?" I say.

"Hush, it's a good move."

"I'm starting to think it's your only move."

"Now, now, ciaróg, you know that isn't true."

The way he looks at me makes me blush. "Oh, all right."

"Let's see . . ." His index finger drifts lightly along the center of my palm. "Well, that's not good."

I narrow my eyes at him. "What's not?"

"Says here that you are very bad at Jenga."

"Oh, come on."

"I just say what I see. Don't shoot the messenger." He looks at my hand again, then frowns. "Mm."

"What?"

He shakes his head. "Don't worry about it."

I kick his boot with one of mine. "Jack Dunne, don't tease me."

"I'm not teasing! Some things are just better left unsaid." I roll my eyes, and he leans in closer. "It's about the wedding."

I raise my eyebrows. "Now you have my attention."

He looks over my palm. "Your palm says planning a wedding sounds like a nightmare and we should just get married at the fecking registry office on Monday."

"Hmm." We've been engaged for a month, and I'm already sick of people asking me about the wedding. "Good idea, hand. Count me in."

He grins, then eyes my hand again. "It also says your fiancé is scared of your sister finding out there won't be a ceremony and that you should be the one to tell her."

"Clara's so focused on kicking med school's ass that she won't notice."

Jack laughs. "Don't be ridiculous, Lorraine."

"You're right. But I'll only tell Clara if my fiancé agrees to tell a certain party planner he is related to first."

Jack hisses. "I dunno about that. Your hand says no one should tell Nina. Oh, and it also says your new Christmas tree is waiting for you upstairs."

Jack laughs when I can't help but dance a little in my seat. He leans away but keeps my hand in his. "I'm glad you're home," he says.

After the last few weeks of traveling, it's nice to be here in this place that's mine, where I belong, where I can be myself with someone who understands me and likes me just the way I am. With a pub full of people who don't wish I was someone else.

"Me too."

Jack fiddles with the coaster in front of him. Spins it once, twice, then stops it. "Did you mean it? About getting married on Monday?"

I look him over. He seems like he really wants to know. And why shouldn't I marry him on Monday? I've never been one for planning anything. I don't understand why people wait so long after already deciding to be together. And besides, after two years of traveling, I've gotten pretty good at knowing exactly what I want. *This is awful fast*, the voice of reason warns. But I tell the voice of reason to suck it. Sometimes one beetle recognizes another, and it doesn't matter if it's been five minutes or five years.

And this Jack . . . I love him.

APRIL

# Twenty-Nine

## JACK

When Raine peers over the wall into the canal, my instinct is to grab her by the sleeve and pull her upright so she doesn't fall into the river. She turns over her shoulder and flashes me a smile, and I can't believe I'm here. I can't believe I'm in Tokyo with her.

"It is pink! Come look," she says.

*Don't go over there. What if you push her over the side? What if she falls into the river?*

Good thing she knows how to swim, I tell my OCD.

The park is filled with people. I stand beside Raine. She loops her arm through mine and pulls me tight to her side, resting her head on my shoulder. When I peer into the water, I see that she's right, most of it is pink, transformed by a flurry of cherry blossoms.

"Are you okay?" she says.

Raine travels on her own all the time, but we've visited a few places together—London was the first. Then Paris. I went to Boston for Thanksgiving and met her parents. But this is the biggest trip we've done. All of them have been hard, but the good has outweighed the bad. I've done more than I ever thought I could.

"My OCD suggests I'm going to push you over the edge of this bridge and into the river," I tell her.

Raine laughs, and it makes me smile. "Well, tell your OCD that if you do, I'm taking you with me."

"We'd be quite the spectacle, wouldn't we?"

"We always are," she says. "Let me know if you need a break, okay? All our plans are flexible. I've built in plenty of downtime."

"Thank you," I say. "I'm okay right now."

I press a kiss to her temple, and when I pull away, notice a cherry blossom in her hair. A flash of pink in a sea of red. I pluck it from her hair and balance it on a fingertip. "Make a wish, ciaróg."

She looks up at the cherry tree above us. "If we stay here long enough, I'm going to have a million wishes," she says.

She squeezes her eyes shut, and when she opens them again, blows the cherry blossom away. It flies from my finger and over the edge of the canal and into the river.

"What did you wish for?" I ask.

"Don't be nosy. If I tell you, it won't come true."

"Nonsense. I'm Irish. I'm lucky. If you tell me, it'll be *more* likely to come true."

She squints at me. "I think you're making that up."

I shrug. "Go ahead and risk it, if you like."

Her cheeks turn pink, and she looks away. "It's silly. I was just wishing for the meeting with that agent to go well."

"What's silly about that?"

She shrugs, and then her eyes dart to the top of my head. "Oh!" She stretches up onto her toes and her fingers brush my hair. "Your turn."

She holds out the cherry blossom on her fingertip, but before I can make my wish, the wind carries it away.

Raine's face falls. "Oh, shoot," she says. "Sorry. I'm sure there will be another one."

I pull her closer and she wraps her arms around my middle. "I don't need any wishes," I say. "And the meeting is going to be amazing."

"How do you know?" Raine mumbles.

"The luck of the Irish. We just know."

I kiss the top of her head. "And also because you are incredibly charming and talented. And your music is incredible. I'm proud of you, you know."

She sighs against my chest. "I know."

She tilts her face up to mine. "I'm proud of you too."

"For what?"

She raises her eyebrows and looks around the park. I follow her gaze. Cherry blossoms swirl around us, and that's when it hits me that I'm really here. When my eyes land on hers again, she's grinning up at me. I don't think I've ever loved her more.

I hold her tighter. We stand like that for a while and watch the wind carry cherry blossoms into the river. I resist the compulsion to count the cherry blossoms that get caught in her hair and on her coat, fearful that if I don't, something bad will happen to her. Raine must sense my anxiety, because she steps back from my arms to rummage through the backpack she's wearing.

"You look like you could use some drawing time," she says, and passes a pen and a pad of Post-its into my hands.

"I really could," I say.

Raine sits on the grass with the river to her back. She pats the ground in front of her, and I mirror her cross-legged pose when I sit opposite her. The way she looks with the cherry blossoms in her hair and the river at her back has me putting pen to paper without a moment's hesitation. I wish I had something better than a Post-it to capture it.

Raine gazes around the park. "What's caught your eye?"

"My wife, of course," I say. "Sit still, will you?"

Raine laughs, but does her best to sit still. As I draw, she asks me about the tattoo appointments I have when we get back home, and when that topic is exhausted, starts talking about the agent who emailed her when a snippet of one of her original songs unexpectedly became a viral sound on social media after an influencer posted a video of Raine busking on Grafton Street.

I hang on to her every word until the anxiety eases into something tolerable, until so many cherry blossoms get caught in her hair that if they really granted wishes, we'd have more than a person could ever need.

# ACKNOWLEDGMENTS

This book would not have been possible without the love, support, and hard work of so many. Thanks to my agent, Wendy Sherman, for always telling it like it is. To my brilliant editor, Kerry Donovan, who I wholeheartedly trust to understand my vision and guide me in achieving it. To my entire team at Berkley, especially Mary Baker, Kristin Cipolla, Jessica Mangicaro, Christine Legon, George Towne, and Alaina Christensen. Thank you to Colleen Reinhart and Guy Shield for a gorgeous cover.

To my dearest friends, Raven, Danielle, Emelia, and Krystal, who read my work when it isn't pretty and put up with my constant voice notes. A special thanks to Kelly MacPherson for her insight on the sensitive matters in this book. Thank you to the friends and family who shared their experiences with me. Any errors in my portrayal of OCD and ADHD are my own.

Thank you to the Berkletes and all the wonderful authors who have supported me, not just in publishing, but also in the ups and downs of life. You mean so much to me.

To the staff and supporters of my favorite place in the whole world, the Weymouth Center for the Arts & Humanities, thank you for all you do. My time at Weymouth each summer refreshes my soul and my creativity.

Huge thanks to all the lovely influencers and readers who helped to reveal the cover for this book. To anyone who has read, loved, and shared my books: Thank you, thank you, thank you. I can't express what you mean to me. You're why I love this business.

Thank you to the lovely and generous people of Cobh, especially the kind folks at the Cobh Tourist Office and Steve from Kelly's Bar, who may be the most delightful bartender in all of Ireland.

To Marco, Carolina, and Nicolas, I am grateful to so many, but most of all to you. If it weren't for your love and support, I wouldn't be chasing my dreams. There is no one else I'd rather have by my side.

## JUNE

Returning home from months at sea is like waking up from one dream right into another. Charter season is four months of sunshine, the bluest water that has ever existed, and lots and lots of money. But it's also sixteen-hour shifts, sleep deprivation, and late nights scrubbing the vomit of hungover billionaires from white carpet. At the end of the season, we always come to Mitch's, an Irish pub that puts the *dive* in dive bar. Mitch's is dirtier than someone who cleans a twenty-million-dollar yacht for a living would like, and the dust on the bookcase beside our table is likely a health violation, but seeing as it's the first mess in months that isn't my responsibility to clean, I couldn't care less.

Some people never experience déjà vu, but I feel it all the time. More and more as the years pass. Every time I slip into this booth at Mitch's, for instance. Jo, the *Serendipity*'s second stew and my soon-to-be *former* best friend, says I'm just bored. But I disagree. How can I be bored when I work on a giant boat and run away to the

Caribbean four months a year? How can I be bored when I get paid to see the places most people only dream of? As Jo's nieces would say, I am *living the dream*. Usually, I don't disagree.

Usually.

But as I stare across the table at Jo, *nightmare* is the word that comes to mind. I can see her mouth moving, but I don't hear a word. I'm distracted by the ache in my bad knee, which, after the last four months working barefoot, is aggravated by even the lowest of low-heeled wedges. In a few days, my knee will adjust to life on land along with the rest of me. All I have to do is ignore the pain until it fades. But what Jo's just told me? I won't adjust to it. I refuse.

"Nina?" Jo's voice comes back into focus, and the feeling of déjà vu slips away. Her gaze darts from me to her fiancé, Alex, beside her.

"It's an awful idea." It's all I can manage, because this is the most ridiculous thing I've ever heard. Jo quitting the yacht? To help Alex run a restaurant?

Jo frowns into her drink. "That's all you have to say?"

"You can't even cook, Josephine. They don't pass out Michelin stars for knowing how to operate a microwave. How are you going to help this man run a restaurant? Sure, he makes a good cheese Danish, but the sex can't be that good."

"I'll try to focus on the part where you compliment my cooking," Alex says.

I shoot him a glare. "Don't."

Jo twirls the straw in her glass. "I won't be cooking. I'll help manage the place," she says.

Alex puts an arm around Jo's shoulders, and though I love him for loving Jo, I also want to punch him in the ribs. Not hard enough to break one, but enough for him to understand how all this is making me feel.

A better friend would smile, buy a round of shots, celebrate this new phase of her friend's life. But I am not Jo's better friend. I'm her *best* friend. And as such, I can't help but think of all the things I'm losing. *You're upset because she's choosing him over you*, the voice in my head says. The voice isn't wrong. Of course Jo is choosing Alex over me. He's the fiancé. I'm the best friend. That's what happens when people get engaged, or land their dream job, or find something else they can't resist.

"This is worse than a secret fetus," I whisper into my drink.

Alex tenses. "A what?"

I wave a hand at Jo. "I thought you may have impregnated her. She's been acting weird all week."

Beer dribbles down Alex's chin when he turns to look at her.

"I'm not pregnant," she says. "You've seen me drinking all season, Nina. We shared a fishbowl at that weird pirate bar—"

"Davy Jones's Locker is *festive*, not weird." I fiddle with one of the dangling unicorn earrings I take off only to shower and sleep. "You could've been pregnant. I don't know your life. How am I supposed to know if you adhere to CDC guidelines?"

"You *do* know my life," Jo says. "Which means you also know I never planned to work in yachting forever. I never planned to work in yachting at all."

The three of us fall silent. Mitch's walls are littered with photographs, and ticket stubs, and dollar bills, making me feel as if I've stepped into a stripper's scrapbook. I glance at the wall beside us, my heart cartwheeling in my chest when I spot the Polaroid of me, Jo, and Ollie, the *Serendipity*'s chef before Alex. I decide that our current chef, Amir, is my new favorite. His food isn't as good as Ollie's or Alex's, but at least Amir has never broken my heart.

Ollie and I started on the *Serendipity* the same year, when both of us were new to yachting. We worked together for eight charter seasons, and it was in this very bar, almost a year ago to the day, that I'd found out he was leaving to become sous chef at Miami's illustrious Il Gabbiano.

*Don't think about him*, the voice in my head chides. But how can I avoid it when he's staring right at me from that damn Polaroid? I lean over and grab the photo, yanking it free from the wall with one sure pull.

"Nina," Jo says. "What are you doing?"

I shove the photo into my bra. "Souvenir," I say. I'm not sure what I'll do with it: burn it, tuck it into a book, sneak back here in a week and staple it to the wall again.

"Shots!" Britt, the *Serendipity*'s third stew, appears beside the table with four shot glasses crowded in her hands. She grins at us, completely oblivious to the tension she's walked into.

I take two of the shot glasses and glare at Jo. "I need this more than you." I tip Jo's shot down my throat before chasing it with mine.

Britt scoots into the booth energetically, nudging me against the wall and blocking me into this hellscape.

"Leave some room for the Holy Spirit, won't you?" I shove Britt over until half her ass hangs out of the booth. "Lord help me sitting next to you all night. Where's RJ? He'd let a girl have some peace and quiet."

Britt snorts. "I doubt it."

I've never heard RJ, the *Serendipity*'s bosun, string more than one sentence together at a time, and I've known him for as long as I've been in yachting. Jo and I exchange a look that says, *What's that supposed to mean?* But I look away when I remember she is now my *former* best friend.

"Shouldn't you be somewhere mooning over Amir anyway?" I ask Britt. Their love affair had done nothing positive for the efficiency of the interior crew this season.

"I'm letting him miss me," Britt says. Her gaze is unfocused, and I wonder how many shots she's had already. "What is it with stews and chefs?" she muses. "Is it the knives? I mean, it's got to be more than a coincidence. Me and Amir, Jo and Alex, you and—" I raise an eyebrow. She mimics my expression and realizes her mistake. "Uh, Chrissy Teigen."

I twirl the two empty shot glasses before me on the table. "Is Chrissy technically a chef? There was a robust debate about it on Twitter a few weeks ago, and I don't remember what the consensus was." Alex opens his mouth to answer, but I cut him off. "Rhetorical question, Alex. I don't want to hear anything from you. It's bad enough you've stolen away my former best friend."

Jo looks stricken. "Former?"

Britt sighs unsteadily against the table and nearly topples out of the booth. "They told you, huh?"

"You knew about this?" I say.

"Britt!" Jo hisses.

Britt flashes drunken jazz hands at me and shouts, "Surprise!"

"She's taking over for me," Jo explains.

Which means Xav, our captain, already knows too. "Next you'll tell me RJ found out before me."

"That may be my fault," Britt slurs. She grabs Jo's unfinished margarita, but I pry it from her hands and pass her my water instead.

"She wasn't supposed to tell anyone," Jo says.

"RJ made me tell him." Britt leans forward to catch the water's straw in her mouth and misses.

I ignore the revelation that RJ actually converses with someone and turn to Jo. "When?"

"Why would I know when she told him?"

"When are you *leaving me*?" I say.

Jo bites her lip but doesn't answer.

"Two weeks," Alex says, putting Jo out of her misery.

*Two weeks?* No, no. Clearly, she hasn't thought this through. "Britt can't take over for you," I say. "She always does Med season." Almost every photo Britt posts is of her on either the *Serendipity* or the *Talisman*, the superyacht she works on in the Mediterranean Sea after we finish charter season in the Caribbean. The woman is only on land four months a year. I nudge her with my elbow. "Tell them," I say.

Britt rests her head on the table and mumbles, "Screw Med season."

As I look from Britt to Jo, the cartwheels in my chest become back handsprings. "You're drunk," I tell her. "You're all drunk!" I look at Britt and sigh. "But she's the drunkest. Seriously, she needs to hydrate." I make her sit up so I can shove the straw in her mouth.

Jo worries her bottom lip, and I realize my reaction is hurting her. I take a slow breath and tell myself I can walk this back. I can still save the post-charter-season celebration and Jo and Alex's big announcement. I can be Jo's better friend *and* her best friend.

"I'm just teasing," I say. I force a smile on my face I'm not sure Jo buys. "You're my past, present, and future best friend. I'm happy for you, Jo. Really."

It's true. I'm happy for Jo, even if I'm not *happy*.

Jo grabs my hand from across the table. "You don't have to worry about you and me, you know. Just because I won't be around at work doesn't mean—"

"I'm not worried!" I squeeze her hand before letting it go to fidget with my empty shot glass. "I never worry. I don't know how. We're on land, and on land, I only know how to have fun."

"And are you happy for me?" Alex says. "Getting my own place. Lifelong dream coming true and all."

I squint at him. "Depends on how many cheese Danish I get out of it."

Alex tilts his head as if lost in thought. "How about two dozen?"

"Make it three and you've got yourself a deal," I say.

"Done."

Jo rolls her eyes. "Three dozen cheese Danish? That's all I'm worth to you?"

I shrug. "They're really good cheese Danish."

Jo drops her gaze to her drink. "And you're fine with this. Really?"

I don't know if I'm *fine* with it, exactly. It's not like I have any other choice. I don't love the idea of not having Jo at work anymore, but I don't actually expect her to plan her life around me. "I'm not fine *now*, but I will be."

I hope I seem calm on the outside, because inside, I'm freaking out. I have always known my emotions are bigger than most people's. Years of gymnastics training helped me to develop the discipline necessary to keep them in check, a useful skill when your job requires catering to the whims of the wealthy. Normally I do better than this. But Jo and I have been through everything together over the last six years. Now she has Alex and his fourteen-year-old daughter, Greyson—a real family to go through everything with. I know Jo and I will still be best friends, but things are changing, although I was perfectly fine with how they've been. I thought I'd at least have her at work, even if her life outside of it became a bit more complicated. It never crossed my mind that she'd quit, that one change would ripple outward, washing over everything.

*Too much*, I think. I need to step away for a minute. I force Britt to sit up and move out of my way so I can escape the booth.

"Where are you going?" Jo says.

"I'm getting champagne, of course," I say. "This is a celebration, is it not?"

Jo looks at me for a moment, but she must believe me, because the hesitation on her face eases. "Thanks, Nina."

"Don't thank me," I say. "I have plenty to celebrate myself. Like the three dozen cheese Danish in my future."

When I leave the table, I don't go to the bar right away. Instead, I prowl the perimeter of Mitch's, running a hand over the dozens of dollar bills that jump out at me from the mess of photographs on the walls. What a shame to leave all this money here, stuck but still valu-able. I look around the pub and wonder how much money has been left here. I certainly hope Mitch doesn't plan to use it as his retire-ment fund. It seems a rather risky investment strategy.

A corner of the Polaroid of me, Ollie, and Jo jabs into my skin. I face the wall and discreetly adjust the photo inside my bra. As I do, I spot a dollar bill that's been defaced to make George Washington look like a zombie. When I reach out to touch it, the dollar is so worn, it feels like fabric beneath my fingertips. I think of how good it felt to rip that photo from the wall, and without checking to see if anyone is watching, I tug at the thumbtack pinning Zombie George in place, then fold the dollar in half and stuff it into my bra beside the photograph.

Maybe I should feel bad, but I don't. It feels good to take some-thing for myself, something that would be useless otherwise. It's what I love about thrifting. One woman's trash is another woman's treasure. I put the thumbtack back in its place and scan the wall again. Perhaps I'll grab a few more. Instead of returning to the table, I'll have the champagne sent over and I'll disappear. I'll go down the street to the gas station and buy a pack of cigarettes even though I haven't smoked in years.

"One charter season without me, and you turn to a life of crime?" a familiar voice says from behind me.

*Ollie.* I didn't know he'd be here, but part of me had hoped. I won't give him the satisfaction of turning to face him, though. I don't want to seem too eager. "What are you doing here? You aren't part of the crew," I say.

"Alex invited me. He's not crew anymore either. Mitch's is open to the public, yeah?"

I should've known this was Alex's doing. He and Ollie have be-come *buds* over the last year. They even have matching T-shirts with

Gordon Ramsay's face on them that say *Where's the lamb sauce?* I don't get the joke, and I don't want to. All I know is Ollie talks to Alex about me, and I don't like it.

"How's the form, Neen?" Ollie says.

His breath is warm against my skin, and he smells like the mint tea he drinks obsessively. My instinct is to lean into him, but I'm not sure if being around him will make tonight better or worse, so I try not to move.

"I used to be a professional gymnast, Oliver," I say. "My form is excellent." I know that's not what he means. I've picked up more Irish slang over the years than I let on. This is just part of the game we play.

"You know I don't like being called Oliver," he says, like he often does when I use his full name.

"And you know I don't care," I reply, like I have hundreds of times. Thousands, maybe. Same old barbs. Same old reactions. I like to think of them as the grooves of our relationship. We settle into them when we're around each other just to remind ourselves they exist. If we stick to the lines, we can play this game for as long as we like. If we follow the rules, no one gets hurt.

Ollie wraps his arms around me and rests his chin on my shoulder. I hate how I don't mind it. How I can't help but rest my weight against his chest. Before Jo, it was just me and Ollie. A whole lifetime ago, it seems. He and I have more history than I care to admit. And though Jo is my best friend, my relationship with Ollie means just as much, albeit in a vastly different and infinitely more complicated way.

Ollie's barely-there stubble scratches my cheek when he speaks. "You good, Neen?"

I keep my eyes on the wall ahead of me. "Why wouldn't I be?" I say. *Better*, I think. *Being around him will make tonight better.*

"Heard you might've got some bad news," he says.

So even Ollie found out about Jo and Alex's plans before me? *Worse*, I decide. "I'm marvelous," I say.

Ollie's nose nudges my neck. I ignore the way it makes me weak in the knees, and not just the bad one. "I've missed you," he says, not at all the way you tell your ex-coworker you miss them.

I want to put some space between us, but Ollie is too comfortable, and I can't drag myself away. "Where's your girlfriend?" I ask. Sondra? Samantha? Tall. Redhead. I like her.

"Don't have one anymore."

No surprise there. The man goes through girlfriends faster than I can snap up a pair of vintage Levi's off the rack. "What was wrong with this one?"

"She wasn't you," he says. His breath raises goose bumps on my neck. So, he wants to play *that* version of our game.

I pull his arms off me with a sigh. "Not tonight," I say.

"It's true."

I turn, getting the first good look at him I've had since I left for charter season. He's unchanged, everything about him as in-between as ever. His hair, between blond and brown, between straight and curly, short on the sides and longer on top. He isn't tall, but he isn't short either. Even his outfit, a navy button-down, jeans, and white sneakers, falls somewhere between formal and informal. That's not to say Ollie is plain, because he isn't. There's something striking about the balance of him. Beautiful, really.

The only out-of-balance feature on Oliver Dunne is his eyes. Blue, but not like the sky or the ocean. They're an intense, impossible blue that reminds me of the blue-raspberry Slurpees I shared with my father after gymnastics practice when I was a kid. We'd stop at the 7-Eleven, and I'd stay in the truck while my father disappeared inside. He kept a lucky quarter in the cupholder between our seats, and I'd warm it between my palms while I waited for him.

When he returned, I'd pass him the quarter for his scratch-off ticket in exchange for the Slurpee. Every now and then, the smell of quarters and scratch-off dust washes over me, making me sick. I thought my father and I were playing a game. I suppose we were. But that didn't mean there weren't consequences.

All this is to say, I've encountered many attractive people in my life, ones who wanted exactly what I did—no feelings, no strings attached—but none of them drove me wild like Ollie does. At first I thought it was the accent. But even with his mouth shut I want to kiss him. I tell Jo I don't love him. I tell *him* I don't love him. But of course I do. If soul mates exist, Oliver Dunne is the closest thing I have to one. But that doesn't mean we're good for each other. It doesn't make either of us immune to the damage we can inflict on one another. It doesn't change the rules.

Ollie looks me up and down. "Nice dress," he says. It is nice. A knee-length color-block dress with matching buttons down the front. Vintage Liz Claiborne. One hundred percent silk. He catches the hem between his fingers, and his knuckles brush against my thigh. "Where'd you get it?"

"Do you really care?" I should step back, but my muscles are frozen. I blame the bad knee.

"Maybe I do," Ollie says, his eyes on the fabric between his fingers.

"Butch, of course." Butch, the owner of my favorite thrift store, knows exactly what I like.

"The one and only Butch. You make me jealous when you talk about him."

When he lifts his gaze to mine, I force myself not to look away. I hate when he looks at me that way. It makes me feel stark naked when I'm obviously overdressed.

"You *should* be jealous. Butch is the man of my heart."

"And Jo is the woman, I know."

"Not anymore." I look beyond Ollie. Amir, RJ, and some of the other deckhands have joined Jo, Alex, and Britt at the table. Amir says something that makes everyone but RJ laugh. The look RJ gives him could fillet him alive. At least I'm not the only one who's miserable tonight.

Ollie doesn't say anything else. When I look up at him again, I catch the soft smile he saves only for me. Being near him is like sighing into my couch when I first get home from charter season. We haven't spent much time together since he moved from Palm Beach to Miami. He's only an hour and a half away, but the restaurant keeps him busy, and I've avoided driving down to see him ever since the last time I ended up in his bed.

For the last year, my friendship with Ollie has consisted of phone calls on his drive home from work. Most nights, unless I'm working late on the boat, he calls just as I've gotten into bed. I always put the phone on speaker and close my eyes as we talk, mostly about nothing. The restaurant, the yacht, weird Craigslist listings. By the time I hear Ollie unlock his apartment door, I'm half-asleep, lulled there by the sound of his voice.

It sounds like a capital-$R$ Relationship, but it's not. I don't know what to call it. The phone calls and occasional hook-ups are all I can give. They're enough for me. But this phase, the one in which we can be friends, lasts only so long before Ollie is itching for more, something with a label. And when I refuse, he'll pull away from me again. We won't talk for months, maybe a year. He always says he's done, and sometimes he finds someone else, someone he really likes. But it's no use. We always find ourselves back here, walking this in-between place like a balance beam.

"Did you miss me?" he asks.

"We spoke yesterday. Though you failed to mention you'd be here."

"Wasn't sure I'd come. But I like to see the faces you make when you tease me."

"Teasing? Me? Never." I rest my hands on his shoulders. "You're built like a hunky fridge," I say. My hands slide down his arms to give his biceps a squeeze. He laughs, and I shoot him a glare. "What? You're frigid, and bulky, and occasionally provide food." I'm making quite the spectacle of myself tonight. Maybe it's time to give up the tequila.

"That face. Right there," Ollie says. He presses his thumb to my mouth. "And you say you don't tease me."

My heart is doing moves now that would be physically impossible for anyone but Simone Biles. I take Ollie's hand in mine and squint at his palm like a fortune-teller. I know the callus at the base of his forefinger. I can map out the small scars and discolored burns that run up his hands and arms. Even when I don't want to, I think of them whenever someone else touches me. It's a real mood killer.

"No new injuries, I see."

"Not on this hand."

"And the other?"

He puts his other hand in mine, and I spot a new burn right away, just behind the knuckle of his pinky finger. "New line cook doesn't look where he's fecking going," he says.

"I wish you'd be more careful," I say, but I regret it as soon as Ollie's smile becomes a smirk.

"So, you did miss me."

"I didn't say that." And really, what does he care if I missed him or not? What would it change about anything?

"I'm seventy percent sure you did," Ollie says.

Ollie's hands feel so good in mine after months apart that I don't care that what I'm about to suggest will only make the situation between us murkier. "Do you want to play a game?" I ask.

"What game?"

"Truth or dare."

He raises his eyebrows. "Oh. Sure." He squints at me. "Truth or dare, Nina Lejeune?"

"No," I say. "I go first."

Ollie rolls his eyes. "Why do you always get to make the rules?"

"Because I suggested the game."

"All right, all right. You go."

"Truth or dare?" I ask.

Ollie's eyes are bright with mischief. "Dare," he says.

"I dare you to come outside with me," I say.

"Done."

"Marvelous." I drop one of his hands, keeping a tight grip on the other as I pull him through Mitch's and toward the door that leads to the back parking lot. I'm only distracting myself from one problem by blowing up another. I know that. But I'm not very good at listening to reason, especially my own.

As soon as we step outside, I press my hands to Ollie's chest and push him against the brick exterior of Mitch's.

"You smell like a tin of Altoids," I say.

"Probably taste like them too."

"This means nothing."

"Sure thing, kitten."

When I lift myself onto my toes and kiss him, Jo's news and the ache in my bad knee are all but forgotten. Kissing Ollie is like working a charter—familiar, but never boring. At first the kiss is soft, almost sweet. He tastes exactly as I remember. I'd bet all my tips from the season he has a still-warm tumbler of mint tea in his car. When Ollie slides his fingers into my hair and pulls me closer, my hands find his shoulders again. Really, does the man do anything besides swear, and cook, and work out?

When we pull apart, Ollie grins. "Now I'm ninety-nine percent sure you missed me."

I roll my eyes and lean in to kiss him again, but Ollie catches my shoulders and holds me back. "Uh-uh," he says. "It's my turn."

I sigh. "Fine. Go."

"Truth or dare?" he says.

"Truth," I say.

Ollie's expression turns serious. He caresses my cheek with the back of his hand. "What's this really about?"

I glare up at him. *This* is not part of the game. We don't talk about *why* we do things. We just do them. "I've been at sea for four months; what else could it be about?"

"Come on, kitten. You're obviously upset. Talk to me." His voice is so gentle it makes my chest ache.

When I don't say anything, Ollie pushes my hair, down from its usual high ponytail for once, over one shoulder. He tugs gently at one of my unicorn earrings. "These give a man false hope, you know."

My eyes leave Ollie's to run over his gently sloping nose, his mouth, the wrinkle between his eyebrows. "Please don't," I say, surprised to find myself blinking back tears.

How do I always end up kissing Oliver Dunne in secret? Despite what he says about missing me and breaking up with his girlfriend, this thing between us is not serious. It shouldn't be, anyway. And I should be inside celebrating the next chapter of my best friend's life. But instead, I'm in a bar parking lot making out with Ollie so I can forget about it.

Ollie's hand drops from my ear. He pulls me to him, and I think he's going to kiss me, but instead he tucks my head beneath his chin and holds me against his chest. "It's all right," he whispers. "Nothing has to change. You and Jo will be the same as ever."

I want to believe him, but Ollie is wrong. I can feel it. My entire universe is being reordered, just like when he quit the boat last year.

The distance between us grew, and these days we hardly see each other. My bad knee is throbbing now. It's the same feeling I get when I'm on the *Serendipity* and know a storm is coming. The sky may be cloudless and calm, and RJ and Xav can tell me there's nothing on the radar until they're blue in the face, but I'm never wrong about storms. It's like they're part of me.

Ollie can pretend he doesn't feel it too, but I know he does.

Everything is about to change.

Photo by Joanna Sue Photography

**Sarah Grunder Ruiz** is a writer, educator, and karaoke enthusiast. Originally from South Florida, she now lives in Raleigh, North Carolina, with her husband and two children. She holds an MFA in creative writing from North Carolina State University, where she now teaches First-Year Writing.

Ready to find
your next great read?

Let us help.

**Visit prh.com/nextread**

Penguin
Random
House